P9-CAN-113

A Song
in the
Air

Other Books by
Catherine Ritch Guess

In the Garden

EAGLE'S WINGS TRILOGY
Love Lifted Me
Higher Ground

SHOOTING STAR SERIES
In the Bleak Midwinter

SANDMAN SERIES
Old Rugged Cross

A Song in the Air

♪ ♪ ♪ ♪

Catherine Ritch Guess

CRM BOOKS

Copyright © 2004 by Catherine Ritch Guess. All rights reserved.

Questions & Reflections Foreword written by C.J. Didymus

Cover artwork by Madeleine Nagy. All rights reserved.

Cover design by Jerry DeCeglio. All rights reserved.

Author photograph by Mark Barden. All rights reserved.

CRM BOOKS, P.O. Box 2124, Hendersonville, NC 28793

Visit our Web site at www.ciridmus.com

The Reality Fiction name and logo are registered trademarks of CRM BOOKS.

No part of this book may be reproduced or utilized in any form or by any means, electronic or mechanical, including photocopying, recording, or by any information storage or retrieval system, or transmitted, without prior written permission from the publisher, except by a reviewer who may quote brief passages in a review.

This book is a work of fiction. Except for recognized historical figures, all names, characters, places, and incidents either are the product of the author's imagination or are used fictitiously. Any resemblance to actual events, locales, or persons, living or dead, is coincidental and beyond the intent of either the author or publisher.

Printed in the United States of America

ISBN: 0-9713534-6-8
LCCN: 2004094539

In Memory
of
Madeline Tyson

A True Saint
whose ever-present
radiant eyes,
joyous smile
and effervescent spirit
guided me through
each page of
this story

In Memory

of

Tara Howell
Parker

In Memory

of

Dawn Marie
Finfrock

Special Thanks

to Dale A. Jarrett, NASCAR driver, for his support and permission to use his real name in this book, and its sequel, *The Midnight Clear*. I believed you to be the ideal family role model, and after a year of research, I've found you to be that, plus a whole lot more. Your example, both on and off the track, made you the perfect character to fictionally portray as the hero of *A Song in the Air*. Most especially, thank you for making a difference in the lives of so many through the Dale Jarrett Foundation.

An added word of appreciation goes to James Gaither, Mr. Jarrett's business manager/general counsel for his support, gracious assistance and diligence in making my research possible.

My sincere thanks to the crewmen of Dale Jarrett who patiently introduced me to the "pits"; to Laura Kouns, UPS Motorsports Marketing Manager, for your support, permissions and pleasantly helpful attitude; to Eddie and Sharon Comstock and Steve Lavender, who answered numerous questions and shared experienced insights at the various tracks; and to Ellen Patterson (former Ned Jarrett scorer), Genie and Debbie and the many NASCAR and DJ fans who so willingly allowed helpful interviews

Lastly, and most inspirational, my sincerest appreciation to Larry McReynolds, NASCAR Fox Race Analyst, who unknowingly introduced me to the "real" world of NASCAR through the eyes of Brooke and Brandon

Acknowledgments

To Isaac Rogers, the face of inspiration for my main character; to his parents Michael J. and Connie Rogers for consent and support in this project; and to brothers Micah, Christian and Noah for giving me the "real" scoop on Isaac

To Madeleine Nagy for a most inspiring cover; to her parents, Chris and Jille Nagy, for permission and support; and to Julie Langley, Cannon School Art Teacher, for co-ordination; and to Jerry DeCeglio, whose covers always make me look good

To my former students, the staff, and administration of Cannon School, Concord, NC, who made teaching a most rewarding experience for me; with special thanks to Richard Snyder - Headmaster; Gay Roberts - Lower School Administrator; and Dot Monroe - second-grade teacher and tutor of many, who taught my younger son cursive handwriting. Your pleasant smile and energetic spirit have touched countless students.

To NorthEast Medical Center, Concord, NC, and the following individuals who gave permissions and helped with numerous details: Jim Monroe (husband of Dot) - Executive Director, NEMC Foundation, and secretary Donna Harless; Barry W. Hawthorne - VP, Patient Care Services & Chief Nurse Executive; Cindy Fink - Clinical Director, Pediatrics and Child Advocacy Center; Carol Lovin - VP, Strategic Planning and Market Development; Gayle Deal - Executive Director, Business Health Services; and Cookie Stafford, Care Partner of 35 years - a "character" all to herself; and lastly, deepest appreciation to Dr. George Engstrom, retired pediatrician of Concord, NC, whose support, expertise and genteel charm were invaluable in creating this story

To Emeril's - Orlando, FL - for providing the perfect "Parents' Night Out" and Mauricio, my illustrious waiter

To the following students from St. Micheal's Middle School, Findlay, OH, for use of their stories and to their teachers Michelle Fox and Janice Brumbaugh for coordination: *Coming Home for Christmas*, Alyssa Logsdon; *What Does Christmas Mean, Mommy?*, Alisha Riley; *An Elf's Christmas*, Molly Boes; and *Aria*, Kari Hohman

To John Letterle, Amanda Ledford and Josh Santiago, and all the rest of my "Staple's family" (Staple's - Hendersonville, NC) who make my life much easier and take great care of me

To the Dean Osborne Band (Dean, Matt DeSpain, John Widener and Richard Bennett) - my favorite bluegrass band - and the Moron Brothers, Lardo and Burley, for a night of laughs and a rousing musical Renfro Valley experience

To Reverend Mark Barden - Director of Missions and Outreach for the Western NC Conference of the UMC, and wife, Barbara, and son, Chris. Words can never express my thanks for the many ways you help and support me.

To Ruth Wiertzema - Conference Director of Connectional Ministries, Red Bird Missionary Conference, KY; to Jamie Reviere - Director of Christian Education, FUMC, Brevard, NC; to A. J. Moore, Otis Snow, Mickey Harrison and Chris Morgan of Methodist Motorsports Evangelism; and to Joy Barton, Child Welfare Supervisor - Transylvania County, NC

To Give Kids the World - Kissimmee, FL - for granting wishes for children all over the world and for allowing me to use your facility for this story; with special thanks to the following GKTW individuals: Henri Landwirth, Founder; Pamela Landwirth, President; and Kristin Weissman, Director of Communications; and father/daughter volunteers - Jeff and Jaime Frank

To the Breakfast Club of the Red Pig Cafe for use of *A Red Pig Christmas Carol*; and for the life you've added to mornings at the restaurant for over two decades; special thanks to Marijke and Ike for the use of your names

And most especially, to Randy, Jean and Cory Lyle - owners of the Red Pig Cafe, Concord, NC; and waitresses Jan McGee, Tami Galbreath and Jennifer Hauss; Chelmo Bustos and the entire kitchen staff; and special recognition to Gail Horne, who has taken care of the "regulars" for over thirty years. You have all made my every wish your command. As 11-year-old Chris Barden aptly said, "The Red Pig's a friendly restaurant that is like a family in itself. And each new relative has more to add to the family tree."
I love you all - *and* the bread pudding and squash casserole!

AN INSPIRING CHARACTER and A NOVEL LUNCH

People often ask where I find the inspiration and ideas for my books.Usually, the book comes to me like a bolt of lightning. Such was the case with this book, the second in the *Shooting Star* series.

While I was reading the final proof for *In the Bleak Midwinter*, the first book of this series, I went to Staple's to get a copy of the cover. The original copy had traveled so much with me around the country that it had gotten scratched diagonally across the upper left corner.

John Letterle, the copy technician, looked at the cover, pointing to the scratch, and asked, "Is that a shooting star?"

I looked at him, looked at the scratch, and stared back at him. "No, but it's going to be."

This Staple's employee had just become the latest messenger of inspiration for me. I drove home as quickly as I could, called the editor and publisher and informed them that I was making an adjustment, explaining what had happened. Thank goodness they trusted my creativity, for a shooting star appeared at the end of *In the Bleak Midwinter*, adding the connecting touch to begin a series.

It was the following week that I wandered into Kelly's Restaurant in Brevard, North Carolina (which spawned a whole book, *Church in the Wildwood*, and my move to Cedar Mountain, NC), and met Isaac Rogers, my "real-life" main character. Through the eyes of that child came the rest of the story that you'll read in the pages that follow.

And may you find your own shooting star.

John Letterle, blessings!

CR?

CHAPTER 1

No school tomorrow, the music teacher reasoned, looking out the front door of her cozy home on Union Street at the rare accumulation of snow and ice for Concord, North Carolina. *Good! I need the day to get some planning done for my new position.*

She looked up at the sky. *How similar this looks to the evening that we did the live nativity at the academy.* The woman reached her foot out to feel the ice that had formed on her sidewalk. *Thank goodness it wasn't this cold that night.*

Suddenly, she heard a tree limb breaking from the weight of the ice that had formed on it. Her eyes moved upward just in time to see the star streaking across the sky in all its radiant glory before it disappeared against the black sky.

I wish I may, I wish I might, she instinctively whispered, remembering the verse she had taught her students in a song recently. Then she made her own wish regarding her newly appointed role as Director of Outreach for the prestigious Tillman Academy, located on the rolling outskirts of town.

Thank goodness we're flying to Daytona. I'd hate to have to make the whole trek in this mess.

The driver of the car passed Lowe's Motor Speedway as he entered Concord. *Feels like home,* he noted as he looked up at the sky. *At least the clouds appear to have moved out. Should be a good flight. And if we're lucky, maybe the clear weather will hold out all week. We could certainly use some breaks this year.*

Suddenly, he saw the star take off across the sky. He laughed aloud as he wished that he could move that fast this season.

Fast as a streak of greased lightnin'! he thought, recalling one of the phrases from his childhood.

♪ ♪ ♪ ♪

Great! Just what I need. Another snow day tomorrow. At this rate, our tennis team will never be ready for the start of the season.

The physical education coach of Tillman Academy threw salt on his steps and sidewalk. *Maybe we should take up ice hockey at the school instead,* he chuckled sarcastically. *Or maybe I should move to sunny Florida. Then we could play tennis all year round.*

He looked up at the sky. *You know I'm not complaining, God. It's nothing more than my way of getting out my frustrations.*

The man, who was on his way toward a professional tennis career until an unfortunate knee injury, stepped out onto the ice and slid all the way down the sidewalk. *The kids would love doing this tomorrow. It'd mean I wouldn't have to come up with a lesson plan.*

Speaking of lesson plans, maybe I should plan to have a dinner date tomorrow night. I really enjoyed going out with a "certain someone" back at Christmas.

He took another glance at the sky to see if the clouds had passed. *Something good might come out of this snow day after all.*

As he started to slide back down the sidewalk toward his apartment, the coach caught a glimpse of something in the sky. The shooting star was almost gone before he noticed it, but he saw enough of its tail to make a wish – a wish that involved a change in his life during the next year.

A Song in the Air

♪ ♪ ♪ ♪

Holding tightly to her son's hand, the mother looked up at the clear night sky, the calm after the winter's storm. *Dear God, thank You for this precious child. Please help him to stay warm through this cold night. He's had so many colds and earaches lately. And be with the baby boy to whom he gave his only belonging, his blue blanket, so that infant, too, may stay well and be warm.* With her eyes still turned toward the heavens, she saw the white flash.

"Quick, son, make a wish! It's a shooting star!"

The boy swiftly thought of a wish as he looked up and watched the star take off across the night sky. Then he closed his eyes tightly. *Oh God, Momma would be so happy if You would let my wish come true.*

"Did you make your wish?"

"I sure did, Momma. I made a wish for you."

"You're such a sweetheart," she smiled, gazing into his huge blue-violet eyes – eyes that were the inspiration for his name. "I hope we're together for a very long time."

"We're going to be together forever, Momma. Forever!" the boy pealed with delight, his voice ringing in the cold blackness of the night as he shivered and moved up next to her.

She wrapped her shawl around his shoulders and held him close as they walked the familiar path. The child stretched both arms around her, making it possible for the mother to feel the kernels that had formed in his neck and under his arms.

"Watch out for the ice. It's slippery out tonight." His recent weight loss seemed to cause his steps to be a little slower. "We're almost home, son. Only a little bit farther."

"I can make it, Momma. Don't you worry about me. I'm a big boy, remember?"

"My baby, the big boy. Always taking care of his mother."

"I love you, Momma."

"I love you, too, son."

CHAPTER 2

Dale Jarrett was on his way to the Concord Regional Airport to meet his racing teammate. Rather than each driver taking his own plane, they had decided to go to the Daytona track together. That way, they could utilize the flight time to discuss all the changes for the new season and hopefully plan some strategies for the upcoming year. And by flying from Concord - home of Lowe's Motor Speedway - instead of Hickory, it provided a built-in excuse to get away from town and pick up Valentine presents for his wife and children, given the first "official" race this year fell on February 15th. *And the preliminary Bud Shoot-Out on the 7th left no time for shopping.*

He often wondered whose idea it was to make the NASCAR season begin right at that time of year. It had made it rough over his career to show his family how much he appreciated their support in his absence for approximately four-fifths of the weekends out of each year.

Dale was hoping the ice, remaining from the past couple of days' storms, wouldn't delay their flight to Daytona. There had been some significant changes in his car's body and engine, as well as a Goodyear tire change, and even though he had been to several of the tracks to test, getting ready for the first race of the season was crucial. Not only was this the season starter, it was the first race of the Nextel Cup Series. This was a most significant race, even though the legendary Daytona 500 fell on the following weekend.

His mind blocked out any of the details that involved work. There would be enough time for that once he reached the airport. Besides, the last two days' weather had taken a turn that was much worse than had been anticipated by the forecasters of the media.

Ah, the media. Can't live with them and can't live without them, he grinned, thinking how that statement was so similar to the age-old joke about women. The media had become a regular part of his life, which didn't really bother him. He, like his father, had gone about his everyday business in the same manner on-the-track as off-the-track.

Dale was looking forward to comparing a few notes with his teammate on the way down so that he could get a good night's rest before jumping straight into practices the next morning. They were both looking forward to an exciting season.

As usual, he had spent a lot of time in the off-season thinking through the next season, and working hard to stay in top athletic shape, a must in order to be a serious competitor. One look at his personal gym inside his corporate offices would attest to that.

He felt ready and rested for the new season, determined that he could handle anything the upcoming weeks threw into his path.

SCREECH! He heard the Jake brakes of the eighteen-wheeler in front of him and saw the trailer of the truck skidding from one side to another. Realizing there must be a patch of black ice on the road, he put all of his professional skills to use, avoiding the huge metal rig slinging from side to side directly in front of him.

Dale's car also began to slide once it hit the bridge, making it difficult to control the direction of the vehicle. His steady eyes stayed on the truck in front of him, one eye glued to that situation, while the other eye measured the distance between his car and the bridge embankment.

Ready for anything, huh? God, I need a little help down here. Then he saw the terror of the situation in front of him. Staring into the headlights of the rig was a woman. There was a child holding onto her, but just before the impact, he saw her give the child a shove, struggling to push him to safety.

He'd seen, and even been in, numerous accidents, but the professional racer couldn't bear to watch as he saw the wheels on the left side of the truck leave the pavement and began to jackknife onto its side.

The child fell right in front of Dale's path, causing him to swerve sharply as he tried to steer in another direction, knowing he was at the mercy of the ice and nature more than his own skills. And then he saw the cab of the truck fall, propped against the concrete wall of the bridge, its edge hanging over the child, ready to come crashing farther down with the slightest movement.

Dear God . . .

Dale's car came to a slow halt. Jerking the door open with one hand, he dialed 911 on his cell phone with the other. He turned on his flashers to alert the drivers behind him to slow down and that there had been an accident.

His years of growing up in a mountainous area came in handy as he tried to maneuver on foot through the ice and snow and make his way to the bridge to see if there were any survivors of the crash. He was afraid flames would burst from the truck at any minute, and he was determined to get its driver and the pedestrians out of more danger.

He could detect a car stopping behind him, and he could hear a voice as another man made his way to the scene. The ice had caused the truck to skid even more after it fell on its side and Dale feared the boy, as the mother, had been struck or penned against the bridge.

Dale's long legs enabled him to grab hold of the cab and pull himself up to see inside. He tried to open the door, but it was locked. One look inside the window told him there was little hope for the body slumped over the steering wheel.

Aware that the rescue vehicles would be on the scene within minutes, he searched for the woman who had looked like a scared deer blinded by the truck's headlights. His heart raced, for fear of what he would find when he checked the front of the cab that was lying penned against the railing of the overpass.

The sight was worse than what he had imagined. His

only hope was that the poor woman, who was not clothed warmly enough to be out battling this weather, died instantly.

He was afraid to even look at the child, terrified that he had met the same fate as the woman, whom he assumed was the child's mother.

The man from the other stopped vehicle followed Jarrett's steps, first looking into the truck, then at the woman. His cries of helplessness and panic were a continuous rambling of "Oh, my God! Oh, my God!"

He walked up behind Dale's tall and well-built frame and burst out, "Man, that was a pretty fancy piece of driving. About the only time I've seen driving that good was at . . ."

The racer turned to look at the man. His face became visible in the headlights of his car, which were facing the bridge and the truck's cab.

The cries into space were flying again. "Oh, my God! Oh, my God! You're . . . you're . . . you're . . . "

"Yes, I am. Do you have a flashlight?"

"You're one of NASCAR's greats!"

"Thank you. I'll grab the flashlight from *my* car."

Dale rushed to his vehicle and pulled an emergency light from under the seat, his every move being watched by the other man.

As the racer got down on his hands and knees with the flashlight, he caught a glimpse of the child. It appeared that the boy's jacket was the only thing penned by the corner of the cab. He scurried to reach underneath the part of the cab propped against the rail and tried to drag the child's body out from under it.

The man knelt down and gaped into the racer's face, his eyes still as big as saucers, not looking much different from those of the woman who had minutes earlier been staring into the truck's headlights.

"You're Dale Jarrett!"

"I know that. Now will you *please* help me pull this child out from under the truck's cab? It could still slip and fall right on top of him."

"Uh, uh . . . yes . . . of course."

The man, too, got down on his belly against the cold ground and tried to help Dale shift the child around to where they could pull him to safety.

Dale could see a tiny movement on the child's chest. That was all it took for his long arm to give enough of a pull to rip the child's jacket in two. He knew the dangers of moving the body, but he was more concerned about what could happen if he didn't move it. The experienced driver thought back to the afternoon his father pulled "Fireball" Roberts from a burning race car. He silently prayed that this rescue would not end the same way.

He gave the man with him instructions on how to carefully pull the boy out from under the leaning cab. The man had finally calmed down enough to be of some assistance. Dale removed his coat and used it for a gurney to pull the child out of the way of the truck should the vehicle slip and come crashing to the pavement.

Sirens were just beginning to blare in the distance. Cars had lined the emergency lane and drivers and passengers alike were rushing to see if they could help.

Dale skillfully felt for a pulse and listened to the child's chest.

The man who had helped Dale pull the child to safety was once again sputtering, this time to the people gathering around him. "He handled that like a pro. I mean, he *is* a pro. Well . . . you know what I mean."

Dale stood and went to shake hands with the man.

"Thank you for your assistance. Why don't you clear this crowd out of here so the emergency teams can get in now?"

"Yeah, yeah . . . that's a great idea." The man turned back to the crowd. "Okay, you heard the man. Let's get back into our cars and give the fire trucks and emergency vehicles some room to get in here." He still couldn't resist the urge to add, "That's Dale Jarrett, you know. He's a NASCAR driver. One of the best. He learned from his dad, he did. I used to watch his dad . . ."

CHAPTER 3

"Hello. May I please speak with Celia Brinkley?"

The woman did not recognize the voice on the other end of the line. "This is Celia."

"Miss Brinkley, my name is Dale Jarrett. I'm a,"

"Mr. Jarrett," she gasped, recognizing the voice that went with the name from the many commercials and interviews she had seen on television. "I know *exactly* who you are. Ever since our school's Christmas project for the Little family, and your most generous contribution, I've become NASCAR's, or should I say *your*, biggest fan."

A muffled grin came over the phone accompanied by a softly humbled "Thanks." He paused long enough to find the right words to speak to this stranger. "That's kind of why I'm calling. I understand that you're wonderful with children and that you're also now over the outreach program for Tillman Academy."

"Yes." There was a slight hesitation in her voice, with a curiosity of how and why he would care to have that information. She pulled a piece of her shoulder-length dark-brunette hair behind her ear, a habit of the music teacher's when something was amiss.

"There has been a horrendous accident on I-85 and I just happened to be driving behind the vehicle involved. A young boy was severely injured and his mother was killed. As far as authorities can tell, he's homeless and has no family. At the moment, they don't even have an identity for him. They had to rush him to NorthEast Medical Center in Concord. I've been with him, but I'm supposed to be meeting my teammate to fly to Daytona.

"I understand from one of the guys on my crew, whose children you teach, that you have a phenomenal way with kids. After all the effort you went to for that Little family at the school this past Christmas, and given your new position, I was hoping that maybe you would consider coming to the hospital and staying with this little guy until some arrangements can be made."

Celia's heart was already breaking for the child, and her admiration for this public figure was growing. "I'll be right there. Where exactly in the hospital are you?"

"Right now, we're still in the emergency room. It seems there are several injuries so he'll be in radiology for a while. The Department of Social Services has been contacted, and someone from that agency is on their way here, but I thought that you being here might be a little more personable."

"I agree. I should be there within twenty minutes, even with the icy conditions."

"There will probably be a slew of detectives and reporters in here soon, too."

"Thanks for the warning. I'll try to beat them."

Racing to get there first! Celia smirked, grabbing her coat from the front closet. *That's Jarrett's job.* She rushed out the door, not even taking time to change clothes or freshen her face. As the Director of Outreach's tall, slender body shivered in the cold, all she could think about was a child in need and how honored she felt to have been called to help.

On her way to NorthEast Medical Center – NEMC to the community – the woman's prayers were already being raised for this child. Celia was full of questions, all of which she hoped could be answered once she got to the emergency room. Luckily, she had recently attended an art show at the hospital - featuring work by Tillman Academy students - so she knew the quickest way to park and get into the medical facility.

A student's father, Dr. Patrick Marlowe, was on call and recognized the teacher as she came through the door.

"Miss Brinkley," he called. "Mr. Jarrett is waiting for you. I'll take you to meet him."

"Thanks," she acknowledged, following at a quick pace. "Do you know anything about what's going on?"

"Not much. This little guy, I'd say about five or six, was brought in by ambulance with multiple injuries as the result of an eighteen-wheeler running into the bridge where some of the homeless people of the area hang out. His mother, at least that's who we assume she was, was crushed between the truck and the bridge. She was apparently killed instantly. The boy managed to escape being penned completely by the truck, but was apparently knocked up against the concrete by the impact."

Celia stared at Dr. Marlowe, speechless.

"Seems the driver of the rig nodded off. Mr. Jarrett was behind him, and from what I understand, was able to skillfully keep from hitting the truck or the boy. He's stayed right by the child's side except for the few minutes that he took to call you, and that's while they took the boy back for x-rays."

They turned down a hall lined with small cubicles on each side.

"The child's unconscious. We think probably from shock and pain, but the pictures will give us more information."

Celia was most impressed by what she heard of the driver. "I've heard Mr. Jarrett is a fine family man. Now I believe it."

"Well, I can certainly attest to the fact that he's made quite a few more fans tonight, myself included," confessed Dr. Marlowe.

He stopped and pulled back the curtain in front of one of the cubicles. "Mr. Jarrett, this is Celia Brinkley. Now, if you two will excuse me, I have to get back to our young patient."

The racer extended his hand. "Thanks for getting here so quickly, Miss Brinkley."

She saw that he was as tall in person as he appeared on the television screen. His silver hair added to his look of distinction as she immediately noticed the reason that women raved about his eyes. They were filled with an expression of genuine sincerity that would make any female melt.

"I feel honored that you called me, Mr. Jarrrett. And please, call me Celia."

"Okay, Celia, and I'm Dale."

The teacher had been so busy seeing her role in regards to a needy child that she had not once thought of the man who phoned her, or that she was on her way to meet a celebrity. For the first time, it struck Celia as to the magnitude of the public figure shaking her hand. *Whoa! How many women wouldn't die to change places with me tonight?*

The minute the words raced through her mind, she was instantly sorry. For one woman had died this night and that was the very reason she was standing in this small cubicle with the celebrity.

She smiled at his personable and relaxed manner, one that set the tone for her to be the same. He motioned for her to walk with him to a private room down the hall.

"I apologize for calling you on such short notice."

CHAPTER 4

"Mr. Jarrett?"

The driver turned toward the door.

"My name is Stan Britten. I'm a detective with the Concord Police Department. Do you mind if I ask you a few questions?"

"Not at all. I'm on my way to Daytona, but I'm sure this won't take long."

"No, it won't." The officer glanced over at Celia. "Is she family?"

"No. But I felt like it might be nice for the boy to have someone here with him when he comes to rather than an officer guarding the door, and someone asking him a bunch of questions . . . if you don't mind me saying so."

"No, I don't mind at all. Knowing the kind of family man you are, I'd expect that from you. I have kids myself."

"Hello," came another voice, that of a woman, from the door. "Mind if I join you? The reporters are trying to get in the hospital now. I thought maybe we could take care of some initial steps in here before facing them."

Officer Britten nodded. "This is Norma Schell. She is the coordinator between the hospital and the Department of Social Services," he explained to Mr. Jarrett.

"I'm sure you recognize Dale Jarrett, the race car driver. And this is . . ." he said, glancing at Celia. "I'm sorry, I didn't catch your name."

Mrs. Schell recognized the woman as the academy's

Director of Outreach. They had met a few weeks earlier when Celia was organizing each grade's project.

"Celia Brinkley," the young woman introduced herself.

"We've met, I believe," Mrs. Schell interjected.

"Yes, when I first started my new position last month."

After several routine questions by Officer Britten, Mrs. Schell explained the procedure taken by the DSS in a situation of this nature. "If his relatives do not care to accept responsibility of temporary custody for the child, or we cannot locate any family members, he will be placed in the care of the court, which means he will live in a foster home."

"A foster home?" questioned the driver. "If there's no family and there's a person who is willing to see that the boy receives proper medical attention and a home, could they not be allowed to be his guardian?"

"That could happen," the woman answered, "but it would take months. And it's very unlikely. It would have to be with a person who already has a strong bond with the child, there would be checks on the person and the home, and a judge would have to sign an order for that to happen. In the state of North Carolina, we are extremely concerned with a child's welfare, so either foster home guardians or adoptive parents must go through our program of the Model Approach to Partnerships in Parenting, known as MAPP training, to ensure that they will be suitable parents."

Celia listened closely to the conversation. *Just another case to her,* she observed, realizing that the woman saw numerous cases of homeless and abused children daily and that she could not afford to become too connected. *Yet, it's like music,* she reasoned about parenting. *"True" musicians are born with that talent, that desire, that natural ability. I've never seen one yet that got it all from a book or a class. And my training as Director of Outreach didn't come from a step-by-step manual.* She pondered on the driver's words and his obvious concern. *There has to be another way.*

"The results of the x-rays and the MRI of the head are back." Dr. Marlowe entered the room, followed by another physician, and disrupted the discussion. "The radiological studies show a fractured leg that will require surgery and a concussion, however there is no significant brain injury. In addition to his trauma injuries, the child's exam in the emergency department found him to be underweight, his spleen and liver are somewhat enlarged, and there are multiple enlarged lymph nodes in his neck, armpits and groin. This raises the possibility of additional problems of a medical nature unrelated to this accident." He looked up from his notes to make sure his words were understood. "For that reason I have called in a pediatric consult, Dr. Ellis Teague, one of Concord's finest pediatricians."

Dr. Teague nodded to the people congregated in the room. "I've ordered some preliminary blood work necessary as pre-op lab and in addition, tests to try to define the cause of the enlarged nodes and other problems. Once that has been completed, the child will be prepped for surgery."

He looked at Officer Britten and Mrs. Schell, both of whom he apparently recognized. "You'd better get busy looking to see if this boy has any family. It would be a good thing if there's someone here to be with him besides hospital staff and the two of you."

Dale Jarrett reached over and squeezed Celia's hand. "Miss Brinkley has said that she will be willing to stay here in my stead while I'm in Daytona. I will do whatever I can to take care of this child until you have some answers." He paused as his face took on a tenderly solemn expression. "And longer, if necessary. Just make sure he gets the best care possible."

Dr. Teague extended his hand to the racer. "Thank you, Mr. Jarrett. I will personally see to that myself."

A nurse appeared at the door. "The press is lining up outside like crazy."

Jarrett looked at Dr. Teague. "Is there any way I can get out a back door to the Concord Airport? My teammate is waiting on me, as we speak, to fly to Daytona."

"Does he have a helicopter there?"

"Yes," answered the driver. "But we're taking his jet."

"Not from here." Dr. Teague turned to the nurse. "I am giving you strict orders to contact the helipad and tell them there will be a helicopter landing in a few minutes. Make sure it can get clearance. And nurse, you're not to mention this to anyone. Do you understand?"

She glanced at the racer. "Yes, I do. But can I have an autograph for my son?"

Mr. Jarrett grinned. "What's his name? I'll send him a signed picture."

She jotted a name on a piece of paper from her pocket, handed it to the driver and took off down the hall.

"You'd better call your teammate. He'll need to get his helicopter over here," smiled the doctor, enjoying his role in this plot.

Officer Britten spoke up. "I'll escort you to the helipad." He turned to the social services worker. "Mrs. Schell, why don't you go down with the hospital spokesperson in a few minutes and talk to the press?"

"Why do I always get all the fun jobs?" she retorted with a congenial smile.

"Look at it this way," answered the officer. "You can get a head start on finding out if the boy has any family. You'll get all sorts of publicity."

"Is there any way I could see the boy one last time before I leave?" Mr. Jarrett asked.

"Not a problem." Dr. Teague turned to Celia. "Perhaps you'd like to come along since you're going to be staying with him during his recovery."

She quickly fell in line behind the three men and listened to all the details regarding the accident and the boy's care. They turned into the surgical suite and wound their way down a long hallway until they darted into a small side room.

Celia gasped and fell backwards, catching herself against the wall.

All three of the men turned to look at her.

"Is anything wrong?" the doctor asked.

"I . . . I . . . I know . . . this child," she stammered.

Celia explained how she had met the child at the live

nativity the year before when he showed up with a woman. Now she wondered if the woman involved in the accident was the same woman, and if she was the boy's mother.

"It's quite possible that you may be our primary lead here, Miss Brinkley. I think it's a good thing that you'll be with him when he awakes," replied Officer Britten.

Dale Jarrett looked at Celia. "Do you have someone to come and stay here with you? It looks like it's going to be a long night."

"Yes, I do."

The driver gave the woman a hug. "Thank you again for coming to rescue me." He reached in his pocket and retrieved a card. "This is my private cell phone number. Please call me the minute you know anything and keep me posted on his recovery."

"Thank *you* for rescuing this child. And thank you for calling me. I'm deeply honored."

"This child is quite fortunate," he told her as he started toward the door.

"To have both of you," Dr. Teague added as he followed Officer Britten and Jarrett out the door, leaving Celia alone.

She found her way back to the nurses' station on the hall where she had been earlier. "May I borrow the phone and the phone book?"

"There's a public phone down in the," began the rehearsed response from one of the nurses.

"Here," offered the nurse who had asked for the autograph a few minutes earlier, as she handed Celia a phone book and reached the phone to her.

After finding the number she wanted, Celia dialed the phone. "Brad," she responded when she got an answer, "I have a favor to ask."

CHAPTER 5

"What's going on?"

Brad's wrinkled khaki shorts and navy-blue sweatshirt told her that he had rushed straight to the hospital when he got the call. His tousled brown hair looked like it had not been combed since before he left for his normal day of coaching at Tillman Academy.

"Do you remember that little boy who appeared with his mother at the nativity scene and gave Bobby Little his blue blanket?" she inquired.

"Yes. No one there could have forgotten that little guy. He was the hit of the evening."

"He was involved in an accident this evening with an eighteen-wheeler out on the interstate and has a broken leg and a concussion. He's in surgery right now."

"Dear God!" Brad gasped.

"It gets worse." Years of experience in working with people had not prepared her for the next four words. But they had taught her that saying them that first time would be the most difficult, for they would be packed with all the emotion of the tragedy. Her instincts told her just to spit them out as fast as she could. "His mother was killed."

Brad Sell's usual strong athletic build turned limp as his handsomely tanned face went white. Celia could tell that he was as devastated as she was. In fact, she was not sure that her body had suffered the full impact yet, having to act as the child's "unofficial" caretaker until other arrangements could be made.

"How . . . how did you find out? And what,"

Celia saw this man, the one whom only months earlier she had accused of being a dumb jock, struggling for words.

He took a deep sigh and tried again. "How did you get here? I mean, how did you find out? Did the hospital call you or something since you're the Director of Outreach?"

Suddenly, she felt like the tower of strength that she had called him to be for her. And then she realized that his presence and his questions were giving her an outlet to release her emotions. "Why don't we go and sit in the surgical waiting room and get some coffee or something?"

"Yeah, I agree we'd better sit for this. It sounds like the making of a long story."

♪ ♪ ♪ ♪

"Miss Brinkley?"

Celia and Brad both stood as Dr. Teague entered the waiting room for the pediatric surgical area. He acknowledged the man beside her.

"It isn't customary to discuss the case of a patient to someone who isn't family, but since you're the only person here who recognizes this child, and we have no clue as to whether there *is* a family, I feel I should share our findings with you."

"Yes, please do. And I'm to call Mr. Jarrett the minute I've heard something."

Brad looked at her sharply when he heard the racer's name come from her lips. It was like that was the switch that told him this was all real.

"The surgeries went fine. We feel that given his young age, the fracture will begin healing immediately and that he'll be up and about in no time."

"Thank God!"

"However, during the pre-op preparation, we found

an abnormality in the blood count. We've discovered that the boy has borderline anemia and leukopenia." Dr. Teague caught the look of confusion on the couple's face. "That's a low white count."

They both nodded.

"Mainly what it does is alert us that something else is going on."

"Something serious?" Celia asked.

"It's too early to tell. For now, we've had to correct the immediate injuries. The surgeon and I both feel that the child needs to rest this evening. But given his social background, I'll order more blood work tomorrow morning. I feel it's best to stay on top of this."

"Will he be able to eat?"

"Yes, absolutely. That will probably be the best thing for him. In fact, you can find out his room number and go there now. They'll bring him up as soon as he comes out of recovery. At that time, they should give him something light to eat."

"It will no doubt be the best meal the child's had in a while," Celia uttered.

"I hate to agree, but I fear you're right," replied Dr. Teague. "Due to the situation, I've ordered sedatives to help him rest once they've gotten something in him. He should sleep uninterrupted well into the morning."

It suddenly dawned on her that she had not introduced the man in the room with her. "Doctor, this is Brad Sells. He's the PE teacher at Tillman Academy. He saw this boy and his mother back in December at the school, too."

"Ellis Teague," the pediatrician said, holding out his hand. "Will you be helping Miss Brinkley watch the boy while he's here?"

This question had not come up during their earlier discussion in the waiting room, but Brad quickly answered, "Yes. I'll stay with her, or let her go home and I'll stay." Brad placed his arm around Celia's shoulder. "But we'll make sure the child has someone here, if only to be a friendly face."

"Young man, I think that, along with a good night's

sleep and some food, is the best thing for that little guy right now. I hope the woman with him was not his mother, but that is extremely likely. In any case, it's going to be the responsibility of someone to tell him that she was killed when he's cohesive enough to understand."

The doctor's confident expression disappeared. "And that's not going to be easy on anyone."

Celia felt like a ton of bricks came crashing down on the bottom of her stomach.

CHAPTER 6

"Third floor. We're here," announced Brad.

The elevator doors opened to bright-green walls with the words "Welcome to Pediatrics" greeting the visitors. Painted frogs dotted the walls adding a vibrant touch of life.

Celia and Brad stepped out and looked around them at the menagerie of color.

"Boy, they sure didn't make them like this when I had my tonsils taken out!" he blurted.

"Mine, either."

"Big Frog Mountain," he read. "That would explain all the frogs."

"Pediatrics to the left, Pediatric Intensive Care Unit to the right," Celia noted. "Why don't we take a walk through the halls before we go to his room? I'm sure we've still got a while to wait."

"Sounds like a winner to me. This place looks like tons of fun. Can you imagine what it looks like to a child?"

Celia laughed. "What *does* it look like?" she asked, enjoying the childlike energy of Brad's perception.

"Very funny. I can't help it if I'm still a child at heart."

"So that's why you play games with the children all day? I knew there was a reason for the PE coach not being a dumb jock."

"Okay, I didn't come here to be ridiculed all evening," he jeered.

"I know. I was simply getting even for last December.

Sorry. I really *do* appreciate you coming here to be with me."

Brad stood looking at Celia. "Hey, there's a child at stake here. And you're a fellow teacher at the . . . well, maybe not a *fellow* teacher, but a co-worker. We have a responsibility to stand by each other."

"Thanks. I appreciate your devout dedication to your job." There was a hint of disappointment in her voice.

"Besides, I had a great time helping you at Christmas with the live nativity and the project to help the Little's. And we haven't seen much of each other since then with your new job. I was glad for the chance to spend a little time with you."

They began to walk toward the pediatric unit.

"So how is the new job going?" Brad asked, neglecting to inform Celia that he had already planned to ask her to dinner the following evening.

"Great. I love coordinating all the classes with the various outreach facilities. It seems that the children are having as much fun with all the projects as I am. And it hasn't taken me away from my art. I still use music in each of the projects with the students."

"After watching you at Christmas, I knew that was the job for you." Brad took Celia's hand and stopped her. "But I have missed seeing you. I really *am* glad you called me." The usual playfulness disappeared from his eyes and in its place lingered a deep sincerity that she had not seen since the evening they had dinner and he shared his past with her.

"Oh, look at all the caterpillars on the wall." Celia was ready to change back to the playful mood.

"Caterpillar Court."

They walked to another corridor, taking in all the pictures of playful creatures on the walls.

"Dragonfly Drive," Brad said, rounding the corner.

"And Pediatric Park," Celia read, looking ahead.

"They sure try to keep it lively up here for the kids. This is really neat."

"But can you imagine what it will seem like to a child who's lived outdoors?"

He sighed. "I'm afraid it might seem pretty fake given

his background. After all, this little guy's been out with the real frogs, caterpillars and dragonflies."

"That sounds like a guy thing to me. Seriously, don't you think this will seem like a wonderland to him?"

Brad turned to look directly into Celia's eyes. "Celi," he said in a serious tone, using the name he had called her back at Christmas, "you're forgetting one thing. When that child is alert and out of danger, someone is going to have to tell him what happened to his mother."

Her head fell. "If that's who she really was."

"We both know the odds for that are pretty good."

Celia raised her head and stared back into Brad's eyes. "Who do you think will have to tell him?"

"I don't know, but we are both going to be here for him when that happens."

She fell into Brad's arms, exhausted from concern and emotion. "Thank you for being here. Mr. Jarrett was right. I did need someone with me."

Brad gently lifted her chin so that she could see his eyes again. "And I'm glad that someone is me." He allowed her a good cry before suggesting they find the child's room.

♪ ♪ ♪ ♪

"Thanks for the call. Please keep me posted on his progress. Is there anything I can do for you while you're there? And did you get someone to come and be with you?"

Celia could hear the driver's heartfelt concern for the boy through the phone.

"No, I'm fine and I did get someone to come here with me during the surgery. I'm going to try to catch some sleep while the little guy's sedated. I just wish I knew his name instead of feeling like he's 'that child.'"

"I know. But hopefully, when he comes around, he can give you and the doctor some answers. Call me the minute that happens so I can see he's taken care of. I don't want him lacking for anything he might need. And I'll have some bright balloons sent to his room in the morning."

"Mr. Jarrett, thank you. Thank you for being there, and thank you for everything. You are a true hero."

"No, but I am glad I was there right at that moment. I don't think it was a coincidence."

"Me, either."

"I'm used to people running into the wall, but nothing ever prepares you for something like that. Hopefully, my ability for thinking fast in the car helped. I just wish I could have done something . . . *anything* to help his mother."

Celia could detect the sorrow in his voice.

"And please," he continued, "call me back the minute you find out if that was for sure his mother, and let me know how it goes when he's told about last night."

"I will."

"Thank you, Miss Brinkley, for helping out with this little guy. I know you're not there for a reward, but I will make sure you don't go without during all this."

"I appreciate that, but I'm fine. Like you, I'm sure my being here is not by coincidence. And remember," she added, "the name's Celia."

The driver chuckled. "Yes, ma'am. Talk to you later."

"Yes, sir."

Celia hung up the phone feeling like she were in some dream and she was going to wake up to find that none of this had happened. But as she turned and walked back down the corridor and touched the dragonflies on the wall, it was like pinching her arm. She knew this was the "real thing."

She wanted so desperately to question God, to be mad at the truck driver or somebody. But the way she saw it, it was all an unfortunate situation . . . *for everyone.*

♪ ♪ ♪ ♪

"It feels curiously odd talking so personally to a man that women all over the world drool over."

"Why, thank you! I'm glad you think so highly of me,"

Brad said, taking a bow.

Celia looked at him and realized how her comment must have sounded.

"Oh! I'm sorry if I offended you. It's just . . . he's . . . well, you know."

"I do know. Dale Jarrett doesn't fit your role model of a dumb jock any more than I do. He and I really *do* have a lot in common," he joked.

"That's probably the most accurate thing you've said all evening," she stated, turning his humor into seriousness. "You and Mr. Jarrett both have an interest in this child that you know nothing about. You don't even know his name."

"But we both know that he needs someone," came Brad's reply.

Celia went over and kissed Brad's cheek. "I do feel honored to know *both* of you, and I'm really glad that the three of us are in this together."

"A peace offering, huh?" he grinned.

She looked at him, appreciative of his teaching and psychological skills at the moment. Celia knew that Brad was doing his part to lightly take the edge off a highly emotional situation, and still be the source of strength that she needed.

"You're doing a good job, you know. You're a fine person and the students and Tillman Academy are extremely fortunate to have you."

"I'm just like you, Celi. It's not about the money. It's the love and enjoyment of what we do, not to mention the reward of working with the people."

Aware that they had reached a common ground again, one that had been slightly unearthed back in December, Celia basked in the comfort that came with this friendship.

"It's getting late and you look tired. Why don't you go home and get some sleep?" Brad suggested.

"No, you go and get some sleep. Even though school will be out, it'll still be a teacher's workday tomorrow. I'm going to take the day off and I can sleep fine right here. This recliner is as comfortable as my bed. Besides, it's your job to go in and tell Dr. Lacey about this in the morning and inform him that I may be out a few days. Once I know what's going on here, I'll get in touch with him myself."

His heart told him that he didn't want to leave Celia alone with the child in this situation, but his head told him she was right. She was going to need him worse later and the look on her face told him they both knew it.

Brad looked at the child who was still heavily sedated. "I guess you're right. But if you need anything, I can be here in less than fifteen minutes." He took Celia's hand. "God put you here, Celi. I can feel it."

She nodded, a tear surfacing. "I've sensed that, too."

He gave her a big hug. "Don't forget that if He put you here, He's here with you."

"I know that, but thanks for reminding me."

"I'll come back first thing in the morning to check on you. Both of you," he added, walking out the door.

CHAPTER 7

"Knock-knock." A lab technician strolled into the room as quickly and sprightly as if she had been on roller skates at the Sonic Burger.

Celia was the only one who opened her eyes.

"I'm here to do the daily bloodwork."

"I think they're supposed to be running some tests on him later today," managed Celia, repositioning herself in the recliner. "Will he have to go through this twice?"

"This will check to see if there are any changes from the time he was admitted. It will give the doctor a more in-depth look at what's going on." She gave an encouraging smile to Celia. "*If* there's anything going on." The technician pricked the child's finger. "Are you his mother?"

"No." The overnight caretaker stalled. "I, uh,"

"Good morning!" A middle-aged African-American woman walked into the room, bringing a wave of relief and cheerfulness with her.

I've heard that the hospitals wake you up to ask if you're sleeping and then give you sleeping pills, but this is ridiculous. Celia glanced at the clock on the wall. *Five o'clock?*

"What are you doing here so early, Cookie? I didn't think you got here until seven."

"I woke up this morning and couldn't sleep."

She's the one who needs the sleeping pill! I was sleeping just fine.

"Turned on the news and heard about this little guy. Thought maybe he might need a little Cookie this morning."

The woman, whose eyes were as large and full of sparkle as the child's who lay asleep, beamed at Celia. "From the sound of things, it appears I got here right on time."

Celia was amazed that this care partner had wandered in on the question about the child's mother and acted like she knew exactly when to make her grand entrance.

"Why don't you go on to your next victim?" Cookie suggested to the technician. "I'll catch up with you in a minute. I've got some business to take care of here first."

Finishing up with the boy, the lab technician packed up her carrier and exited as Celia watched, now fully awake and wondering about the "angel" who had jubilantly floated into the room.

The care partner pulled up a chair and sat down right beside the recliner. "My name is Cookie. I've worked here as a nurse's assistant for thirty-five years. My job is to do whatever needs to be done at any particular moment with a patient, whether that means taking vital signs, bathing and cleaning them, or changing their underclothes, socks or hospital shirts."

She looked straight at Celia. "And honey, after what I saw on that news this morning, I knew this is where I was needed."

"I guess they told the whole story, huh?"

"You haven't seen it?"

"No, I was so concerned with the child and the situation that I didn't even think to watch the TV."

"It's just as well. You know how the media can be. They were determined they were going to have a story here. I think it's really cool how that driver, Jarrett, got in and out of here without the press catching him. They were all after him bad. Huh!" she grunted. "I'll bet they're all over him at Daytona once this word gets out."

Celia pursed her lips and looked at the child. "What I hope they'll do is ask for prayers for this child and make a plea to find his family."

"Do you think the woman with him was his mother?"

"I think so." She gave a shiver under the blanket. "Like

everyone else, I have tons of questions that will probably go forever unanswered, but I did see him back in December with the woman Mr. Jarrett described. If she wasn't his mother, she was probably his guardian."

"He'll be awake later this morning. There's a good possibility that we can get enough answers then to get the ball rolling here and find someone to take this guy."

"Cookie, I take it you're a believer?"

"What?"

"I take it you believe there's a God."

"Honey, I've seen Him at work too many times in this place *not* to."

"Good. Then will you pray with me that I will be allowed to be this child's temporary guardian until they find out about his family?"

Cookie stared at the woman. It appeared the nurse's assistant had already formed her opinion of this situation during their short talk together. "Let me tell you this much. I think that same God who woke me up and told me to turn on the news is the same one who put you here. Now go on back to sleep for a couple more hours and I'll come back and check on you. This little guy's my Number One priority today, so if he, *or* you, needs anything, you push that buzzer. I'll be listening for you."

"Thank you, Cookie. You were just the medicine I needed this morning." *Better than a sleeping pill to make me go back to sleep.*

CHAPTER 8

"Thank you for talking with us, Miss Brinkley. I do appreciate your concern and eagerness to help the child, but as I discussed with you last night, I'm sure you understand that the Department of Social Services has to be sure the child receives proper care. It would take months to get you through the entire legal process of qualifying as a foster parent."

"Would it help if I told you that I've gone through the preliminary classes for MAPP?"

Mrs. Schell, surprised by the question, glanced at the detective then back to Celia. "You're familiar with our MAPP process?"

"Yes. While I was in college, I took a double major, one being sociology, and became interested in being a foster parent should I ever get married. I looked into the classes and began the process, but when my teaching career started and I stayed single, I decided that must not be my calling."

"I'd think that between Dale Jarrett and this woman with her credentials with children, you'd be hard pressed to find better temporary guardians," Officer Britten interjected.

"You know the rules as well as I do. We have to treat everyone the same and they all have to go through the same process."

Bureaucratic red tape! Celia wanted to scream, but knew better. "I would do whatever it takes to care for this child . . . even if it means taking a leave of absence from my job."

"You could afford to do that?" the social worker asked, raising her eyebrows.

"If I had to."

Celia sat in the room where Mrs. Schell normally interrogated abused children as a part of the hospital's Children's Advocacy Program. It was a special unit with a two-way mirror that usually had a policemen and a specially-trained social worker sitting on the other side. The cozy "conference" room was equipped with a basket of markers, Play-Doh and dollhouse furniture. It was carpeted in a pattern of little houses, sailboats and stick people and furnished with a comfortable purple-covered love seat for the adults.

She knew, for the moment though, her place on the love seat had turned into the proverbial "hot seat" as Mrs. Schell sat in a chair on the opposite wall sizing her up. Suddenly, Celia was glad for the breakfast biscuit Brad had brought her. *I'm not sure I could have handled this on an empty stomach.*

"I need to make a stop by that bridge and try to catch a couple of people who will talk to me about the boy and the deceased woman. I'm going to have to investigate to see if there's a father." Officer Britten picked up his overcoat and headed for the door.

"I think I'll go with you," offered Mrs. Schell. "You know how those folks are. If they see too many different 'official' vehicles, or get too many callers, they'll clam up. And then we won't get anything."

"Right," agreed the policeman. "We both know they're not supposed to congregate under that bridge, but they're causing no problems down there. Or at least they weren't until now."

"Officer Britten," interrupted Celia. "I don't mean to be disrespectful, but it seems to me they didn't cause this, either. That truck driver could have nodded off anywhere on the interstate. Had it not been that this couple happened to be there right at that moment, he could have struck another car or plowed into the countryside. If it had not been for Mr. Jarrett's skills, the trucker could have even hit him. I think it's a little unfair to blame this on the homeless."

She took a breath to see if her comment had aroused

anger. Seeing none, she continued, "It seems to me that those homeless people could be on the streets, in front of shops and on benches like in many downtown areas. Sure, you'd be running them off all the time, but they'd find a way to get back. At least these people are trying to stay warm in an out-of-the-way area and not causing harm to the public." Biting her lip before concluding, she gathered the stamina to make a final statement. "If you ask me, this child and his mother have done a lot for the town of Concord. Are you familiar with the project, the live nativity, that Tillman Academy did for the Little family this past Christmas?"

"Oh, I remember that," chimed Mrs. Schell, her professional curtness giving way to a slight hint of emotion. "Don't tell me that little fellow and his mother was the couple that appeared in all the nearby newspapers and on the TV stations."

"That would be them. They appeared from nowhere, having walked to the school, and this boy gave his blanket to baby Bobby. He taught my students more about love and giving than I ever could have."

"I remember reading that story. In fact, I cut it out and saved it, thinking how touching it was." Mrs. Schell's look of remorse turned into a faint smile. "That's the kind of stuff you like to come across in my profession. And believe me, those examples are few and far between."

"Now I know what you're talking about," joined Officer Britten. "Some of the off-duty officers went to the school and helped direct traffic that night. And I remember making a donation when the notice about the Little's came through the office. My dad went to school with Donnie's dad. He said they were fine people and he wished he could tell the teacher who planned all that what a wonderful gesture it was for one of the county's oldest families."

"You're talking to her. You can relay that message for your dad personally." Mrs. Schell had thought back to the story and remembered that the teacher was the school's musician. Her face showed that her respect for the woman on the "hot seat" had just increased a couple of notches.

"Is that right?" the policeman asked the teacher in a

casual, non-businesslike tone.

"Yes, it is," admitted Celia. "That's how Mr. Jarrett remembered me, too. He, his crew and his car dealership gave a car to the Little's. When the accident happened, he called his crew chief to get my name. You see, I taught the children of the crew chief. The driver knew from the story that I loved children, so he took the initiative to see if I might help with *this* 'project,' also."

She took the nodding heads of her listeners as an invitation to the next question. "Do you mind if I go with you to that bridge? I'd really like to get a feel of the boy's home and friends for myself. And Dr. Teague said that the child will be in tests until sometime after lunch."

"Normally, we aren't allowed to take outsiders with us on interrogations," stated Officer Britten.

"But since you've shown such an interest in caring for the child, I think this might be permissible. It would definitely give you an insight into his prior environment." Mrs. Schell glanced at the policeman in hopes that her words were persuasive enough to allow this extra passenger.

Officer Britten paused only briefly. "I think that under the circumstances it would be alright. It appears to me that you've earned this privilege, both with taking it upon yourself to help the Little's last Christmas, and now with offering this boy a temporary home. Besides, we may need you to give us a positive identity on the woman. You know, whether or not she's the one who was with the kid in December."

"I'll get my coat." Celia ducked by the nurses' station to let them know she would be gone for a while. "Please call me if you need me."

Cookie passed by the desk. "I've got it all under control. You go and take care of what you need to with Britten and Schell."

"But how did you know . . .?"

"Cookie knows everything. We all think she's got some kind of built-in radar," laughed one of the nurses.

"When it comes to her patients, she really *does* seem to know everything," agreed one of the other nurses.

Cookie winked at Celia. "I'll never tell all my secrets."

Celia ran to the child's room and grabbed her coat. As she rushed back down the hallway to the conference room to meet Officer Britten and Mrs. Schell, a prayer came from nowhere. *Dear God, I know all children need a parent, but please, if this boy's father is a bad person, don't let us find him. This child's surrounded by persons that love and care about him now.* She didn't even bother to conclude with an "Amen" as she threw on her coat.

CHAPTER 9

"Yeah, I knowed 'em. They'd lived 'ere nigh on six years. Ever since shortly after she 'ad 'at baby," stated one of the homeless men, proud that he'd been chosen for information. *I must'a looked like th' smart one in th' bunch,* he reasoned to himself.

"She'uz crazy, 'at one. Al'ays goin' on 'bout what a big mansion she'uz gonna live in someday. I al'ays did think it wuz cruel fer her t' be promisin' 'at boy stuff like 'at. Huh! Any fool'd a'knowed it wadn't ever gonna happen. Why, look at what kind'a mansion she done gone an' got herself now!"

What a mansion she did gone and got herself now, Celia wanted to cry aloud.

"An' 'at boy, Isaac."

Ah, we now have a name, Celia told herself as she watched both Officer Britten and Mrs. Schell start taking notes.

"She raised 'im t' be just as crazy as she wuz. All 'at boy ever 'ad t' 'is name wuz some ol' blanket 'e got frum th' Salvation Army when 'e'uz a baby. Carried it ever'whur 'e went. Full'a 'oles an' nasty frum 'im a-layin' on it. An' 'en back at Christmas, when it wuz freezin' col', 'e done went an' give it t' some poor fam'ly fer thur baby.

"Say, ya ain't got no cigarette, do ya?" the man asked Officer Britten.

"King of the Road," Celia sang in her mind.

The policemen reached into his pocket and handed the guy a cigarette, then pulled a lighter from his pocket to give the homeless man his nicotine fix.

"Why, I ain't never see'd anybody any poorer 'an 'at boy wuz. An' 'en 'e give away th' only thing 'e 'ad!"

He looked at Celia, who up until this point had gone unnoticed by him. "Wouldn't ya call 'at crazy?"

His gaze turned to Mrs. Schell. "It's a wonder th' youngun' didn't freeze t' death after 'at. Prob'ly's just as well he'll be in th' nice, warm 'ospital now."

The homeless man threw the cigarette butt on the ground, not bothering to extinguish it.

Officer Britten stomped it out with his foot. "Ever hear anything about his daddy?"

"Maureen didn't never talk 'bout 'im, but one'a th' other fellas 'at use' t' come 'roun' said 'e knowed 'im."

Maureen? Good, now we have a mother's name, too, Celia deduced from the witness.

"Said 'e died frum AIDS, but I never b'lieved it."

Celia's heart sank. *Is that why the blood work showed something else?* Suddenly, there was a sickening feeling in the pit of her stomach. She wanted this interview to hurry up and be over so that she could hear the test results. The next words gravitated over her head as she struggled to listen to this man.

"Said 'e 'ad a bad needle 'abit, but 'at wuzn't 'at woman's type. She might'a been crazy, but she just didn't 'ave 'at in 'er. 'Sides, 'at woman didn't seem t' be sick a day in 'er life. Her nor 'at boy. They'uz al'ays walkin' 'roun' like 'ey 'ad some reason t' be 'appy they'uz poor an' 'ungry. An' Isaac, 'e'uz gettin' punier an' punier ever'day. Starvin' t' death, I reckon."

Mrs. Schell glanced at Officer Britten, then at Celia. No one said a word nor changed their blank expressions, but they knew this man had just unknowingly answered their one big question.

This time it was the woman from social services who asked the question. "Do you know if they had any family?"

"Got any more cigarettes?" asked the man.

Again, the officer reached in his pocket, mimicking the same actions as before.

I wonder if those are for him or all the people he interrogates? Celia questioned. *At this rate, it would be one big tax write-off.*

"Same dude tol' me 'bout 'is daddy said somethin' 'bout Maureen 'avin' gone t' college. Never b'lieved 'at, either. Huh! Who knows whether 'er real name wuz Fuller? Mos' people 'ere calls 'emselves somethin' diff'rent."

"Did the guy happen to mention the college?"

"Called its name once er twice. I think it wuz one o' 'em Yankee schools. Started with a P er somethin'."

"Here," Officer Britten said, handing the rest of the pack of cigarettes to the man.

"Thanks, pal," he yelled. "Come back anytime."

♪ ♪ ♪ ♪

"So what do you think?" Mrs. Schell asked Officer Britten.

"If the guy was right, she could have been carrying the HIV virus and passed it on to the kid unknowingly. Happens all the time in these kinds of conditions."

"Exactly what I thought. She could have never known anything about it if she had no contact with the child's father and she wasn't affected herself."

Celia listened from the back seat of the patrol car. All she could think about was how horrible this would have been for Isaac's mother had she known.

"Do you think she even suspected the child was sick?" wondered Officer Britten aloud.

The music teacher piped up from the back seat. "I can answer that. I watched that child and his mother at the live nativity with the Little's. I can't believe she would have allowed him to give his blanket away to the baby of that poverty-stricken family had she known. From the impact they made on the crowd at the nativity, it was like he was an angel specifically sent to relay God's message of unconditional love."

"I agree, from all indications of what I've seen and

heard," voiced the social worker.

"That makes three of us. Now what about the family?" conferred Officer Britten.

"If she gave that boy as much attention as it appears and taught him the things about life that she did, I'd say there either *is* no family, or she got absolutely no support," offered Mrs. Schell.

"In which case it would be disastrous for the child. Probably another episode where the parents disowned their perfect little daughter because she was pregnant by someone of whom they didn't approve."

How familiar that sounds, mused Celia, thinking of her father and her older sister, Beth. *Should I mention that now?* she wondered, knowing how hard she was working to see that situation resolved. Then she recalled how long she had carried that burden of not being wanted herself, and then watching Beth's rejection from their father once he learned she wasn't "his perfect darling." *Forget it*, she decided, not wanting this child to share in that fate.

"And how many colleges and universities begin with a 'P?'" inquired Mrs. Schell.

"I'll do the routine search for 'Fuller' to see if there are any cases of missing young women," reported the officer.

"Isn't it odd that we have all the faces on milk cartons with people wanting to find those who don't care to be found, and here we are trying to locate a missing family who probably never cared?" asked the social worker. The question sounded more like her subconscious speaking, rather than her seeking an answer.

♪ ♪ ♪ ♪

"Mrs. Schell, if there's *any* way possible, I would definitely like to be the temporary guardian for Isaac," Celia voiced, glad to know a name for him. "And I know that Dale Jarrett will do whatever necessary to make sure the child receives proper care. He's already told me as much."

"I know you think you'd like to have him now, but what about when he's ill or there are problems? And most importantly, what do you know about parenting, given you didn't complete the MAPP training?"

The music teacher prodded forward, speaking her heart. "I don't intend to ever have children of my own, but I love children and would like to give a child a home with someone who actually 'wants' him or her." She paused. "I was an unwanted child . . . at least by my father," Celia confessed. "I know that pain."

Mrs. Schell and Officer Britten looked at each other.

"I realize it may be difficult for me to qualify for a guardian since I'm single, but my mother raised me to know that at least one parent loved me. The way I see it, one loving person is better than two who don't really care all that much."

Celia lowered her head and missed the look that the officer gave the social worker. She felt the hurt of being an unwanted child come back to her, and prayed that young Isaac would not have to endure the same pain.

♪ ♪ ♪ ♪

Officer Britten pulled into the back entrance of the hospital parking lot. "Miss Brinkley, would it be too difficult for you to go to the morgue with us? I feel that you can give us an identity of whether the woman killed in the accident is the same one who was with Isaac in December."

Celia knew there were a million other things she would rather be doing right now, but she also knew that she needed to do this. She had to be sure for herself. "I'll go," she agreed hesitantly.

The threesome was allowed access to the locked morgue and led to the woman's body. Officer Britten pulled the body out for Celia to identify. Without saying a word, her expression told the police detective all he needed to know.

She stared at the floor for a brief moment before making a statement. "Although I've never had a child of my own,

I recognize this face as the face of a mother. Even without the testimony of the homeless man, I'd know this was Isaac's mother. And yes, she is the woman who was with him at the academy in December." Celia turned away and took several deep breaths. "This is . . . 'Maureen.'"

Officer Britten was sincerely moved by the teacher's sympathetic intuition. "Thank you for doing this. It was a big help with our case."

He led Celia and Mrs. Schell from the morgue and back toward the hospital's entrance. "I'll see you two later, I'm sure. I've got some looking to do for Ms. Fuller's family." He pursed his lips. "If that indeed *is* her name."

"Could you please let me know what you find out?" questioned Celia.

"Normally, you'd see it in the papers like everyone else." He looked at Mrs. Schell, again his thoughts coming across loud and clear. "But this is not your normal case."

"Oh, thank you," she said, her anxiousness showing.

"I'll try to keep you abreast as much as possible, too," offered Mrs. Schell.

"I can't thank either of you enough for letting me go with you today. I'm glad I had that experience. It helps me to see things from Isaac's perspective much more clearly."

The policemen turned to Mrs. Schell. "Any more questions?" he asked, hoping she caught his drift.

"No, I think that about covers everything. I think I'll walk upstairs with Miss Brinkley to see how Isaac is for a second before I go and fill out my report."

And see how Isaac responds to Ms. Brinkley is more like it, he figured. "You know, maybe I'd better go and check on the boy myself." *I'd like to see the two of them together for my own report.*

CHAPTER 10

Celia peeked in the door to see Cookie taking Isaac's vital signs. *How good it feels to know a name rather than "and here we have John Doe."*

"He's just beginning to come around," the nurse's assistant informed her. "Why don't you come on over here so he can see you when he wakes up?"

The teacher, followed by the social worker and detective, moved closer to the child, praying for the right words to say, with an anxiousness clouding around her as she wondered what his first words would be. *Will he ask about his mother? Does he even remember about last night?*

"Good timing, Dr. Teague," Cookie welcomed.

Celia turned to see the pediatrician acknowledge Mrs. Schell and Officer Britten. Then he walked over to the bed and looked at the child.

Isaac opened his eyes, slowly at first, falling back and forth between the last traces of sedation.

Dr. Teague stood quietly until the child fully opened his eyes and looked up.

Celia saw immediately that those eyes – the same giant blue-violet ones that she remembered from December – sparkled as the child's face grew into a huge smile to match. He didn't appear at all frightened, either by the room full of strangers or the unfamiliar cast and tubes. *It's still the effect of the sedation, I'm sure.*

"Hello," greeted the doctor. "I'm Dr. Ellis Teague. How are you feeling this morning?"

The boy's smile never wavered. "I'm Isaac. I feel fine."
Good! No questions yet, she joyfully sighed. *And Isaac is his real name.* Celia loved the energy that was already a part of the atmosphere now that the child was awake. And she could sense from the doctor's mannerisms with the child why he was a successful pediatrician.

"Isaac, it's nice to meet you. I'd like to introduce you to a few people." Dr. Teague motioned for Celia to move closer.

"Hi, Isaac. My name is Celia Brinkley. I teach children that are your age. I love children." The teacher could feel the magnetism of his eyes as she caught herself being drawn to him already. She wanted to add that she remembered seeing him at the live nativity, but she found herself at a loss for more words.

With a voice that was weakened by the surgery and medications, not to mention the trauma, the child spoke. "I know who you are. You're the only person who has ever kissed me besides my momma."

The teacher felt her mouth open, but not from words.

"I saw you with all the children at the school where I took my blanket. You were beautiful and the boys and girls sang so pretty. Momma said they sounded like angels."

Did she also tell you that you were the star of the evening? Did she tell you that you were plastered on all the newspapers and TV stations? Did she tell you that you were the angel of the nativity? Celia stopped her rambling. *How do we tell him about Momma?*

Officer Britten nudged Mrs. Schell. "Sounds close enough to an aunt for me. You'd better get to work on that kinship placement if you want to do the best thing for this boy."

As badly as Mrs. Schell didn't want to agree with him, she, too, saw the bond that was already present between the child and Miss Brinkley.

"That's the way, boy!" cheered Cookie silently.

Dr. Teague knew that the dreaded time had come. He felt that the responsibility of breaking the news of the accident fell on his shoulders, so he took the child's hand that was free of tubes.

"Isaac, do you remember anything about coming here last night?"

"Yes."

All eyes were on the child as every person in the room anxiously awaited any information he could give them – each one for a varied need.

"A big truck came sliding toward Momma and me. It hit Momma, but she pushed me away. I fell asleep, but I did see a bus bring me here. It had bright lights."

"Son, I need to tell you about your mother. Something happened last night. Something,"

"I know!" Isaac interrupted. "Momma went to live with Jesus. I saw him take her to heaven." The child smiled at everyone as if he had just proclaimed the greatest news on earth.

Not a word was spoken by anyone as eyes darted back and forth from one person to another.

Maybe he had a dream, Celia tried to explain to herself.

Well, that certainly took a major burden off the old doc, sighed the policeman.

What a case! How am I ever going to write this one up? wondered Mrs. Schell.

The nursing assistant exited the room, having heard enough. *I see I'm not the only smart Cookie on this floor,* she beamed.

"How about something to eat?" inquired the physician.

It was obvious that he, as well as the others, needed to go and regroup before making any kind of recommendation or conclusion on this case.

"We'll leave you for a few minutes and someone will be back to stay with you shortly."

"I hope it's Celia. She's a nice lady. Momma said so."

Dr. Teague led the group down the hallway to the Children's Advocacy Room and took his place on Celia's earlier "hot seat." "I'd say that about wraps this up. We know the child's real name, he knows his mother is dead, and he recognizes the one person who wants to care for him."

"You know we can't stop here," Mrs. Schell complained. "How am I to tell my supervisor that he thinks that angels and Jesus took his "Momma" to heaven?"

"You tell her that there are phenomena that none of us understand," dictated the doctor. "Surely in this profession, she's run across them before." He turned to face the social worker. "And you can also tell her that we were all very blessed that we didn't have to tell the child anything. He seems to be a wealth of information."

"And you heard the kid say he wants Miss Brinkley to stay with him. He already knows her. How are you going to do any better than that?" asked Officer Britten.

"I'm not saying that I disagree with any of you. It's just that . . . well . . . you all know the rules as well as I do. There's a ton of paperwork and legalities."

"That sometimes gets in the way of a patient's best care." The doctor stared at the professionals seated around him with eyes and a voice of earnest. "As I see it, we have a young boy here that society owes a responsibility. And I do not intend to let anyone get in the way of that happening. I promised Mr. Jarrett last night that I would do everything in my power to make sure this boy gets the best care possible. I intend to do exactly that. That's why I became a doctor and that's how I read my Code of Ethics."

You tell 'em, Doctor Teague. I knew there was a reason I liked you so much, Cookie nodded as she kept walking down the hall toward another patient.

The pediatrician rose from the purple loveseat. "Miss Brinkley, would you like to call Mr. Jarrett or shall I?"

"I will, but I was hoping to have the test results before I called him."

"It may be a couple of more days before I have all the results back. Why don't you alert him to the child's condition, which I would decipher as extremely good? But there's still something that's not matching up here."

Officer Britten spoke up. "Dr. Teague, I'm afraid I have some news that you may not want to hear."

Oh, no! The moment we've all not been waiting for, feared Celia.

"While I was talking to a guy under that bridge where the homeless hang out, I got a tip on the boy's father. This guy says he heard that Isaac's dad died with AIDS."

Dr. Teague sat back on the loveseat. "That's exactly what I was afraid of when that blood test showed an abnormality." He leaned over, put his head in his hands and took a deep breath. Gathering his thoughts, he proceeded. "It's too soon to make a conclusive diagnosis, but if that is indeed the findings of this morning's tests, he'll need to be referred to an AIDS clinic, what we call a tertiary care center, for evaluation immediately. There's a very good one in Winston-Salem."

Who will go with him? wondered Celia.

"Miss Brinkley, I think you'd better call and give Mr. Jarrett the heads-up on this. I'm sure he'll want to know. Make sure you emphasize that we're awaiting the test results, but early indications point toward that."

"Are you saying that I need to find out if he would take financial responsibility?" she asked.

"No, absolutely not. They will not turn Isaac away, especially in his indigent situation. But I want Jarrett to know that this boy is going to get the *very* best care there is. I give my word on that."

The pediatrician stood and started toward the door again. "And one more thing, Miss Brinkley. Did you kiss Isaac?"

"Yes, I did. On the forehead when he came to the school."

"Good. That kiss may be the best thing you ever did for that boy." Dr. Teague glanced at her. "And for you."

"Boy, that really gives our case a new twist." Officer Britten looked at Celia and then to Mrs. Schell. "I'd say that you both have your work cut out for you."

The discomfort of the situation was written all over the social worker's face. "Miss Brinkley, this adds a whole other set of problems to this case. Are you still interested in being the caregiver for this child?"

"Mrs. Schell, this makes me want the boy all the more."

Resting her chin on her fist, Mrs. Schell sat back in her chair and gave a long scrutinizing look at the woman in front of her.

Great! The "hot seat" again.

"I'm not making any promises, but I will consider you for a temporary placement for the child. He may be appointed to a foster home in the future, but that will be up to the judge. I can make certain recommendations. For the moment, it appears that Isaac needs someone immediately. Someone who can take off and go with him at a moment's notice."

Officer Britten decided to sit back and see which direction this scenario went. He was a betting man and he'd already made his wager.

"Are you in a position to do that?"

"I can be."

"Can you financially support this child?"

"Mr. Jarrett and I have already had this discussion. He has instructed me that he will make sure Isaac is provided for, in every way."

Mrs. Schell looked at Officer Britten. "May I speak with you for a minute, Stan?"

He nodded. *Too bad I don't have some money laying on this.*

"Miss Brinkley, could I ask you to excuse us for a few minutes?"

"Sure. Why don't I go back to Isaac's room?"

"I think I'd rather go back down there with you. This will only take a minute or so."

"Okay, I'll go to the snack bar."

"Oh, no, you won't," smiled Cookie as she came around the corner. "I'm going to show you the nourishment room. We've got all kinds of cookies and drinks. What'll it be, milk or juice?"

"Cookie, you're too much."

"Thanks, but I'll settle for just enough."

Celia laughed.

"You sit in here and relax for a minute. Everything's going to be alright."

♪ ♪ ♪ ♪

"Miss Brinkley, they're ready for you in the consultation room."

Celia felt like a music major again with final juries. She tried not to let the pressure show as she followed Cookie back down the hall.

Mrs. Schell and Officer Britten were standing when she arrived.

"Miss Brinkley," questioned the social worker, "do you feel absolutely confident that you can give this child the kind of attention and care that he needs, especially given the possible issue at hand?"

"One-hundred percent."

"And are you willing for us to do a thorough investigation on you and your home?"

Celia looked at Officer Britten and Mrs. Schell, her face totally unflinching, as she spoke to them. "I only have two questions. What do you need from me and how soon can you start?"

That gal's a surefire winner. Officer Britten started toward the door.

"I believe that's all I need for now, Miss Brinkley. I'll be back in touch with you shortly," responded the social worker.

"See you soon, ladies. I'll let you know if I find anything," promised Britten.

As Mrs. Schell and the detective headed for the elevator, Celia dropped onto the purple loveseat with a heavy sigh. She laid her head against the back and closed her eyes. *Thank you, God.* She was too intelligent to think that her troubles were

over, but she at least had made her point strongly enough to
be in consideration for temporary custody of the child.

"That's a great start, Celia."

The teacher opened her eyes to see Cookie standing in
front of her holding a plate of food.

"I thought, after that, you might need a little more nourishment than a cookie and some juice." She reached into her
jacket pocket. "And here's a note for you."

Celia unfolded the paper to see a message from Brad.
"I'll be by in about thirty minutes. Just called to make sure
you're still there."

"Thanks, Cookie. I am starving, but I don't want to
leave Isaac for too long. How's he doing?"

"He's asleep again right now. Why don't you take this
downstairs and relax for a few minutes? You'll have plenty of
time to get back before he's awake."

"I think I'll take you up on that. This has been a most
draining day."

♪ ♪ ♪ ♪

Celia used the time to call Dale Jarrett. She could hear
the shock in his voice, but more than that, the compassion for
a young boy left with no one, lying in a hospital surrounded
by strangers. And now, possibly the target of a terminal illness.

"Should I come there? What's going to happen now?"

She explained the course of the day's events and agreed
to call him the minute she had any word on the tests.

"If those people have any sense, they'll leave that boy
with someone who has any connection with him. And after
you recognized him and told me the story behind him last
night, I could see the concern and affection you held for the
child. Excuse me, for Isaac. You let me know if there's any
way I can help with that process."

"I appreciate the vote of confidence, but I think it's out
of my hands. I guess I'll get to see how well I believe that

verse of scripture about waiting on the Lord."

"Well, you *and* that boy are in my prayers, and I've got our MRO, the Motor Racing Outreach, here praying for him, too. And, if there's a big enough break in my schedule tomorrow, I'll be there to see Isaac. You call me the minute you know *anything* else."

"I will."

♪ ♪ ♪ ♪

"Brought you something."

Celia wheeled around to see Brad.

He was carrying a cup of ice cream from Cabarrus Creamery. "Thought this might give you a little boost of energy. I even remembered the right flavors."

"Oh, Brad. This is perfect. You just won't believe everything that's happened today."

She proceeded to give him the same run-down that she had the racer, only to get the same reaction.

"Let's go see the little guy . . . Isaac," Brad added, glad to know the child's identity. "But then you're going home for a while and sleep. No arguments if you want me to let you stay the night."

"Since when are you the boss?"

"Since I promised myself that I was going to help you get that child. I'm on your team, but don't forget who's the coach."

Celia's face radiated. "Thanks, Brad. I knew I could count on you. That's why I called you last night."

♪ ♪ ♪ ♪

Dr. Teague passed the couple in the hall, his head in a folder of notes.

"Any news on Isaac yet?" Celia called to him.

"No, but I do expect to have something by tomorrow

afternoon. Why don't you go home tonight? He'll be asleep the entire time and the nurses will keep a good check on him. That little fellow's the star of the floor for now, so they'll all be taking extra special care of him. There's going to be a greater need for you tomorrow when he's awake and the pain and reality begin to set in."

"Excellent suggestion," agreed Brad. "I'll see to it that she follows your advice." He smiled at Celia.

"If you're sure," she replied to the physician, a doubtful hesitation in her voice.

"I am sure."

She looked at Dr. Teague and realized that he, too, was on her side. "Okay. I'd like to go see him for a minute before I leave."

"I'll be checking in on him myself soon, so why don't you go on up?"

♪ ♪ ♪ ♪

"Just as I suspected," Dr. Teague said when he saw the sleeping child. "This injury took more of a toll on Isaac than the x-rays showed. Not to mention the fact of the trauma involved. No matter what he saw, or didn't see, last night, this boy knows his mother is gone, and that's going to be a great loss. Think of it. With him homeless, he was with her constantly."

Celia's heart hurt even more seeing Isaac's situation in that light.

"He's going to need a female presence for a while. One that can be with him a good bit of the time. I'm going to make that suggestion to Mrs. Schell."

Do I dare ask? Celia questioned herself. But before she had time to answer, Brad intervened.

"Dr. Teague, what are the chances of Celia getting temporary custody of this child? I've seen her in action with children and with Isaac, and no one could be better for him. And with the backing of Dale Jarrett and his reputation, I don't see why there's an issue."

"I appreciate your opinion. And frankly, I agree. Regretfully, though, I didn't write the rules when it comes to this area of his well-being."

"But aren't you the doctor, the specialist? Don't your years of training and experience account for something in this situation?"

Celia was relieved that Brad had tackled the dilemma. He was making a much better play for her cause than she could have. *Tackle. Play. Yes, he is the coach!*

"Let's see what happens tomorrow. Hopefully, I'll have some answers then and we can get to work on our gameplan."

Gameplan? Now I know this doctor's on my team. He likes to play ball, too.

And then Celia thought of the other player in the scenario. *Great! A NASCAR driver!* She smiled. *I might as well sit back and enjoy the ride.*

CHAPTER 11

Isaac sat in his hospital bed looking out the window. *I wonder how odd it must seem to him to be looking at the world from this side of the glass.* Celia looked at his perfectly rounded face with those huge eyes and saw the most beautiful child she had ever encountered. She was so busy watching him that she missed the foot steps behind her until Isaac's head turned.

Celia turned around and saw Dale Jarrett peeking in at the door.

The racer walked into the room and nodded at Celia as he went over and sat on the edge of Isaac's bed. "Hello, young man," he said, his face flashing that same characteristic grin seen in many of the television commercials.

"Hello," the boy replied.

"Isaac," Celia began, "I'd like to introduce you to someone. This is,"

"I know who he is, Celia. He's an angel," the boy declared.

"Huh?" she asked, startled that the child had enough recognition to know that this man had truly been the angel that saved his life.

"He's an angel. He's the angel who stayed with Momma until Jesus came and took her away."

Both the racer and Celia glared at the child, then at each other, neither quite sure how to respond.

As was already becoming a habit, Cookie walked in to save the moment.

"Hello, Mr. Jarrett. I understand you're the man responsible for saving this child's life."

"I wouldn't say that," he denied modestly. "Let's just say I happened to be in the right place at the right time, a lucky coincidence."

"You know what they say about coincidences. Coincidences only happen when God wants to remain anonymous."

This time the eyes of both Celia and Dale were on Cookie, again neither knowing how to respond to that profound statement.

"He's the angel who stayed with Momma until Jesus came to take her," Isaac insisted.

Dr. Teague, hearing the child's proclamation, entered the room carrying Isaac's chart. "Is that so?"

The boy's head nodded. "Uh-huh." Isaac flashed a huge appreciative smile at the racer. "And he pulled me out from under the truck and stayed with me until the big bus came to get me. Then he rode with me here." The child's face, still exuberant, turned into an inquisitive expression. "Did Jesus send you to come and get me, too?"

Dale Jarrett sat dumbfounded on the bed as the other three adults joined his expression. "No, son," he finally managed.

"How's Momma? Does she like her new mansion?"

The driver looked at the trio behind him and felt their collective strength and support as he slowly stumbled forward. He took a deep breath, as if gathering all the adrenalin and concentration that he used on the track and proceeded. "She's doing fine, Isaac. And she's got a wonderful new home."

Isaac looked satisfied as he eyed the other adults, giving each a big smile and waving to Brad, who quietly entered the room.

Celia continued with the introduction she had tried to make earlier. "Isaac, this man's name is Dale Jarrett. He drives race cars."

"In Concord?" fired the rapid response.

"Sometimes," answered the driver.

"I've heard you."

The eyes of the adults took on the saucer-shaped appearance of Isaac's with that statement.

"We could hear the cars from under the bridge. The first time I heard the cars, the ground was shaking so bad, I thought the bridge was falling down. But Momma told me it was only the race starting up. She taught me to tell when the green flag started the race, when there was a yellow caution flag, and when the checkered flag dropped, all by the loud roar of the cars."

Celia stared at Isaac in amazement. *He lived under a bridge and knows more about racing than I do.*

"Would you like to go to a race sometime, Isaac?" asked Dale.

"I sure would!"

"Well, I'll tell you what. As soon as Dr. Teague says you're able, I'll see that you get to come and watch me."

"Oh, boy!"

Again, the trio of onlookers stood dumbfounded, but this time from the opposite end of the spectrum of emotions.

Dr. Teague moved over to the bed. "How's my little patient today?"

"Good. This is a very nice bed."

"I'm glad you think so. Are you having any pain, Isaac, either in your leg or your head?"

"No, sir."

"That's great." Dr. Teague checked over Isaac's small body as he talked to the child, building up a trust. He looked over his shoulder. "You're very lucky to have all these friends."

"I know," replied Isaac.

Dr. Teague smiled at the boy. "I think you do know, Isaac."

As the pediatrician turned to exit the room, he glanced at the child's visitors. "If you don't mind, I'd like to see the three of you in the conference room for a few minutes."

He knows something. The results are back. Celia's body shuddered in fear of the doctor's upcoming words.

♪ ♪ ♪ ♪

Dr. Teague looked at the individuals who sat in the consultation room. "The results from our tests have come back. I'm deeply saddened to tell you that Isaac tested positive for the HIV virus.

"I want to emphasize that he is *not* contagious. From what we can gather, the father transmitted the disease to the mother sexually, and it was passed on to Isaac through vertical transmission from his mother. Due to her homeless state and lack of access to health care, she received no pre-natal care. Had she received such care and the routine screening that goes with it, her infection with the HIV would have been detected before Isaac's birth.

"There are a few other things that I could tell you, but we are not equipped to handle the disease. As I had feared, Isaac needs to be transported to another facility. But the good news is that we have one of the finest tertiary care centers in the country right here in Winston-Salem, North Carolina. I've taken the liberty to contact Dr. Tony Shepherd, one of their pediatric infectious disease specialists.

"It is my feeling that the sooner we can get Isaac to Winston, the better we can control his illness. There are several other assertions I could make, but it would be best if we go ahead and make arrangements to transport him and let Dr. Shepherd make a more conclusive diagnosis. I simply felt it my obligation to tell the three of you since you seem to be the current "family," if you would, of the patient."

Although there were many questions, no one spoke in anticipation of the outstanding comment that was still written on the pediatrician's face.

"Miss Brinkley, Celia . . . I know you have an interest in getting custody of this child. I must now ask you if that is still the case given this new information."

The eyes of Brad and Dale fell on her, along with their prayers.

She looked directly into the eyes of the physician. "Dr.

Teague, your report changes nothing except the fact that I feel this child needs me even more now. If there was any doubt before, now there is none."

"Dr. Teague, if I may speak," interjected the NASCAR driver. "I called Miss Brinkley because of what I had been told about her by someone on my crew. From the moment I met her on the night of the accident, I saw nothing but total concern and compassion for that child. I am prepared to take care of any financial responsibilities that she might incur if given custody of this child."

Dr. Teague nodded in appreciation to both Celia and Dale. "Very well. Then if you don't mind, I'd like to call in Mrs. Schell. I saw her earlier working on another case, so she's in the hospital. She must be informed of my decisions since Isaac is at present in the care of the state of North Carolina."

He excused himself and disappeared down the hall.

"Mr. Jarrett! I've been looking for you and Miss Brinkley. One of the nurses told me I'd find you here." Officer Britten took a seat in the consultation room. "How are things going down in Daytona with all the changes and those new Fords?"

"They're going great, but I'm sure that's not why you came looking for us."

"No, it isn't. Where's Dr. Teague? I was told he was here with you."

"He's gone to find Mrs. Schell and speak briefly with her. They'll be back shortly."

"Good, good. I actually need to see both of them, so since we're all together, it will make my job that much easier."

"Officer Britten, glad you could join us. Since you, also,

are working on this case, we can go through this all at one time," greeted Dr. Teague.

"I've got some information that I wanted to share with you and Mrs. Schell, too. Since these three are also involved in this case, I think it would be alright to discuss it in front of them."

Dr. Teague nodded. "Why don't you go first? What you have to say may have some bearing on my recommendation."

The detective pulled out his pad. "I've gone through all our databases and contacts and have found no missing reports for either Maureen or Isaac. They were known in the chain of shelters and soup kitchens around town, so I feel certain that the deceased was the child's real mother.

"And we've tried to find out about the father. None of the people I asked about the mother and child had ever seen a male with them. I did verify that a Joe Dan Fuller died in jail on the eastern side of the state about eighteen months ago, and he had the HIV virus. He was in on drug charges."

He looked up from his notes. "As of yet, we've found no relatives for either Joe Dan, Maureen or Isaac."

Numbed reactions floated through the room as the listeners wondered whether to be glad that the child wouldn't have to return to his former world, or be saddened by the situation.

It was Jarrett who finally broke the silence. "I think it would be fitting for us to have a short prayer regarding this child." He bowed his head, a signal for the others to do the same. "Heavenly Father, we have few answers here about Isaac's past, and those we have are not leading us forward. So we look to your desires for this child so that we can all band together and give him a fair chance at life. Touch Isaac and these doctors that they may be guided by you. And we pray the issue of his custody will be in his best interest. Amen."

There was still an aura of emptiness throughout the room, but to Celia, she felt that the spirit of God had filtered into their presence. She wondered if any of the others felt it.

"Well," Dr. Teague began, heaving a great sigh, "as

I've indicated, Isaac tested positive with the HIV virus. He needs to be transported to the tertiary care center in Winston-Salem, and the sooner, the better. Dr. Tony Shepherd is making arrangements, as we speak, for the child's arrival."

The pediatrician then looked around the room, allowing his eyes to make contact with each individual before coming to rest on Celia. "I've also taken the liberty to ask a couple of my friends and colleagues about Miss Brinkley."

His eyes shifted to Mrs. Schell and Officer Britten. "In understanding and trying to care for Isaac's physical needs and also his psychological and emotional needs, I am making a proposal to you. It is my belief that given how Miss Brinkley has been entrusted with students, whom she has taken abroad, by their parents, she has earned a tremendous vote of confidence from people who are extremely selective with their children's associates. She was required to take a number of sociology and psychology classes in dealing with children to prepare her for her twelve-year tenure in working at Tillman Academy, giving her, as I perceive it, more preparation than a MAPP training course.

"In the best interest of the child, I'd say those qualifications deem her suitable to serve as Isaac's guardian for his transport to Winston-Salem." He saw Mrs. Schell prepare to speak. "I've already spoken with Miss Brinkley and she is willing to make the sacrifices necessary to accompany him." Dr. Teague looked at the social worker. "Now *and* later."

"Is that correct?" questioned Mrs. Schell, looking intensely at Celia.

"Yes," came the solid affirmation.

"Seeing that the boy is still under your care," she responded to the pediatrician, "I think this is your call. I will be working on things from this end to ensure a safe home upon his release."

It was then that Mrs. Schell looked at Celia. "Miss Brinkley, I, too have been looking into your past and credentials. I must add that we have seen nothing to hinder your approval. However, this is a very unlikely placement by our state's guidelines. We can make a recommendation, but as I stated before, the final say will be up to the judge."

"Didn't you hear Mr. Jarrett's prayer?" Brad's diversion took everyone in the room by surprise. "Mrs. Schell, I don't mean to be rude, but is the state interested in closing a case, red-tape guidelines or doing what's best for the child?"

Muted admissions of agreement were heralded in the air. Mutedly silent but deafeningly loud enough for the social worker to denote the opinions of those surrounding her.

"Please know that I understand and appreciate your viewpoints. But also, please understand that I do not have the final word on this matter. I, too, agree that Miss Brinkley," she turned to look at the teacher, "Celia, would be an excellent choice as a caregiver for Isaac. But there are many ramifications and qualifications to be met in the state's eyes."

Mrs. Schell looked around the room. "All I can do at this point is observe the relationship between Celia and Isaac and hopefully communicate something that will catch the attention of the board to persuade them to recommend a kinship placement to the court."

"Thank you, Mrs. Schell. That's all anyone can ask. I'm sure I speak for all of us when I say that we appreciate your efforts," Mr. Jarrett commended.

It was a positive comfort for the social worker to see the nods and smiles of all those gathered in the room.

"I think it's time to go back and talk to Isaac. Due to the nature of this situation, I'd greatly appreciate the presence of everyone involved for this young guy's support." Dr. Teague led the procession back to the patient's room.

♪ ♪ ♪ ♪

"Isaac," Dr. Teague began, "we'd like to talk to you. Some things have happened and we've had to make some decisions and we need to share those with you now."

"Is Celia going to be my new momma?" the child asked enthusiastically, reaching his hand out to take hers.

"I think your problem has just been solved," Officer

Britten whispered, leaning over to Mrs. Schell.

Brad reached down and squeezed Celia's other hand in support.

Dr. Teague looked at Celia with a smile that matched Isaac's, and then turned back to the boy. "Not exactly, but we have to send you to another hospital and she will be going with you."

"Will we have to stay there?"

"No, not for long. There are some things I'd like for them to check. When they are through working with you, you will be allowed to come back to Concord."

"Will I have to go back and live under the bridge?" came the melancholic query.

"No, Isaac, absolutely not," interjected Mrs. Schell. "I will be making some arrangements for you to have a place to live when you return."

"Can't I live with Celia?" The child's eyes were filled with trepidation. "I want to be one of her children."

"I'll talk to my supervisor and the court and see what we can do," offered the social worker, giving Isaac her word and her smile.

Each of the adults in the room knew that Isaac had just become the mediator for the case of his own custody.

CHAPTER 12

It was the day of the greatly publicized Budweiser Shoot-Out. Daytona was filled with fans that had been waiting for nearly three months to see the fury created by the cars on the track and hear the roar of their engines with this infamous prelude to another NASCAR season. There was much anticipation as the traditional Winston Cup passed to a new generation, the Nextel Cup.

And in a hospital in Winston-Salem, North Carolina, lay a six-year-old boy watching his very first race on the television in his room.

After what seemed hours as Celia anxiously sat on pins and needles, Dale Jarrett unexpectedly whipped around the lead car in the final moments of the race to become a third-time winner of the annual race.

"Oh, no, Celia. His car's on fire," yelled Isaac, so loudly that the hall nurse ran to his room.

"No, Isaac, that's smoke from his tires. The race winner gets to take what they call a Victory Lap and the driver always does that to show his appreciation to the fans."

"To impress the fans is more like it," laughed the nurse, seeing what all the commotion was about.

"That's the driver who saved Isaac's life," informed Celia.

Suddenly the nurse's laughter turned to a silent stare at the screen.

Reporters were now racing to interview Jarrett. After

thanking his new crew chief and all the guys on his crew and Ford Racing, and making all the normal accolades for the car's owner and sponsors, the racer paused and took a huge gulp of Coca-Cola before looking into the television cameras. "And I'd like to thank Isaac Fuller for giving me the inspiration to win today's race. Isaac is a six-year-old boy who lost his mother this week in a fatal accident in Concord, North Carolina. He's now hospitalized in Winston-Salem undergoing diagnostic tests and I'd like to ask not only my fans, but all of NASCAR, to join me in keeping this little guy in their prayers."

A huge cheer went up through the stands, a cheer so loud that the reporters' next comments were unable to be heard. Tears filled the eyes of many of the spectators.

Celia turned to the nurse to also see her eyes filled with tears.

"He said my name, Celia. DJ said my name on television."

The child called the racer by the abbreviation he'd heard all afternoon during the course of the laps. *As if they were best friends*, sighed the guardian.

♪ ♪ ♪ ♪

"Thanks to both of you for your time."

Celia sat across the desk from Dr. Tony Shepherd as he made the conference call to Dale Jarrett.

"After a thorough work-up of Isaac, I'd like to share our findings and our diagnosis with you. I understand that the two of you have been the ones to care for the child. And just so that you know, Mr. Jarrett, I'll be going over some details with Miss Brinkley following our conversation that will equip her to know what to expect and how best to care for him.

"I've spoken with Dr. Teague and understand the dilemma with social services, but I think after today, she will be the most prepared person to care for Isaac. I'm going to write a letter to that effect for the social worker and the judge. Miss

Brinkley has observed and heard all of the details regarding him, in all areas of his well-being, so I feel that there is definitely a bond and a knowledge that would be hard to replicate at this point with another individual or family."

"I'm glad to hear you say that, Dr. Shepherd. I can assure you that everyone involved on this end feels the same."

Celia felt a boost simply knowing that she had the support of so many people regarding the custody of this child. She silently prayed that the judge and the Department of Social Services would see and feel the same way that everyone else did.

"Oh, and congratulations on your win, Mr. Jarrett. That was an exciting finish, and a most personable interview. I'd like to both commend and thank you for what you did for Isaac. He's on Cloud Nine. People sometimes don't realize the healing that comes from outside forces such as that."

"Thank you."

Celia detected the humbleness in the racer's voice that she had come to recognize.

"First, let me reiterate what you've learned from Dr. Teague. We don't have Isaac's mother here to confer with us, but gathering from his social situation and background, this is the probable scenario. In any case, the bottom line for the child is still the same."

The specialist turned to his notes. "It is important to understand the difference between HIV infection and the disease known as Acquired Immunodeficiency Syndrome, AIDS, and it is important to understand that there are some differences between pediatric AIDS and the adult disease. In teenagers and adults, the incubation period between infection with the virus and the onset of disease can be up to ten to fifteen years. Pediatric AIDS usually begins with infection at the time of delivery or during breastfeeding and has a much shorter incubation period."

As Dr. Shepherd glanced away from his notes, his affable eyes fell on Celia, making sure she absorbed and understood every word. "Isaac is infected with HIV and he now is showing signs that he is developing AIDS. His infection, I suspect, goes back to his father whose illness probably started with a needle shared with an infected fellow drug addict. His father infected Isaac's mother through sexual activity and she in turn passed the virus on to Isaac at the time of birth."

Seeing the distraught look on Celia's face, the specialist tried to assure her as much as possible. "It is important for you to know that Isaac is not contagious. The course of his illness depends on how his body responds to the virus and his response to the medication we use.

"Some children do not survive to their first birthday while others have a much longer active life, particularly with our present-day cocktail drugs - as we call them. In addition, as time goes on, these children are at risk for a variety of unusual infections, some of which are very difficult to treat. Some children also develop a degenerative brain disorder which shortens their life and all eventually show poor growth, or 'wasting.' The key to success is diagnosis at birth and early treatment."

Suddenly, the last six words were the only ones that mattered to Celia. She wondered if Dale caught that phrase through the telephone.

"How long are you talking about?" came the question from Jarrett.

Celia was relieved that the racer inquired about the one thing she could not bring herself to ask.

"It could be as long as two to three years, maybe more depending on how he responds to the drugs. Unfortunately, however, the missed opportunities of detection at birth and early treatment were two extremely costly strikes against Isaac. Death could come quickly or may be more drawn out by dementia and wasting."

The urge to bury her head in her hands was warded off by the strength Celia was determined to exhibit if she expected to be a suitable guardian for this young child. And the bleeding of her heart was forced to stay hidden until she had done what was necessary to give this child the "longer active life" that the doctor had referenced.

"Dr. Shepherd, thank you for your report, and thank

you for everything that you are doing for Isaac. I wish I could say I'm pleased with the outcome of your findings, but . . ."

"I understand completely, Mr. Jarrett. Unfortunately, that's the nature of being in my field."

Dr. Shepherd's statement gave Celia the realization that Isaac was not the only child in the world dealing with this illness.

The racer hung up and left Celia to finish with the specialist.

"I do have one last question. Will Isaac need to stay here, or return for future care?"

"We've done about all we can do. I'll be in charge of his medicines, and I will see him for follow-up visits and certain lab tests, but in this case, there's nothing that cannot be handled by NEMC and Dr. Teague." He paused. "Isaac is most fortunate to be under the care of Dr. Teague. He has dealt with similar cases and knows the ropes and appropriate follow-up care. We want to make this as easy as possible on both the child and you."

"Thank you, Dr. Shepherd. Does that mean he'll be going back to Concord soon?"

"Yes. I'd like to keep him here long enough to see the initial effects of the medicines, but then he'll be allowed to return to NEMC and then home."

He realized the implication of the final word. "I'm sorry. Wherever he goes from the hospital."

"I sincerely *do* hope and pray that it's home. *My* home."

Dr. Shepherd smiled knowingly as he stood and shook Celia's hand.

CHAPTER 13

"Is your name *really* Cookie?" Isaac quizzed, munching on the chocolate chip cookie the care partner had brought him.

"As far as everyone here is concerned, it's really Cookie," answered a young nurse who walked in the room. "We loved Cookie when we were student nurses. And we loved Cookie when we were real nurses." She laughed. "*Everybody* loves Cookie!"

Cookie laughed and hugged her co-worker.

"How *did* you get that name?" asked the young nurse.

"I was really named after my mama. But I got my nickname from my uncle. I only weighed 4 pounds, 13 ounces when I was born. And when my uncle came to the hospital to see me, he said I wasn't as big as a cookie. I've been called that ever since."

"I think they should have called you 'Purple Sunshine,'" Isaac squealed with delight. "You're always bright and shiny in your purple clothes."

Both of the women erupted into laughter with the child.

"You're right, Isaac. 'Purple Sunshine,'" repeated the young nurse, going to check on her next patient.

Isaac was responding positively to the medicines and his injuries were healing well. The long leg cast had been traded for a shorter cast. He was now able to take steps with his short crutches and was free of the I-V lines.

His light-brown hair complimented his young tanned and slightly freckled face, which surprisingly didn't appear weather-beaten. The huge blue-violet eyes, which stood in stark contrast to his other features, were what called attention to his face. From the moment Celia first saw him open his eyes at NEMC, she recognized the same sparkle that she had seen from them on that night at the live nativity.

Dr. Teague walked in with Dr. Marlowe. "Well, if it isn't our prize patient, all rearing and ready to go," the pediatrician grinned.

"I like staying here. They have pets and games and television and movies."

Isaac's remark was not much different from that of the other children who loved the safe haven that had been created at the hospital for them. But, in his case, this "haven" was the home he'd never had.

"Would you like it if I told you that you might be going home with Celia?"

"Can I?" The blue-violet eyes grew wide with anticipation.

"She's at a hearing right now to see if the judge will let you live with her. But when you leave here in a couple of days, you will be going to a home where you will be very comfortable and you'll have a bed of your own. And Celia will get to visit you."

"Can I ask the judge if I can live with Celia?"

"Isaac, son, you already did. Mrs. Schell took down your request and has relayed that to the court. We'll know something within the hour. But at any rate, you'll be going 'home.'"

CHAPTER 14

Celia beat the nurses in to see Isaac. Since he was "going home," the technicians who normally came in poking and prodding did not darken his door this Saturday morning. But they did all make a pass to his room to wish him well and say "good-bye."

Naturally it was Cookie who led the procession of hospital personnel that visited their young patient, all dabbing their eyes as they left the room.

♪ ♪ ♪ ♪

Isaac walked cautiously toward the room where each wall had been painted with one of the primary colors and a NASCAR border was running around the room, about two-thirds of the way up from the floor. He stood in the doorway, his eyes as vibrant as the colors on the walls. "This is the coolest thing I have ever seen. Did you do this all by yourself?"

"I did have a little help," she admitted.

"From Brad?"

"Well, yes, as a matter of fact." Her answer left her feeling a little sheepish. For what reason, she didn't know, but it made her take an honest look at how much time they had spent together on the project of painting this room and gathering all its accessories. It was the first time she had ever thought any more of him than as a co-worker who shared the same interests.

"Look at all the posters of DJ!"

"He sent those to you himself. And look at this," Celia bragged, opening the closet door. "I waited to see where you wanted to put it."

"Is that a *real* hood?"

"It sure is," she grinned.

"Was it really on DJ's race car?'

"It sure was." Celia grabbed a camera to take a shot of the child's excited face to send to the driver.

On the bed lay a DJ shirt that matched the racer's uniform and an action figure doll of Jarrett. The child immediately grabbed the figure and tucked it under his arm. "Can I wear the shirt now?"

"Yes, you can," his guardian answered, deciding against correcting his grammar with "may."

As they walked through the house with Celia giving Isaac the same grand tour that she had given Brad only four months earlier, it suddenly hit her that those four months felt like years in many ways. She realized how much she had learned about the man who had seemed like "the dumb jock" on the other side of the campus in those hundred-and-twenty days.

"Hello. Anyone home?" A familiar voice shot through the air as they heard a rap at the front door.

"It's Brad," Isaac acknowledged, his eyes shining even brighter. "Celia and I are here," he yelled, taking off toward the front door as fast as he could with his crutches.

"What are you two up to?"

"I was giving Isaac the nickel tour."

"I'll take it from here." He turned to Celia. "Why don't you go and make yourself beautiful? You're taking the two of us to the Red Pig for dinner. Remember your promise from Christmas?"

Celia crossed her arms in front of her and shot the visitor a playful "How dare you?" look.

"She's already beautiful, Brad," came the quiet, sincere voice of the child.

"I know," Brad said, squatting so that his face was on

the same level as the child's. "But never admit that to her. She might think we like her."

"But *don't* you like her?" questioned the lad.

Brad's surprised expression as he looked at the child, to Celia, and back to the child said that Isaac's question had caught him as off guard as the one to Celia had moments earlier.

Celia stared at her startled guest, earnestly waiting for a response.

"Why don't you go and get ready? I'll take care of this," he suggested, trying to wiggle his way out of an uncomfortable situation.

This may not be as easy as I had suspected, Celia warned herself as she climbed the stairs. *How could one little child leave two educated adults totally speechless?* She made up her mind to choose her words carefully as the evening progressed.

♪ ♪ ♪ ♪

Celia had brought one of her favorite CDs for children home with her. She had an entire collection of children's songs, but with no children of her own, she kept them in her office at the school where they got plenty of use. It now seemed odd to be driving down the road, in the PE coach's car, no less, listening to the songs she had learned as a child.

Brad joined her elated surprise when Isaac sang most of the songs.

"Momma liked music. We used to sing lots. It made the time go by during the day and on our long walks." His voice faded out with the last words.

Celia wondered where the child and his mother had been on their last walk together. She wondered how things might have been different had they arrived ten minutes earlier or later in their destination of the homeless "home" under the interstate's bridge. She wondered about the child's future. And she looked into the back seat and wondered whether Isaac was wondering about all of the same things.

"Hey, look!" he exclaimed from the back seat. "A McDonald's! I got to eat there once. A man stopped along the road and handed Momma a bag from there. Momma said he was a very kind man because he even bought apple pies and gave me an ice cream."

Luckily, the stoplight in front of them turned red for Brad slammed on the brakes. He and Celia stared at each other. They both knew that Isaac had been raised in a homeless situation. They were aware of the many things, including necessities, which he had been without. But that one statement instantly made both of them aware of how many things, things that were as common as getting out of bed each morning, were luxuries to this child in the back seat.

♪ ♪ ♪ ♪

"Why don't we stop and rent a movie?" suggested Brad, seeing a rental store on the right past the light.

"Great idea!" agreed Celia.

He casually glanced over the seat at Isaac. "What's your fav . . . ?" Brad caught himself before he stuck his foot in his mouth.

He turned to Celia and rephrased his question. "What would you like to have with the movie, Celi - popcorn or candy?"

"I have some of both at home, and some sodas. Why don't we let Isaac choose a movie he'd like to see?"

"Another great idea," beamed Brad, glad that his counterpart had helped him out of an awkward situation.

"Why does Brad call you Celi?" came the curious observation from the back seat.

Celia looked at Brad, hoping he could help supply an explanation.

"It's just a special name, sort of like you'd give a pet," he offered lamely.

"Yes," Celia added. "My grandfather called me that for short. He was very special to me. In fact, he was my very favorite person when I was a child."

"Then I'm going to call you Celi, too. A special name for a special person!" He held up the action figure. "Did you hear that, DJ? From now on, our special person is named Celi."

♪ ♪ ♪ ♪

While Isaac ran around the store on his crutches looking exactly like what he was – a kid in the candy store, a kid in the toy store, and a kid in the movie store, all for the first time in his life – Brad grabbed Celia's elbow and pulled her close to him.

"Can you believe he's only eaten at McDonald's once? And that wasn't even *in* the restaurant?"

A tear glistened in her eye. Her words, sounding forlorn, seemed to be going into the air rather than directed at Brad. "It's hard to believe, isn't it? We're in America, the home of the 'golden arches.' 'McDonald's' is one of the first words out of most children's mouths. When Isaac said that, all I could think was how eating at McDonald's is as common as getting out of bed each morning." Celia's head dropped. "And then I realized he didn't have a bed to get out of each morning, either."

"Well, he does now!" Brad lifted Celia's face to look at him. "And guess where we're eating breakfast tomorrow morning?"

"Lunch and dinner, too?"

Isaac came hobbling up the aisle and wiggled his way between them. "Look!" he said proudly, "I found three!"

"I'll bet we can rent all three of them," suggested Brad. "We've got all weekend."

Celia took the boxes from the child's hand. "May I see?" She looked at them, her own face, which had been terribly saddened only a moment before, now beaming with delight. "'Robin Hood!' My very favorite Disney movie!"

"Okay. It looks like I know what I'm watching this evening – for the child in *both* of you!" Brad took the boxes from Celia and turned to the child. "Why don't you go and make sure you can't find any others you'd like to see?"

"How are we going to watch all these movies if we're at McDonald's all day?" asked Celia, wondering aloud.

"It's going to be a long weekend." He looked straight into her eyes. "If you can stand that much of me."

"We're both only doing what we feel is best for this child. I think our own thoughts don't matter very much at the moment."

"So are you telling me that you're only allowing me to be with you for Isaac's sake?"

"Here's another one!" screamed Isaac from down the aisle. He limped as hard as he could toward the couple and held up the box.

Great timing, kid! I owe you one, mused Celia, breathing a little easier.

"'The Fox and the Hound!' Now we're talking," smiled Brad.

Isaac went tearing off down the aisle again toward the children's favorites.

"Brad, I know we both want to make up for all the things that Isaac's missed in his life. But look at him. There's a beautiful purity about him that is absent in many children. He's been unspoiled by all the luxuries of life that children have come to expect."

"I know what you're saying, and I agree. It's just that he deserves a decent life. That's not to say his life with his mother was not wonderful, or that she didn't do a good job."

"How right that is! Look at him. What parent wouldn't want a child as bright and happy and polite as that little guy?"

Brad took Celia's hand. "We've got to be careful not to play God here. Maybe it would be a good idea if we kept a watch out on each other to make sure we don't overdo it."

"I totally agree. Yet, it's difficult when you know the battle that guy's fighting inside. Physically and emotionally. It's so hard not to feel sorry for him."

"No feeling sorry games. We're treating him like we would if he were our own . . ." Brad stopped the words in midstream, wishing he could retreat them, and hoping he had not caused Celia any discomfort.

"Hey, you're holding Celia's hand. How come you're doing that if you don't like her?"

Brad and Celia stared at the child. Neither of them was aware that they were still holding hands. They were so deeply involved in conversation about the child that it seemed the appropriate friendly gesture.

"Time to go. I'm hungry," announced Brad, changing the subject while dropping his hand. "And Celi promised me that the next time we went out to eat, she was going to introduce me to the Red Pig. She says you're not an official resident of Concord until you've eaten there."

"Does that mean I'll be an official resident, too?" came the child's excited, yet naïve voice.

Brad and Celia glanced at each other, clearly sharing the thought of Isaac's homelessness from their conversation moments earlier. "Yes," came the unison response.

"Oh boy! Now Momma and I *both* have a home!"

Celia could see that the tear in her eye was matched by the one in Brad's.

CHAPTER 15

*E*yes flew toward the threesome as they walked in the front door of the Red Pig Cafe. Most of the customers recognized Isaac from the headlines of the local newspaper, and those that didn't heard the story before the trio got from the car to the restaurant.

They chose a table in the back non-smoking section as eyes and whispers followed them.

"Are you sure it's alright for me to be here?" Isaac asked.

"Of course it is." Celia found it both strange and painful that even at this tender age, Isaac recognized the fact that people were staring and talking about him. It was a life to which he had become accustomed. She sensed that there were going to be many hurdles to overcome as this child entered the world not only as a normal part of society, but now as a member of the spotlight due to his rescue by a notable NASCAR legend.

"Well, look who's here!" The brightness of the waitress' smile rounded the corner before she did as she bounded through the door. "What would you two guys like to drink?"

"Can I have a glass of milk?" blurted Isaac.

"You certainly may," answered the waitress.

"And I'll have the same," stated Brad.

"Thank you, Dawn," acknowledged Celia to the familiar waitress.

"Isn't Celi going to have anything to drink?" Isaac asked as the waitress walked away.

"Yes, but they know what she wants. She's obviously a regular," explained Brad.

"Does that mean she's been an official resident for a long time?" the child inquired.

Celia grinned. "Isaac, did you know that our church's Prayer Pigs came here and prayed for you the last two Wednesdays while you were in the hospital?"

"Pigs go to your church?"

Brad burst into laughter, as did Dawn, who appeared with a tray of drinks.

"No," Celia snickered. "We have a group, called the Prayer Pigs, who meets here on Wednesday mornings to pray for people with problems. They eat breakfast while they go over the prayer requests for each week."

"Did they pray for Momma and me when we didn't have a home?"

Brad's laughter halted as he watched to see how Celia chose to respond.

"They sure did!" answered Dawn. "I heard them every Wednesday morning."

Isaac took a large sip of his milk, a contented expression on his face as he scooted back into his chair.

"Do you know what you want to eat yet, or shall I come back?"

"I'll have President's Pie," volunteered Isaac.

Three pairs of surprised eyes fell on the boy.

"I'm sorry, Isaac, but they don't have that item on the menu," responded Celia.

"Isn't that a picture of the President in the other room?"

"We do have a picture of President Bush in the front room," the waitress confessed.

"Is he eating pie?" asked Brad.

"Yes, coconut cream," answered Dawn.

"See, I told you they had President's Pie," the child boasted, giving all the customers a laugh.

"And I thought *you* were the regular," Brad commented to Celia. He leaned across the table, his voiced now hushed. "Did you know they had a picture of the President eating pie?"

"No," she whispered.

Celia turned to Dawn. "I think we may need a few minutes."

Brad went to look at the picture as the waitress explained the story behind it.

"How did you know that was President Bush?" Celia asked.

"Momma showed him to me in the newspapers. Whenever we walked places, she'd tell me all she could about the pictures we saw on the front pages in the newsstands. President Bush had his picture on the front page lots of times."

"A pretty ingenious way to teach a child," Celia confided to Brad as he sat back in his chair.

"I'll say," he agreed. "I wonder what else he knows?"

"Plenty from what I've already seen. He's light years beyond his age in knowing *about* life."

While the waitress took Isaac on a tour of the restaurant, showing him all the pictures and articles and explaining the history of each one, Brad took the opportunity to question Celia about something that had been gnawing at him since he first heard about the child. "Do you think there's any way we could get Dr. Lacey to let Isaac come to school at the academy?"

Celia peered at him in shock. "That's exactly what I've been thinking."

"The child needs to go to school somewhere. He's obviously extremely bright. Since we both teach there, maybe they would give us enough of a break that we could afford to send him."

♪ ♪ ♪ ♪

Isaac downed every bite of the pie, scraping his fork along the plate so as not to miss any of the filling or meringue.

Dawn, who was singing along with the oldies playing on the radio in the background, came by to check on the threesome. "All done?" she asked Isaac.

"Yeah. I think I'm ready for my hot dog now."

"I'll tell you what. Catch hold of my waist and do what I do. We'll go back and give Cory your order."

Dawn began to do the train with Celia and Brad jumping in the line behind Isaac, his crutches left at the table. Other customers, as well as Jan and Tami – two other waitresses - randomly joined the procession as it wound its way through the restaurant. Jennifer – another waitress – began singing harmony to the music.

"Yell out 'one hot dog all the way' when we pass the kitchen window," Dawn instructed the child.

"One hot dog all the way," Isaac yelled, never missing a step.

Cory, the cook who was also one of the restaurant's owners, glanced up, laughed at the party going on in the dining area and yelled back, "One hot dog coming up!"

The human train made its way back to Isaac's seat where it came to a halt.

"This place is fun. Can we come back?" the elated child asked.

Cory bent down, personally delivering the hot dog, and gave Isaac a high-five. "Anytime, Little Man, anytime."

The child looked at Celia. "Can we eat breakfast here?"

Celia looked at Isaac, then to Cory. "I guess we can. Just don't sit in that booth in the back corner. That's where the Breakfast Club meets."

"What's the Breakfast Club?" he questioned.

"It's a group of friends that comes in and solves all the problems of the world," Cory explained.

"Huh?" came Isaac's puzzled expression.

"Eat your hot dog and I'll explain on the way home," offered Brad. "It's time for someone I know to go to bed."

"Do I have to?"

Celia laughed. *How is it that* all *children seem to understand that question of going to bed on time?*

Brad whispered, "Looks like we're down to two meals at McDonald's tomorrow."

"At this rate, we may never get there." Celia's eyes

met Brad's to say thanks for his part in helping Isaac to adjust. She quickly looked away before they were able to reveal anything else.

"Has my daughter been causing problems?" Jan smiled at Isaac as she came over and welcomed him, explaining that she was Dawn's mother.

Tami followed and gave Celia her traditional hug. "How's Miss Celia today? And who is this fine-looking man you have with you?"

"That's Brad, and I'm Isaac," called the child.

Celia's blush was as red as the pig on the front wall. "This is Jan and Tami," she introduced, trying to slide past the remark. "And that's Jennifer," she pointed toward the far corner. "These are the women who take good care of me at the Red Pig."

"Like Brad does at school?"

The waitresses all broke into a fit of laughter.

"I love this little fellow already," spoke Jan, giving Isaac a bear hug.

Jean and Randy came from the kitchen. "These are two people who prayed for you, too. They are Cory's parents. He owns the restaurant with them."

"So everyone here is one big family," announced Isaac from the tidbits he'd gathered.

"Yes, you could say that," agreed Randy.

Celia finished all the introductions, making sure that Isaac knew all the names to go with the faces.

"Since I'm an official resident now, can I be family, too?"

"You sure can, sweetheart," Jean answered with a hug for the boy.

"Miss Jean is the one who made the President's Pie," confessed Dawn.

"And Randy and Cory made everything that Brad and Celia had," explained Tami.

"Except for the bread pudding," added Celia. "Jean makes the best bread pudding in the whole world, and I don't even like bread pudding."

Jean smiled appreciatively. "I have to make it every Tuesday for Celia and the judge. No raisins. Then I make another pan for the customers who want the raisins."

Celia missed the rest of Jean's words. Her concentration stopped on "the judge." Suddenly she realized how she knew the judge who had granted her permission to be Isaac's guardian. For he, too, was one of the Red Pig "family." Over the years, he had watched her at work with her "children." She returned to the conversation, grateful that she had been an "official resident" of Concord and a member of the "family" for so many years.

The customers all joined the party and delighted in telling Isaac tales of the restaurant and about the life that took place inside the Red Pig. Their stories spread to include yarns of Concord and the residents of the town.

By the time Isaac finished his hot dog, he had been warmly initiated into the regulars of the Red Pig – "an official resident."

CHAPTER 16

The school's headmaster propped his elbows on his desk and rested his chin on clasped hands. It was obvious that Dr. George Lacey was deep in thought with the process of making a decision that was good both for the child and the school.

"Before you came in this morning, Dale Jarrett called to inform me that you were coming to discuss Isaac's education. He said that no matter what the tuition was, he would pay it plus any fees and uniform costs."

Brad and Celia looked at each other, both wearing huge smiles on their faces, at the realization that their dream had become a reality. But their smiles were short lived, for Dr. Lacey continued with his decision.

"But I must inform you that after careful consideration and in speaking with the academy's board of directors this morning, we cannot allow this."

Celia's face dropped. She couldn't believe her ears.

"But Dr. Lacey," Brad pleaded for her.

"Hear me out," Dr. Lacey explained. "After a called meeting with Mrs. Gaye and the board this morning, we all agree that Isaac is owed an education, and that given his role in the Little project, and his association with the two of you, Tillman Academy would be the best place for him. And also, it would give us an opportunity to show that children and their needs truly *are* our greatest interest here." He paused, looking into the eyes of both the teachers seated in front of him. "But there's still no way we can allow this."

Noting the mounting confusion on the faces of Brad and Celia, he buzzed his secretary. "Martha, could you ask Mrs. Gaye to come in now? And I'd like for her to bring Dorothy Lee with her."

The three of them sat in silence waiting for the arrival of the other two women.

Celia felt as though she were trapped inside a nightmare where she could see Dr. Lacey's lips moving, but she couldn't believe the words coming from them. She glanced briefly at Brad, whose expression showed that the silent minutes were like hours to him, also.

A knock at the door interrupted the torment for Brad and Celia. Both Mrs. Gaye and Mrs. Lee spoke to their co-workers with bright smiles.

How can they be so cheerful? Celia wondered, knowing they were here to back the headmaster's decision.

"Thank you for joining us," Dr. Lacey welcomed. "Mrs. Gaye, if you would, I'd like you to give Miss Brinkley and Mr. Sells the final words and unanimous vote of the committee.

"My pleasure," she said.

Her pleasure? How can they all treat this like nothing more than some business deal that they've unanimously voted down? Celia felt a sickening queasiness in her stomach.

"The board, along with myself and Dr. Lacey, voted unanimously that Isaac would be a fine asset to Tillman Academy. Such an asset, in fact, that there's no way we can accept any money from either the two of you, or Mr. Jarrett. Therefore, he will be enrolled as of tomorrow on a full scholarship. We appreciate your consideration, but we cannot allow your payment."

Celia's queasiness turned into butterflies of joy as she jumped up and hugged her three mentors, who had now risen to a new level in her respect of them.

Brad followed the Director of Outreach in hugging Mrs. Gaye, Mrs. Lee and then Dr. Lacey.

"I don't know what to say," Celia whimpered through tears of joy.

"What you'd better say is 'good-bye,'" instructed Dr.

Lacey. "I've called in subs for both of you so that you can spend the afternoon getting this list of supplies for Isaac, as well as his new uniforms. And I expect to see all three of you here first thing in the morning at regular time."

"Oh, and by the way," added Mrs. Gaye, "we've asked Mrs. Lee to join us because she will be tutoring Isaac to catch him up on his reading and writing each afternoon while you're doing carpool duty, Miss Brinkley."

She continued, "I'd like to personally test him for the first couple of days to assess his various levels. I understand that this will be a new experience for him, so there will be a social challenge as well as an educational challenge. But we all feel that it will be well worth anything that we can do to help this child. He has certainly already given a lot to our students at the live nativity."

"Thank you. Thank you all so much," the Director of Outreach said, now more composed. "I'll call Mr. Jarrett right away with the good news."

"Don't bother," replied Dr. Lacey. "I called him back this morning. He's made arrangements for you to pick up Isaac's uniforms in the school store once you leave this meeting. He'll also be forwarding a check to you to cover any supplies the boy may need."

"That is one more fine race car driver," rejoiced Brad.

"That is one more fine human being," corrected Dr. Lacey.

"He's certainly a wonderful role model, isn't he?" asked Mrs. Lee.

"That he is," agreed Mrs. Gaye.

"You two had better get going. You've got a lot of work to do before tomorrow." Dr. Lacey reached out and shook hands with Celia and Brad a last time.

"And you two have students waiting on you," he smiled at the other two teachers.

CHAPTER 17

"It's uncanny how that boy can pick up anything that the other children are doing and participate like he was here from the first day of kindergarten," related Mrs. Lee.

Celia listened intently to the woman who had been a strong supporter and treasured mentor over the twelve years that the Director of Outreach had been the school's music teacher. She recalled the first day she met Mrs. Lee's grown daughter and stood amazed that they both possessed the same beautiful blonde hair and pleasant disposition. And the second grade teacher's appearance was so youthful that the pair looked like sisters rather than a mother and daughter.

In all the years of working with Mrs. Lee, she had never once heard her raise her voice or seen a scowl on her face – not even behind the closed doors of the faculty meetings. That demeanor filtered through the students of her class, making it a joyous pleasure on the two days a week they showed up for music class. And her skill for one-on-one tutoring kept her busy with students of all ages who needed extra help.

Celia's thoughts turned to Mrs. Gaye, the academy's lower school administrator, who had proven to be an invaluable supporter and resource during the live nativity and possessed the same wonderful qualities as the second grade teacher. Her tall and slender stature was carried by a graceful poise that gave her a most stately appearance. Yet her gentle smile indicated that she was a most approachable figure for both the students and the teachers. *That's why this woman*, who taught first grade for years before taking the administrative position, *has such a wonderful rapport with everyone,* observed Celia.

Both of these women seemed perfect for their roles at Tillman Academy. So perfect in fact, that the other teachers, *including myself,* were strengthened by their years of expertise.

Now Celia sat learning another side of both Mrs. Gaye and Mrs. Lee. This time, she sat as a parent in a conference concerning the child in question. *My child,* Celia thought, suddenly appreciating the parental support of her students. She couldn't help but say a prayer of gratitude that now Isaac had the privilege of knowing and learning from both of these women.

"I know you told us how Isaac had learned to read and write from his mother, using sticks and rocks on the ground for pencils, and the newspaper stands for reading primers, but I was totally unprepared for his level of understanding and intellect," spoke Mrs. Gaye.

"I find that I'm the student every afternoon when I work with that child," confessed Mrs. Lee. "His comments are always triggering new ways of teaching methods to instill with my own class lessons."

"What we've decided to do is place Isaac in the first grade. His street experience has taught him more than we had expected, and he picks up immediately by watching the other children." Mrs. Gaye glanced over her notes as she summarized her report. "His manners are impeccable and his lack of having things has taught him an invaluable respect for his belongings, as well as those of others."

"The child is filled with the most wonderful stories," expressed Mrs. Lee.

"That's because his life has been quite a story," smiled Celia.

"Yes, and because of that, I would like to include him in the writing assignments for my class. I think he's most capable of handling anything I'll give him. Yet we don't feel it wise to place him with students that much older than him."

"I agree," nodded Celia. "What he needs most now is

to be a child, with children that are his age."

Both Mrs. Gaye and Mrs. Lee agreed, fearing that their plans for Isaac were short-term.

Mrs. Gaye placed her hand reassuringly on the musician's arm. "Celia, this had to be a difficult decision on the part of everyone involved, but I feel you were right in not telling Isaac about the disease. He's bright enough to figure things out on his own and I expect he perceives more than most people give him credit for."

"I agree with you, except that I think most people who've dealt with him truly *do* suspect he perceives quite a lot. That's the reason I think we all concurred not to make an issue out of the illness and simply let it run its course with us doing everything we could to give Isaac the life of any other six-year-old."

"Very wise decision," reiterated Mrs. Lee. "And I think that both you and Mr. Sells are to be commended for the guidance you are offering the boy."

"Did I hear my name?" Brad stuck his head in the door with his usual smirk. "I was hoping to get here before the meeting ended."

"We're all done here, but I'm sure Celia can catch you up on everything," replied Mrs. Gaye. "However, on behalf of not only Mrs. Lee and myself, I'd like to thank you from the entire staff for the time and effort and example you are giving Isaac. He's a fine young man who was most fortunate to be taken in under the wings of you and Miss Brinkley."

Celia resisted the urge to jokingly question the "fine example" set by Brad as she blushed in sincere appreciation of the vote of confidence. Coming from the two women she respected so eminently, it was a compliment of the highest order.

CHAPTER 18

"Tragedy Strikes the Red Pig," read the morning headline of all the nearby papers. The heart-breaking story was accompanied by a photo from the accident scene. Reporters from various local television stations interviewed the employees and customers of the restaurant and showed the clips on the evening newscasts.

♪ ♪ ♪ ♪

Very few people noticed the tall man enter the sanctuary. Celia happened to look back to see if she saw Brad and noticed him. She leaned down and whispered in Isaac's ear, prompting him to go to the narthex and greet the visitor.

The child returned to the pew, quietly leading the man by the hand.

Celia fought back tears at the thought of all this man had given up to attend this memorial service for Dawn. "Thank you for coming," she whispered as the pair sat down, Isaac scooting himself as close as possible to the man.

A nod was her acknowledgment as the congregation stood for the procession of the family.

The three mourners noticed Brad enter with the pall-bearers, but he looked straight ahead, ignoring all eyes.

Celia sensed how tough this was for him, not only because of the tragic ending to this young woman's life - a woman younger in years than either Brad or herself - or because she touched the life of everyone who knew her, but because she had become one of the members of Isaac's "family."

The tall man who had his arm around Isaac reached over to Celia's shoulder and squeezed it, providing strength and comfort as she watched Jan and the rest of the "family" take their seats.

As the minister spoke of the fact that Dawn was the most "found" she had ever been, and offered words of encouragement and hope to the family, Celia glanced down at Isaac. *Please God, don't let it have been a mistake to bring this child today. I know he wanted to come to say good-bye, but don't allow it to be a negative experience for him in his process of grieving for his own mother.* She stopped to snatch a peek of him listening to the minister and recalled his words as she'd tried to discourage him from coming to the service. *"I* want *to be there,"* he had insisted. *"I want to be there for Dawn."*

Before she had a chance to add an *"Amen"* to her own private prayer, Isaac tugged on her sleeve. "Celi, look at Jesus' footprint on the stone wall," he quietly commented.

Celia looked at the stone façade of the altar area, but she saw no shape of a footprint.

The child, catching her confused expression, added, "See the white square box on the wall?"

She nodded.

"Look up three stones. It's Jesus' footprint and his leg."

The woman glared at the wall while listening to every word of the eulogy. Still she saw nothing that resembled either a foot or a leg. Celia glanced back at Isaac, who had retreated to being content at leaning into the figure beside him.

During the entire rest of the service, Celia's eyes diverted between the ministers, the soloist and the wall as her search for the footprint continued. *Perhaps I'm too distraught by the situation. Maybe it's nothing more than his childlike simplicity of faith.*

She heard the minister say, "Jesus meets all of us where we are. God loves us as we are, where we are."

Then it struck her. *I do need to "lose" my adult thinking and see things as simply as Isaac does*, her concentration going back to the wall. But still she saw no footprint. Finally Celia gave up looking at the stone façade and decided to check it again at the conclusion of the service.

She became intent on the thought of Dawn – a servant, one who gave freely to others, one who spent her time waiting on others. *A talented, intelligent woman who could have been successful in any number of careers, but instead she loved people so much that she gave her life serving others.* Celia looked at the family. *A servant whose life ended too soon in an auto accident.*

That thought was the key to her vision. *A servant. A foot-washer.* The image of Christ washing the feet of his disciples at the last supper, a supper where he had acted as their lowest servant, spread before Celia's eyes.

She looked at the stones again, this time with an added insight. It was there, the footprint, plainly as visible as it had been to Isaac. There were three stones that made the image. One, the toes; two, the foot with the heel extended; and three, the leg covered by the hem of Jesus' garment.

How did he ever see that? she pondered, staring at the wall, then looking down at the child's face. *The face of purity.*

As one of the ministers concluded the service, Celia turned her head to catch a glimpse of the large crowd that had gathered to pay their respects. There were people of every age, every social level and every color. She recalled a phrase that Isaac had once told her. *"Poor knows no boundaries,"* he had said, quoting his mother.

Looking around her she saw that Dawn had known no boundaries, either. *What a wonderful tribute to this young woman! No one made these people come. No one cared where she lived, what label of clothes she wore, how many carats her diamond was, how much was in her portfolio. They cared that she loved them and served them.*

Celia remembered the day she had gone to the power company to get help for the Little's last December. She had seen Dawn there paying the bill for an older gentleman who couldn't afford to stay warm for the winter. And then there were those days when she had seen the waitress leave work to go home and cook for families who were hungry.

She loved people where they were, Celia thought to herself. *I wonder what God is thinking as he is looking at this congregation.* Then a slight smile spread across her lips. *"We Are Family,"* she sang in her mind. *That's exactly what God is thinking as he looks at His children gathered here. Rich, poor, black, white, sick, healthy . . .*

"The service will be concluded,"

Celia suddenly realized that like Isaac's mother at the time of her fateful accident, Dawn had been escorted into heaven by the angels in attendance.

"Why don't you ride with me to the cemetery?" the tall man asked when they got outside into the fair May weather. "I'm sure Brad won't mind bringing the two of you back here afterwards."

"Can we please, Celi?" Isaac asked, his eyes full of anticipation.

"Sure we can," she answered, taking the child's hand not held by the man and walking with them to the car.

They rode in silence for a few minutes as the man drove in the slow procession in what seemed an out-of-the-way direction to get to the cemetery.

"I wonder why we're going this way?" inquired Celia, mostly to herself, from the back seat.

"Because we're taking Dawn by the Red Pig one last time!" piped up Isaac.

The driver looked in his rear-view mirror at his passenger.

Celia's eyes caught his to acknowledge the fact that the child was entirely right. *What other way would we have gone?* she laughed to herself.

The procession of cars was incredibly long. People lining the streets were stopped, all of them staring and wondering what VIP was being led through the streets on their final journey. And then some recognized the face of the man driving the car in which Celia and Isaac were riding.

Finally Celia broke the silence. "Thanks again for coming, Dale. I know it's not like you didn't have millions of other things and people requiring your time."

"Luckily, I was testing at Lowe's Motor Speedway. I happened to see the newspaper and read about this." There was a slight pause. "Why didn't you call me?"

Isaac saved the moment. "I told her to, but she said you were too busy. I told her that angels were never too busy." As repeatedly as Mr. Jarrett and Celia had explained to Isaac that the racer was not an angel, the child had repeatedly insisted that he was. "See, Celi, I told you he was there to stay with me when Jesus came for Momma. And he was there for me today when the angels came for Dawn."

Again, she felt the glance of the driver in the mirror.

"And Jesus left his footprint in the church."

"Isaac, dear, that was not really Jesus' footprint. It was a pattern in the stones."

"That made a picture, right? That was a picture of Jesus' foot, right?"

Celia saw she was making no headway. In fact, she felt like Grace going up against Imogene Herdman in *The Best Christmas Pageant Ever.*

"Stop while you're ahead." Celia didn't know whether the small voice she heard in her head was her own conscience or DJ thinking so hard that she heard his thoughts.

When the car finally came to a halt, Isaac jumped out and raced to stand beside his Red Pig "family." "I'll save you a place," he called over his shoulder.

"He certainly has a way of making his point, doesn't he?" snickered Jarrett.

"Which one, God or Isaac?" she grimaced mildly.

The "gentleman of the race track" gently led Celia across the grounds to the burial site.

For the first time of the day, Brad acknowledged her presence when he saw the silhouette of the tall man accompanying her to stand beside Isaac. He nodded his appreciation to the racer. The pallbearer then looked at Isaac surrounded by Celia, DJ, "Uncle Cory," "Mama Jean," "Papa Randy," and the rest of the staff and "regulars" from the restaurant. His heart, knowing the child's future, felt as if it would rip out of his chest.

The ministers each read a short scriptural passage, shared a few parting comments and then spoke to each member of Dawn's family. Once the clerics had made their way through both rows of family members, the pallbearers proudly, yet most somberly, stepped up to the coffin and laid their boutonnieres on top of it.

Celia had seen this done at services in the past as a manner of showing final respect.

As Brad stepped up to the coffin, he looked at Isaac and motioned his head for the child to come to him. The young boy hurriedly slipped through the crowd to Brad's side.

Brad then handed his flower to the child and picked him up so that he could reach the top of the coffin. Isaac kissed the flower and placed it in the same fashion as the others on top of the rounded rose-colored box. They stepped away and the child looked back to Jan and blew her a kiss.

The saddened mother reached her arms out to the boy who leapt from Brad's arms and went running to her.

As Celia took a deep breath, trying not to lose her own composure, she felt the whimpers rising from her chest. Dale placed his arm around her and tried to calm her until Brad made his way to where they stood.

Brad pulled her close to him. "Hold it for just a few more minutes. You can't break down now."

She bit her lip and nodded, knowing the sudden wave of emotion would soon pass. Celia knew the source of that ripple came from watching a boy, a child that she had feared would be broken apart by the day, show the crowd Jesus' love and the hope of a brighter tomorrow.

Just like at the live nativity Tillman Academy had sponsored to help the Little's the past Christmas, it was Isaac's simplistic childlike faith that carried the rest of the crowd on his shoulders.

Oh, that I only knew my Father as he does, she longed. *Here I'm the one who is supposed to be the guardian, the one who is supposed to be setting examples, and it's me who is continually learning the lessons.*

As loved ones walked in a procession past the coffin,

the ministers recognized Dale Jarrett. They stepped out to thank him for the effort he had made to be there.

"She was Isaac's family. I had to be here," he replied simply, walking toward Jan and the other family members.

When Jan looked up and saw the race driver, she let go of Isaac and threw both hands over her mouth. "Oh . . . oh . . ." She tried to express her thanks, but the shock would not allow the words to form. The surprised mother made another futile attempt to say even a word to the man she had watched religiously nearly every Sunday during race season for the past two decades.

Dale took the woman's hands, clasped them in his huge palms, and looked into her eyes. "You must have passed along some wonderful traits to your daughter for her to have touched this many lives in her thirty-four years. You should be very proud of the life she lived and the impact she has obviously made on everyone here." He looked around, noting the large crowd. "It appears she was very loved." Then he hugged the woman and said solemnly, "I'll be praying for you and all of Dawn's family."

"Thank you. Thank you so much." Now Jan was shaking his hand energetically. "I can't believe you came here for this. I just don't know what to say."

"Say only that you'll have Celia contact me if there's anything you need."

Celia hugged the woman with all her might. "I'll talk to you later. You have many people who want to speak to you now." She reached down and took Isaac's hand.

"See you at the Red Pig tomorrow, Jan," he waved ferociously.

A huge smile, the one that everyone was accustomed to seeing on her, broke out on the mother's face. She waved back at the child, Celia, Brad and Dale.

Brad walked up beside the racer. "I want to thank you for making time to come here. I've heard it said that time is the biggest and best gift that a person can give. You certainly gave up a lot to be here."

"Not really. I *was* kind of in the area. Besides, it

wouldn't have mattered where I was. This woman did a lot to give Isaac a happy life over the past two months. The way I see it, it was the least I could do to show my appreciation to her and the family."

Dale reached out his hand to shake Brad's. "I do need to be getting back to the track. Would you mind taking these two back to the church for Celia's car?"

"Since *you* asked, I think I can make the effort," he grinned at Celia while answering the racer.

Isaac stood on his tiptoes, his hands cupped around his mouth, and reached up as high as he could toward Jarrett's ear. "I think he likes her."

"You think so?" asked the driver.

"Uh-huh," smiled the boy. "And you know what? I think she likes him back!"

DJ couldn't resist the urge to burst out in laughter. He looked at Brad and Celia, whose faces were both flushed from embarrassment. *That child can bring one to tears or laughter faster than anyone I've ever seen. Wish I were that quick on the track!* he smirked to himself, his trademark grin written on his face.

"Hey, good luck this afternoon, DJ. Brad says we might get to come watch you practice." The child's anxiousness was written all over his body – a body that looked the picture of health.

"I'll be looking for you," the racer said as he got in his car.

"Can we go to the Red Pig?" Isaac asked. "I'm hungry."

"I'm not sure this is a good time," replied Celia.

"I think this is a grand time," voiced Brad. "I think Isaac may be just what the place needs right now. It seems he's already on the start of a roll," he added, rolling his eyes in regards to the child's earlier pronouncement.

"On second thought," grinned Celia sheepishly, still embarrassed by the child's comment, "perhaps you're right."

CHAPTER 19

The trio found their usual table. Isaac had on his Red Pig cap, a part of his wardrobe that had become a must for every visit to the restaurant.

"C'mon, Jenn." The child grabbed the hand of the young waitress as she passed and pulled her along behind him. He began to step like Dawn had taught him to do the train.

When Brad realized what the boy was doing, he leaned over to Celia. "Why don't you join them?" he asked.

"Only if you'll go," she answered.

"What are you waiting for?" He grabbed her hand, pulling her out of her chair. "It's for a good cause."

Isaac caught hold of Tami as he buzzed past her.

Smiling, the waitress set the stack of dirty dishes in her hand back on the table and jumped in the moving line.

"What's going on out there?" Randy asked Cory as he looked out the window.

The boy, seeing the quizzical look on the faces of the two men, yelled, "We're doing what Dawn would do if she were here!"

Jean, hearing Isaac's voice, stepped from her back kitchen to peek out the window.

"C'mon, Mama Jean. We're doing the train."

"I see that," she called.

"Where are you going?" Randy asked as his wife brushed past him.

"To do the train. Are you coming or not?"

"Certainly n . . . !" Before he could finish his answer, he saw Cory remove his apron and catch up to the end of the line.

All of the customers had joined the action. Celia had no idea whether the unanimous participation, minus Randy, was because of Dawn, or to pacify young Isaac. Then as she saw the man in the kitchen move out to the dining area, throw up his hands, and step behind his son, she knew the reason everyone was involved was to flush out their own pain and hurt. It was a way of therapy.

Through the eyes of a child . . .

"Doesn't this fellow ever stop?" Brad asked, ready to return to his seat and his plate.

"No, I don't think he ever will," smiled Celia, *surprising people* or *leading them in the right direction.* "And a little child shall lead them," she uttered softly.

"Huh?" Brad stepped toward his seat and sat down, pulling his partner behind him. "Did you say something else?"

"No, nothing," she shook her head, pondering all her thoughts in her heart, wondering what it must have felt like to be the mother of Jesus and see the way he led people, even from such a tender age as infancy.

People slowly returned to their seats. Randy, Cory and Jean made their way back to the kitchen. The waitresses resumed taking orders and clearing tables.

"Now, doesn't that feel better?" Celia questioned Brad while patting Isaac on the knee.

"I don't know. I need a double turkey club after all that," he teased and then turned to Isaac. "You really know how to wear a person out."

"What's it going to be for you?" Tami asked the child. "Miss Jean says yours is on the house for building up everyone's appetites."

"Oh, boy! I'll have *two* pieces of President's Pie!"

The waitress glanced at Celia to make sure it was okay for the boy to have that much dessert.

"Sure, why not?" she nodded. "I think he's deserved it."

"Me, too," chimed in others from the tables around the trio.

The mood in the restaurant had changed from a solemn quietness, where everyone was afraid to utter a word, to its usual rollicking spiritedness. Life was beginning to resume to normal for the establishment – *at least for the moment. At least until reality sets in,* sighed Celia.

But for now, we all need to stay busy. We all need to keep moving. Life needs to continue in its circle. She smiled at Isaac and hugged him. *Just like all of us doing the train . . .*

"And I'll have the country style steak, mashed potatoes, squash casserole and bread pudding," she said to Tami.

"Your usual, huh?" beamed the waitress, whose eyes were still swollen from her earlier tears.

"Yes, the usual." *A circle,* she thought, watching the waitress walk away with the order. *Just like doing the train . . .*

CHAPTER 20

"*O*nly one more week till I get to go to the race track," squealed Isaac.

"You don't really want to go to that race next week, do you?" Brad teased.

"I sure do! And if you're not careful, I'll give somebody else your ticket," the child joked back.

Celia came into the den carrying a huge plate of sandwiches. "And if you two get too loud and rowdy during the race on television today, I'm going to give away *both* of your tickets," she grinned.

"Uh-oh. You'd better watch out, Isaac. We don't want the wrath of the 'Mad Musician' on us," Brad advised, using the nickname he'd given Celia.

"Here, let me help you," he offered, following the hostess back to the kitchen for drinks and chips.

"Brad," she bolted insistently, grabbing his arm. "Do you think it will be too much of a culture shock to take Isaac to the Coca-Cola 600? I mean, there will be thousands of people, some of them drunk, some of them doing and wearing who knows what, and let's face it, that child never even had a Big Wheel or a tricycle to ride. Will it be too much for him all at one time?"

The coach gently placed his hands on her arms and gave her a sincere, reassuring smile as if she had indeed turned into the "Mad Musician." "Celi, have you looked out at the world around you lately? It doesn't consist solely of the prim and proper types who spend their time going to operas or art exhibits. In fact, people are doing the same types of things they have through all generations. If you don't believe me, read your Bible a little closer."

He looked into her eyes to see if he was making any sense to her. "You have to choose who and what you will be, and how you want society to remember you and go on with it. There's no way that Miss Celia Brinkley can change everyone in the world to be what she would have him or her to be. You're not God, Celi."

Brad paused, making sure he wasn't offending her with his candor. "But what you can do is give people like the Little's a chance to raise their son in a better environment. You can offer a wonderful slice of life to a young child like Isaac. You can touch the lives of every child with whom you work at Tillman Academy, and you can bring a spark of light to all those people you meet in the various areas of outreach you are doing with the school."

His smile grew. "And you can leave a piece of Miss Celia Brinkley with all of those individuals so that they pass it on to the rest of the world." Brad gave her a huge hug. "Enough of a sermon for today."

He reached around her and picked up a bowl of chips and assorted dips from the counter. "It will be good for him. Do you think DJ would do anything that would harm that little fellow?"

That question, in itself, answered any misgivings she had about taking Isaac to Lowe's Motor Speedway the next weekend. "I guess you're right. Dale's in that scene for how many days out of the year? And it certainly hasn't ruined him yet."

"See, I told you. And just wait. You're going to love it . . . almost as much as Isaac and me."

"If you say so," she smiled, picking up the tray of drinks.

"Besides, they're not called drunks, they're called 'over-beveraged!'"

"What! How did you know that?"

"I can't help it if some of my best friends are dumb

jocks who hang out at the race tracks."

"You're kidding?" she asked, wondering if he might fit that mold.

"No, I'm not kidding. That is what they jokingly call it at the track. And no, my best friends are not dumb jocks who spend their days and nights inebriated. But I do have a friend who works at the track when the race comes to town. He gave me that tidbit of useless trivia."

"Oh," Celia replied, appearing a bit comforted.

"And if you're going to the track, you might as well learn the jargon. I bet you'll be a real NASCAR babe before long. It's a *very* addictive sport, you know."

"Which one isn't?" she laughed, as she pushed the swinging door that led to the den.

"Hurry up, you two! The jets are going over," Isaac called, his face a virtual glow.

"You're right," Celia smiled back at Brad, seeing that the child was already addicted.

"And don't you forget it," he added, putting the bowl on the table and grabbing a sandwich.

"Hey, don't eat that yet," warned the child. "We haven't blessed it."

"Thanks for the reminder," said the coach. "Let's pray. Isaac, do you want to say the blessing?"

"Yeah!" the boy beamed. "Dear God, thank you for this food and for this house and for Brad and Celi. Watch over all of us and keep DJ and all his friends safe. Gentlemen, start your engines! Amen."

Isaac reached for a sandwich and drink while Celia glared over at Brad. "And just where did that come from?"

He sneered apologetically. "I taught him that those words were the most famous words of racing. I didn't know he'd use them in a prayer." Brad waited for any look of understanding, which he didn't get. "But just think, what better place to use them than in a prayer? It's like he's asking for a blessing on *all* the drivers."

"Okay, I'll give you that one," she relinquished. "But watch what you teach that child," she joked, taking a seat and trying a chip.

Never taking his eyes off the television screen, Isaac bolted, "Did I tell you that DJ is taking me to Hickory next week to see his Indian motorcycle? They gave it to him when he won the championship. He said it's painted like an American flag."

"See, DJ and I are giving this boy a *great* education." Brad smiled at Celia.

She grimaced.

"Relax. DJ told me the bike's odometer only has a mile-and-a-half on it." Brad grinned and winked as he bit into his sandwich.

CHAPTER 21

"From the looks of the tags on the vehicles, you'd think this is the World's Fair," Celia said, glancing through the parking lot as they walked toward the track. She listened to the recognizable accents from around the globe and saw all the people milled in a huge crowd, barely able to move.

Isaac's eyes immediately found the hauler loaded with Dale Jarrett merchandise. He grabbed Brad's hand. "That's where *I* want to go."

"How about one of everything?" the guy behind the counter jokingly asked.

"He wishes," responded Brad with a laugh.

"Hey, aren't you," began the question from the salesman when he looked down at Isaac.

The child, now used to hearing the question, nodded his head. He scanned the items in the hauler, his eyes barely tall enough to see inside the case glass.

"Tell you what. Pick out any item you want and it's on me."

Celia and Brad looked at each other, then at the man. Isaac looked back at them to make sure it was alright.

"Go ahead," remarked Brad. Then looking at the salesman, he added, "You don't have to do that."

"I know. But what I love about this job are the people I meet. And in my eyes, it's an honor to meet this little fellow. He deserves one of everything in here and more."

Isaac chose a die-cast replica of Jarrett's car. While

pointing to what he wanted, he asked, "Can I get the truck like this hauler to put it in?"

"I'll get that," spoke Brad.

"No. My treat," smiled the man.

"Here you go, son. I hope you have fun with these." He handed a clear shopping bag to Isaac. "Are you going to any other races?"

"Yes," answered the boy.

"My name's Steve. Look me up. I'll be in the DJ hauler."

"I'm sure you'll be seeing more of him," assured Celia.

"Thanks, Steve." Isaac gave the man a huge grin in return for the car and truck.

"See? I told you they weren't all bad," Brad whispered into Celia's ear as they walked away.

Isaac was already busy combing the other vendors. "Mr. Hot Dog! This looks like a good place to eat."

"This is the *only* place to eat," smiled the guy ringing up orders.

"Here we go again," Celia said, shaking her head. "At this rate, the race will be over before we ever get to our seats."

"This is part of the racing experience," explained Brad. "And this is why we're sitting in the stands instead of a tower suite. You need to see NASCAR at its finest."

"I thought the tower suites *were* the finest," she shrugged, with Brad pulling her hand toward the hot dog stand.

♪ ♪ ♪ ♪

As they finally crossed Highway 29 and made their way toward the track, Celia saw a reporter talking to fans. She was so intent on listening to all the comments that she didn't notice Isaac worm his way through the crowd.

"I see we have a group of Dale Jarrett fans here," announced the reporter. "What brings you to the 600?" He turned the remote microphone toward a woman.

"He's fine, *real* fine!"

"Is this your wife?" smiled the reporter, now pointing the microphone toward a man standing next to the woman.

"Yes," answered the man.

"And you still like DJ?"

The man grinned. "DJ's a class act. He's the champion's champion. He drives clean and hard and his attitude about his family is what keeps me pulling for him."

"Ah, we have a young Jarrett fan. And why do you like DJ?"

It was then that Celia noticed Isaac. She grabbed Brad's arm.

"Because he saved my life."

Suddenly the reporter changed the entire angle of the interview as he realized that he was speaking to the child from February's accident. Fans were straining their necks to get a glimpse of Isaac in person.

"So what's DJ like in real life?" the man asked the child.

"Just like the lady said. He's fine, *real* fine!" exclaimed the boy.

CHAPTER 22

Isaac ran inside the house to answer the phone, a new job that he loved. "Hey, Brad. Are you coming over?"

Celia brought in the last bag of groceries to find the child on the phone. She could tell who was on the other end by the child's voice.

"It's Brad. He wants to take me out this evening. We're going to Lowe's Motor Speedway for the United Methodist Youth Night. Do you want to go?"

"Do I really have a choice?" she asked, loudly enough for Brad to hear.

"He says that one of the students from the academy is racing tonight. Please come with us and watch," coaxed Isaac. "Brad says if we wear our T-shirts from the church, we can get in for four dollars."

Celia looked into the blue-violet eyes that had hooked her from the first time she saw them.

"Okay, if I have to," she playfully consented.

"See you at four-thirty. Bye."

Isaac hung up the phone and wheeled around, helping put away the items on shelves he could reach. "We're going to eat at the Red Pig and then go to the track."

"Let's see. It's Tuesday, President's Pie day. How could I have ever guessed that we'd eat there?"

The child squealed with delight. "And you can have bread pudding."

Celia squatted and hugged Isaac. *What did I ever do without this child? And Brad?*

She sighed, knowing that each day was a precious moment, and decided to dwell on the joyful present rather than the dreaded future.

"And Brad says we don't have to rush home now that school is out for the summer."

"Wasn't that *nice* of him?" Celia scoffed.

♪ ♪ ♪ ♪

"That car has our United Methodist symbol on it," noticed Celia.

"It's called 'the Cross and Flame,'" explained the man standing beside the car. "It's a part of the ministry of the Western North Carolina Conference."

"You're kidding?" she asked.

"Nope." The man pointed to the car's carrier. On the back was painted, "Racing for Jesus."

"What all do you do with the car?" Celia questioned further.

"We actually have several different categories of vehicles that race," answered the man as his wife handed Celia a Fan Guide. "One part of our ministry is handing out Bibles and ice water in the infield during the May and October races here. It puts us in a place to serve people that would never enter a sanctuary. And you wouldn't believe how many responses we get from fans, usually months after a race when they've actually gone home and read the scriptures and studied the questions."

"This looks like a fun job. I'd love to help in some way," expressed Brad.

"We're always accepting new volunteers." The man reached out his hand. "I'm A.J. Moore, a pastor of two churches, but I chair this ministry."

"Too bad my students aren't old enough to help with this," stated Celia. "I'm the Director of Outreach for Tillman Academy, so I'm always on the lookout for community projects suitable for each grade level."

"Then perhaps you need to talk to the man standing over there. Mark," A.J. called out. "He's the Director of Missions and Outreach for the Western North Carolina Conference of the United Methodist Church. One of his responsibilities is overseeing the MRC, or our Mission Response Center. It's in Mooresville, not too far from all the racing shops. That's where we collect items that go all over the world."

"Do people ever volunteer there?" asked Brad.

Having heard his name, Reverend Mark Barden joined the group and the conversation. "That's what we're all about. Groups and individuals come from many places within our conference to help sort donations and send them to either missions around the world or natural disaster areas." He looked down and saw Isaac. "However, I'm afraid we do require that children are at least twelve years old in order to volunteer."

"Sounds like a great possibility for my eighth graders for next year. One of those students is the son of a crew chief. And another's father is an announcer for NASCAR. Having something in the vicinity of the race shops might be of interest to them." Celia continued to explain her interest in the facility and get information while Brad took pictures of Isaac sitting in the #7 Bandolero car.

Rev. Barden handed her a business card. "Give me a call when it's convenient. I know of a project that I think will be perfect for you."

She thanked him for his assistance as Brad helped Isaac from the car. "I never thought I would find out so much about outreach at the racetrack," Celia smiled.

A.J. bent down and spoke to Isaac. "Our driver of that car came in third in the points race last year."

Isaac looked up at Brad. "That driver's a good racer for Jesus."

Everyone in the group adoringly chuckled at the boy's perception.

"Thanks for your time," acknowledged Brad. "I'll be in touch with you."

CHAPTER 23

"Where are you two off to this weekend?" Brad asked, helping cart the luggage out of Celia's house and to the car's trunk.

"We're going to London and then Paris," boasted Isaac.

"You're taking the child out of the country?" Brad's eyes were filled more with fear than amazement.

"No, we're going to Kentucky!" corrected Celia.

"Cute, Celi, real cute."

"I thought you'd think so."

"And what, may I ask, are you going to be doing in London, Kentucky?"

"Do you remember Mark Barden, the minister we met the night we took Isaac to the Legends race at Lowe's Motor Speedway? The one who told us about the Mission Response Center?"

"Yes, the 'MRC,' he called it," Brad responded, placing the last of the bags in the car.

"He told me about a place in Kentucky called the Red Bird Missionary Conference, one of only three United Methodist missionary conferences left in the country. It's a huge comprehensive ministry that consists of twenty-seven mission churches and four mission institutions spread over a ten-county area. Their ministries include a farm, a school, medical and dental clinics, a pastors' school and work camps. They also have a place where special classes are taught, and they've talked to me about a class for the children and youth that will teach self-esteem through music and drama. You know that's all right down my alley."

"So is this a trip for the school?"

"Possibly. I'm not quite sure what it is. But what I do know is that I am supposed to go, and I am supposed to take Isaac. I've cleared this with Dr. Teague. He thinks it's a great idea. So this is what we're doing for summer vacation now that school is out.

"We're even stopping at a church on the way to pick up some supplies that will go to the Conference. Reverend Barden put me in touch with Jamie Reviere, the Director of Christian Education at First United Methodist Church in Brevard, North Carolina. She's meeting us for lunch at a place called Kelly's Restaurant and explaining how her congregation supports the Red Bird Conference as one of their outreach missions."

Brad stood looking at her, making no comments, but his expression indicating that he understood. "It all sounds great, Celi. A part of me wishes I were going with you."

"I'll check it out and see if there is any way you can be involved." She placed a cooler of juice and water in the car. "You know, it's funny, but I couldn't help but think about you, or should I say about your influence, with those children."

"Well then, I totally approve of this place."

"Why, thank you."

"It can't be all bad if it got you thinking about me."

"She thinks of you a lot, Brad," responded Isaac. "We pray for you every night before bedtime."

"Is that so?" he sneered.

"You *are* a part of Isaac's family, you know."

"Okay." Brad buckled Isaac into the car, closed his door and walked around the car. "I really am appreciative of the prayers." He took Celia's hand.

"I knew you would be."

Brad gave her a hug, wishing that he were joining them - for several reasons. "Take care of my boy!"

The trip was more rewarding than Celia had imagined it could be. Isaac immediately related to the children and participated in the Bible School held at the Joy Center, an outreach center of the missionary conference, while Celia spoke to the outreach director and observed the mission's work firsthand. She devised a plan for one of the grades at the academy to collect nutritional snacks and game prizes for the children who would attend day camps and after-school camps at the facility during the next year.

Celia and Isaac went shopping in the mission's thrift store, where churches and businesses from around the country had sent items. The child, who loved the "Queendale Mall" - as he called it, found several toys and outfits of clothing and was very proud that the money he spent would go directly to help the children he had met.

They shared in a scrumptious dinner at the home of Ruth Wiertzema, who hand-stitched a "DJ" shirt for Isaac out of pieces of brown-and-gold fabric she found in the thrift store. She also found a small bear and made it a shirt to match.

"I'll put it on my bed and sleep with it every night," Isaac promised as he waved good-bye.

After their visits of the Joy Center, the Red Bird Mission, Henderson Settlement and The Bennett Center institutions, the pair traveled on to London.

♪ ♪ ♪ ♪

While Celia stopped at a convenience store for gas, Isaac spotted a UPS truck. He immediately ran up to it and peeked inside.

"Can I help you, son?" questioned the driver of the truck, a friendly smile on his face.

"Nah. I was just looking to see if Dale was inside."

"Dale?" The package deliverer got a confused expression on his face. "You mean Dale as in Jarrett?"

"Who else would be inside the big brown truck?"

The man burst into laughter. "I take it you're a DJ fan,

too." Then he eyed the child carefully. "Why, I know who you are. You're little Isaac."

"Yes, sir. DJ saved my life."

"I've seen your picture and read about you. There was a story about you in our corporate newsletter."

The man nodded to Celia, who joined them and placed her hands on Isaac's shoulders.

"I hope he didn't bother you."

"No, no. It's an honor to meet him," he stated, still smiling. The driver held out his hand to Isaac. "My name is Robert Cable, but my friends call me Bob Wire."

Celia laughed at the corniness of his statement, but found it most creative.

"Say, are you two busy this evening? You ought to take in the show at Renfro Valley. I'll bet Isaac would really enjoy it."

"Renfro Valley? Isn't that the place where they do all the bluegrass music?" asked Celia, recalling having heard of it in some of the music circles.

"Sure is. It don't get no better than there. And it's just straight up the interstate at Exit 62."

"Thanks. That might be fun."

Celia took Isaac's hand and walked back to the car. "Would you like to hear a concert?"

"Yeah!" He began to play a pretend guitar as she fastened him in the seat.

They spent the afternoon touring gift shops, antique stores and the Kentucky Music Hall of Fame and Museum of Renfro Valley before grabbing a quick supper.

"This place is great! They even have ice cream!" blared Isaac, still surveying all the shops in the village.

"Just wait. The best is yet to come."

♪ ♪ ♪ ♪

"Can I pay?" Isaac begged as they entered the Red Barn. "I mean, may I?"

"Yes, you certainly may," Celia answered, handing him the money. "Where would you like to sit?"

Isaac took her hand and made his way to a row of folding chairs near the stage where he could easily see.

Celia loved the vision of large barrels catching rain, from an earlier downpour, that was now dripping through cracks in the ceiling. There were old iron bedsteads, with quilts draped over them, hanging on the walls.

Isaac's eyes were glued to the back of the barn where there was a table with candy bars, chips and hot dogs.

"I'm sure there will be an intermission and you can go back there then."

As she watched four men saunter onto the stage with their stringed instruments and break into a rollicking round of "Foggy Mountain Breakdown" and "Wabash Cannonball," while sitting in an old barn with dripping rain, Celia felt as if she had entered Isaac's realm.

The acoustical and bass guitars , dobro and banjo were a far cry from the stringed quartets to which she was accustomed and the environment was a far cry from Tillman Academy. Two other men, one carrying a guitar and the other a harmonica and banjo, joined the group on the stage.

"That's a harmonica. Momma played one of those."

Celia stared down at the child. No wonder his tiny hands had been clapping in perfect rhythm while his feet reached to tap the floor.

The harmonica player began to make a sound that resembled a train whistle before tearing into "Orange Blossom Special."

"Good evening. Welcome to Renfro Valley. Are you having a good time?" called Dean Osborne, leader of the band.

Isaac yelled as loudly as he could in response while he frantically clapped his hands.

The music teacher watched the child wiggle with fascination as he leaned over and called out the name of each tune the band played. Celia found herself mesmerized by the professional musicians whipping out bluegrass and gospel tunes and Isaac's natural responses to the music, singing along on many of the songs. She'd heard of "pickin' and grinnin'" and now she knew why. The band was pickin' and Isaac was grinnin'. The phrase took on a whole new meaning.

Isaac hurriedly downed a cola and a candy bar at intermission. Celia saw him take off toward the band members. Before she could get to him, he had become involved in a conversation with all of the guys.

"This is Dean Osborne, and Matt and Richard and John are his band members. And these are the Moron Brothers, Lardo and Burley. Take my picture with them, Celi." He was so excited that he'd hardly paused to take a breath.

She reached for her camera and flashed the photo. Then she gave Isaac a piece of paper on which to get the autographs of the band members before their return to the stage.

The second half of the show was even more rousing than the first half before winding to a close. *Isn't it strange that no matter what type of music it is, a performance follows the same pattern of getting the crowd's attention, then reeling them into the music before leaving them with an inspirational tidbit before the grand finale?*

The man with the harmonica began to play a crowd pleaser and when the band joined him, Celia noticed they were in two different keys.

Isaac leaned over to her. "He put the D harmonica in the E pocket."

She looked at the man in the overalls and wondered whether Isaac's statement had been factual or whether it was a joke. Either way, Celia burst into laughter at the child's outlook and knowledge of the music and the instruments.

As the show came to a close, Dean leaned into the microphone. "We have a special request by a young man in the audience, Isaac Fuller. Isaac tells me this is the song his momma sang to him every night before he went to sleep."

With that, Dean stepped back and joined the band in *Will the Circle Be Unbroken?* When they came to the final chorus, Dean motioned for Isaac to join the band on the stage.

The child took off and before Celia knew what was going on, he was singing into the microphone with Dean and the other members of the band. "There's a better home a-waitin' in the sky, Lord, in the sky."

There was a rollicking round of applause and Dean had Isaac to bow. Cameras went off in every corner of the barn. But for Celia, the final words of the chorus were going round and round. *No wonder he was not frightened by his mother's death.*

As they exited the building, the man at the concession stand came running up to Isaac. "Here, son. How about a free candy bar and drink? You earned it."

"Thanks!" squealed Isaac, taking the cup and the candy.

"Come back again," invited the man.

"I have a feeling we'll be back tomorrow night," responded Celia, still hearing Isaac's song in her head.

CHAPTER 24

"What's the World's Largest Chicken Festival?" Isaac asked after overhearing the two women in front of him.

"It's where they fry chicken in the world's largest skillet," answered the cashier behind the counter.

Celia had stopped in Corbin, Kentucky, to let Isaac eat in the original Kentucky Fried Chicken restaurant. Besides an order of chicken strips, he got an entire education of how the chain started, as well as the festival created to commemorate it. He had his picture taken with the statue of Colonel Harland Sanders and went through the entire tourist routine.

"You should come back the last weekend of September. That's when the next festival is."

"Can we come, Celi? Maybe then Brad could come with us."

"I can just see Brad at the World's Largest Chicken Festival." Then she laughed. "That may be a great idea. That's the weekend before Talledega."

"I'm going to the race in Talledega in October," announced Isaac.

"Oh, my!" barked one of the women. "You're going to take that little boy to a race? How despicable!"

"There'll be drinking and cussing and, and, and . . . well, you know, all that stuff that goes on at racetracks," chimed the other woman.

"And you don't have all that stuff here in this town?" Celia retorted. "Some of the finest men I know are connected

116

to NASCAR and the racing world."

The foursome walked outside as Celia and Isaac told the women about all the things they had learned and people they had met at the tracks. Celia was pleased to see a change of expression on the ladies' faces as she explained the work of MME and MRO.

The Concord pair left feeling like they had given as much as they had gained when the two women agreed to go to Talledega if Celia and Isaac would come to the World's Largest Chicken Festival and bring Brad.

♪ ♪ ♪ ♪

Isaac sat on the edge of his seat kicking his feet back and forth in anticipation of seeing the Dean Osborne Band again. He had met Dean's grandmother and Matt's mom as he entered the barn and learned that there was an Osborne Brothers Family Festival in August.

"Can we come back?" he pleaded, holding onto his chair and swinging his legs as hard as he could.

Celia began to feel like they were going to spend the rest of their time in Kentucky. *Which wouldn't be so bad*, she reasoned, thinking of all the beautiful scenery.

"How about a hot dog?" she asked, trying to take his mind off the upcoming festival.

"The Osborne Brothers are in the Grand Ole Opry," he bragged.

"What do you know about the Grand Ole Opry?" she questioned.

Within five minutes, Celia learned that her charge knew as much about the Opry as she did about the opera. She thought about the mournful stories in some of the songs and realized that they were words to which the downtrodden and country people could relate.

Dean walked onto the stage with Matt, Richard, John and Bobby, John's son who played banjo. They all waved at Isaac, who was prominently planted on the front row.

As Celia watched the child, seeing him respond to the music in a way that said he understood it, she decided there would be another trip to Hyden, Kentucky, on the first weekend in August for the Osborne Brothers Festival. *If he's able*, she reminded herself.

The concert closed with Isaac joining the band for the final number, which was again *Will the Circle Be Unbroken?* Each of the band members gave him a huge hug, promising to see him in August.

He tore off down the steps of the stage to Celia. "This is the most fun I've ever had in my whole life!" he exclaimed, filled with enchantment.

"Me, too, Isaac. Me, too." She placed her arm around him and led him out of the barn and to the car. *He's introduced me to as many areas of society as I have him*, Celia surmised, finding it hard to differentiate between the student and the teacher.

"Next stop, Paris," she called, as he sang *Are You From Dixie?* at the top of his lungs.

CHAPTER 25

Celia felt like a celebrity in her own right as she escorted Isaac to Florida in the new Ford Thunderbird, a Desert Blue convertible, which had been supplied for their transportation. They were on their way to Daytona for the Pepsi 400, and then on to the Give Kids the World Village located in Kissimmee.

After the diagnosis of the child's life-threatening illness, he had been referred to Concord's local wish-granting chapter, who then handed Isaac's request over to the Village. Give Kids the World Village handled the wishes, received from the more than two-hundred-fifty wish-granting organizations, of all the children from around the world who wanted to visit Central Florida for their dream destination.

"Exit 261A, Isaac. We're finally here."

As they drove down Daytona's Bill France Boulevard, the child's eyes bolted in every direction. "It's bigger than Charlotte's track, Celi."

"We're going down a little farther. I want to show you where DJ's father, Ned, actually raced on the beach years ago."

Isaac had never seen the ocean, so they spent the entire afternoon playing in the sand and surf. *Thank you, God, for the cloud cover.* It was a perfect day for the child to be outdoors. So perfect, in fact, that they stayed there until his bedtime, eating a picnic supper on their towels and overlooking the waves.

They took an evening stroll on the beach gazing up at the stars that were unusually bright over the ocean. Celia thought about the nights, as a child, when she had been outdoors with her mother, who was trying to keep her out of the house and away from her father. Her mother would glance up at the stars and whisper, "Mrs. Claus is baking cookies tonight." And young Celia would think about all the special cookies she was going to get at Christmas.

She looked at Isaac who, following her lead, was staring at the night sky. "Isaac, did your . . . " *No, of course she didn't. Isaac didn't get a chance to know much about* Mr. *Claus, much less,* Mrs. *Claus!*

"Huh?" the child asked, wondering why her words suddenly stopped.

"Nothing, I began thinking about something different and forgot what I wanted to ask."

Isaac looked back up at the stars.

That was the truth. I really did *begin thinking about something else.*

"Momma used to say there were pictures in the stars."He pointed to the sky, using his finger to draw in the air. "She said you could play connect-the-dots with stars and make all kinds of pictures."

Was there anything his mother missed with him? At least anything that really mattered?

♪ ♪ ♪ ♪

"Where are we going?" Isaac asked.

"We have a special infield pass." Celia drove through the black-and-white checkered-flag tunnel and found the first available parking space.

"That tunnel's the coolest. This place is already fun!"

A mother chased three children through the parking lot toward the pits. "Can you believe they'll still have this much energy tonight when the race is over?" she asked, passing Celia.

I wish I could say the same about Isaac. She wondered if she should tell the mother to count her blessings, but decided against it.

They found DJ's pit and saw the crewmen making adjustments on the car. Celia pulled Isaac to a back outside corner where he could watch without getting in the way.

He stood watching the men systematically at work for a minute and then blared out, "Celi, his car is broke. They're putting tape on it."

"That's called two-hundred mile-per-hour duct tape," called one of the crewmen, turning and glancing up at the boy. "Hey, aren't you,"

"Isaac!" called DJ, walking toward his pit area.

The child took off and jumped into the racer's arms, both dressed in their UPS racing attire. "This is the track where you won and said my name on television."

"It sure is."

"Are you gonna do it again?"

"We all hope so," yelled another of the crewman.

The guys took a break and walked outside the pit to meet Isaac and Celia.

"Would you like to see under the hood?" asked the driver.

"You betcha!" Isaac was all eyes as DJ and the crew gave him the ultimate tour of the pit and the car. "Wow!" was all the child could say, repeatedly.

It became clear to Celia that each man's job was extremely important. They were the most organized team she'd ever seen – down to each bolt, rivet and screw. Never before had she even imagined the intense concentration required to make the cars' and drivers' performances their very best.

And I thought backstage at the theater was stressful!

"I hate to break up the party, but it's time for practice. I'll see you for supper." DJ put Isaac back on the ground and got into his car.

Celia watched the energy in Isaac's body and the excitement on his face as the driver started his engine. From the looks of it, the adrenalin level of the child matched the rpm's under the hood.

The crewmen all stood around the car as it vibrated on

the pavement, each one looking and listening for a particular thing. Isaac stood spellbound. Finally, when all the guys were happy with their work, the crew chief gave DJ the thumbs-up sign.

Isaac waved frantically as the driver backed the car out of the pit and wound his way out of the garage area and onto the track. "Have you ever seen anything like that?" he glowed.

"No, I haven't," confessed Celia, afraid to admit that Brad's warning about her addiction to racing had already come true.

CHAPTER 26

"Hi," Celia cordially greeted the woman seated in the small booth outside the gate of the Village. The signs bearing direction from the nearby highway were extremely inconspicuous, allowing the visitors of Give Kids the World to have a truly secluded vacation. She could see very little of what lay beyond, but with only what was visible, she could already tell that inside this barrier, there literally *was* a whole other world that lay readily waiting for the children, its inhabitants.

"Hello," responded the woman. "May I help you?"

Celia turned to her charge, prompting him to answer the question.

"My name is Isaac Fuller. We're here for my wish of a lifetime," Isaac spoke up, as if he had known about this his entire short span on earth.

The young lady inside the booth flashed a huge smile and winked at Celia. "Thank you. You may go right in."

It was clear that the guard was already in love with this child, just like everyone else who had ever met him. The driver of the car suspected that was also the case with most children who had entered this gate.

As the space of the gate's opening increased, so did the size of Isaac's already gaping eyes. "We're here, Celi! Look!" His fingers were wildly pointing from one sight to another. "This is the coolest place I've ever seen!"

How many other children think that very same thing when they arrive here? Celia wondered as she looked at the colorful buildings and all the oversized animated creatures that came into view. With the convertible's top down, they could clearly hear music wafting through the air.

She pulled the T-Bird into a parking spot in front of a yellow building decorated with red hearts and red-and-white striped awnings. There was no doubt this was the House of Hearts where children went to register for their "home away from home" during their six-day vacation in Central Florida. There was a golf cart parked beside the front door with a sheriff's badge painted on it.

"What do the letters say?" Isaac asked.

"Officer Friendly," she chuckled. "And that jalopy belongs to Mayor Clayton." The "official" vehicles were made to look like oversized versions of children's rides, perfect size for the "kid" in every adult.

Isaac looked up at the sign on the top of the entryway. "Give Kids the World," he read aloud.

"Very good, Isaac. You remembered the words."

A huge grin covered his face.

Celia couldn't begin to fathom what this young boy must be feeling, for her own exhilaration at everything around them was far greater than she could have ever imagined. She ran around the car and opened his door, bowing as she did. "Are you ready to be treated like a king?" she asked.

Isaac's shrill laughter was the only answer she received.

She took his hand. "Come along, Sir Isaac. Your wish is everyone's command."

Celia loved the continual change of expressions on the child's face as he peered in every direction, still holding onto his DJ action figure and taking in the most fascinating things he'd seen in all of his young life. *This place is magical from the minute you enter the gate*, she mused, enjoying their surroundings as much as her young charge.

Once inside the House of Hearts, there was a counter to the left with receptionists, and several tables with chairs, all kid-sized, to the right. Celia and Isaac stepped in line behind one other family at the counter. They could already sense the excited wonderment, yet apprehensive enthusiasm, at the many things that would be transpiring within the course of the next week.

"May I help you?" they heard from the next available receptionist.

Celia gave Isaac the same go-ahead she had at the entrance gate.

He peered over the counter and flashed the woman a huge smile, his large eyes beaming. "My name is Isaac Fuller. I'm here for my wish."

The receptionist winked at Celia, letting her know she had trained this child well. Then she looked down at Isaac and said, "Hello, Mr. Fuller. We're glad to have you."

A woman, who appeared to be assigned with the receptionist, came from behind the counter. "Here. This is for you." She placed a black hat with Mickey Mouse ears on Isaac and handed him a stuffed animal of Mickey. Then she pinned a blue star on his shirt. "This is so everyone will know that you are our guest," she explained. "Now when you go in all the buildings, all the volunteers will treat you like the star that you are."

The child turned around and grinned at Celia while squeezing his new plush toy. He was so excited that he could hardly stand still.

"Here are the keys for your villa," stated the receptionist. "It has two bedrooms and two baths, and is completely stocked with everything you'll need for the week, including candy and sodas." She handed Celia a big brown envelope. "And in this packet, you will find your spending money for the week, all your tickets for the local amusement parks and two brass stars. One is for Isaac to write a wish on and leave here, and the other is for him to take home to remind him of that wish.

"If you'll have a seat over there, Anita will be with you in a few minutes to welcome you and give you the tour. There's a video playing about the Give Kids the World Village that will help with your orientation."

"Thank you," said Celia, leading Isaac to one of the

tables in front of the television.

It amazed Celia that this woman still made her spiel about the village with the same fervor as if it were her first time. Given the fact that ninety-six children per week came to the village, she wondered how many times the receptionist had been through this routine. And it was not simply a matter of greeting people as they arrived. It was a job that required patience, love, warmth and breaking through all the barriers that accompanied foreign languages – all with anxious, tired and weary travelers. *Talk about a role of outreach!*

Before the video had finished, Anita arrived. "Well, well, this must be Isaac," she guessed, extending her hand.

He nodded his head.

"It is indeed a pleasure to have you this week." Anita turned to Celia. "And you must be Celia Brinkley."

"Yes, and we are delighted to be here," the child's guardian replied.

"Do you feel up to walking around the grounds this morning as we take our tour?"

Isaac again nodded his head.

"You can leave your car parked here if you'd like, and we'll walk around the village. When we've finished, you can drive to your villa where you'll have your own private driveway." She led them out the back door that opened into a place like neither Celia nor Isaac had ever seen.

There was a walkway of pavers with names on them. "This is our Avenue of Angels. We call our volunteers 'angels' here because they save us 2.5 million dollars in salaries a year. There are also angels who contribute money to purchase a paver. Currently, we have four thousand engraved pavers." Anita turned to Celia, a note of appreciation in her voice. "We have *so* many angels. This place wouldn't exist without angels."

"What's that?" Isaac asked, seeing the bright-blue towering dinosaur that he had noticed as they drove through the front gate.

"He's a part of our mini-golf course. "Would you like to start there?"

Isaac nodded his head veraciously.

"This is Mark's Dino Putt, named after Mark McConnell, one of our past wish children. One of the local theme parks designed it for us, using their animation and visual technology. It has 7-holes, one that has a cave where there are wonderful special effects. You'll have to try it out."

"Now?"

"Let's wait until we've seen the whole place," Celia suggested. "You'll have all week to do anything and everything you want."

A train whistle blew behind a large building. "That's the Amberville train. And this is Amberville." Anita pointed to a huge complex full of all kinds of video games, racing boats, huge stuffed animals and tinker toys, and a large wrap-a-round porch filled with rockers for the family members.

Isaac, who was holding dearly to his plush Mickey Mouse, along with the figure of DJ, saw a child with a gray-and-white stuffed whale. "What's that?"

"That's Shamu. We give those to all the brothers and sisters of the wish children." Anita leaned over and quietly spoke to Celia. "You'll find that the volunteers leave gifts in your villa for each member of the family. Everyone is to feel special while they're here."

No stone unturned, Celia mused. "Well, it's working. Isaac and I already feel *very* special."

"You'll find that we try to treat you like royalty around here," Anita whispered.

Celia thought of her comment to "Sir Isaac" earlier. *Royalty, huh?*

"Look at all the video games, Celi!" the child shrieked, already drawn into the spell of the wonderland. "Can I have a quarter?"

She laughed and started fumbling through her purse for her wallet. *How quickly this lovely homeless child has become acclimated to all the "not-so-finer" things in life – thanks to Brad!*

"You don't need any coins," Anita informed him. "Everything here is free to the families."

Isaac ran toward a pinball machine.

"We never sell anything to the families. Everything here is donated, and the donors are not recognized. Our goal is that the village doesn't become too commercial, that it will always feel like home."

While Isaac ran from game to game, Anita and Celia relaxed in the rockers on the front porch.

The tour guide handed the visitor a sheet of paper. "This is the *Village Voice*. It's our daily newspaper that lists all the activities planned for each day. We try to provide things for the children who don't feel up to going to the big theme parks."

Celia glanced over the day's events.

"You'll see that the entire place is geared to be quiet and whimsical. Notice there are no lines and the only noise, besides the laughter of the children, is the subtle music that is designed to evoke a sense of calm."

The astute teacher had already heard the tones coming out of speakers strategically placed throughout the village. They had a pleasing effect, totally unobtrusive of thoughts, yet a rhythm that captured the soul – one that followed the heartbeat of life.

She had also observed all the plants and flowers that were everywhere. The landscaping hinted at a place that was full of life.

"Do you ever have to turn children away?" Celia asked.

"We've never turned anyone away. In an emergency situation, we can grant a wish within twenty-four hours." Seeing the look of awe on the listener's face, she continued. "That's how the village started. Someone knew that a child was dying and called Mr. Henri Landwirth, who at the time owned lodgings. By the time everyone whittled through all the red tape, the child had died.

"Henri swore that would never happen again. He made it his mission to contact agencies and corporations to help with this dream. And can you believe it's all been done simply by the shake of a hand? No signed contracts – *ever*."

"That's the part that's amazing. That's unheard of these

days," Celia commented.

"You're right. But that's the kind of person Henri Landwirth is. He's as good as his word, and he expects the people he does business with to be the same." Anita pointed to the side of the property. "We have ninety-six villas, all of which are full at any given time. If there's an emergency and we have to do a rush wish, we will place people in the motels near the amusement parks. But they always seem to like staying here better."

"I can see why. Meeting all the other children would be half the fun."

"More than half, actually, according to all the families who've visited the Village. They *want* to be here, to be in a community with the other families."

"About Amberville, I take it Amber was a guest here."

"Yes. She also had a brother who came here as a wish child."

Celia's heart sank. "How devastating that must have been for their family."

"The children's illnesses were devastating, but they at least had the opportunity to come here. And their family saw a vision of the village for the future."

Isaac came back and sat on Celia's lap.

"There's a birthday party held every Saturday in Amberville," Anita informed Isaac. "Mayor Clayton is always on hand to greet all the children."

Celia knew this child had never experienced a birthday party. But she knew that come his next birthday, there was going to be a spectacular celebration to make up for all the birthdays he'd missed.

"Shall we go on?" Anita led them out of Amberville and pointed to a large building on her right. "This is the Safari Theater. It's a movie house with three hundred seats. We show a different movie each day of the week. And it has a regular concession stand with popcorn and frozen drinks. Free, of course," she added. "There's always something to eat around here."

She bent down so that her face was on Isaac's level.

"This is where you'll come on Wednesday evening. Celia will have Parents' Night Out, when she'll get to go out to eat somewhere nearby. Compliments of Give Kids the World Village. And we'll show a special movie just for all of you children. Doesn't that sound like fun?"

"Yes, but who will take care of Celi? I promised Brad I wouldn't let her out of my sight."

Celia blushed. "I'll be fine, Isaac. We won't tell Brad anything about this." She saw the question in Anita's mind, but felt a wave of relief when the woman continued with the tour.

As they walked a little farther, the guide pointed to another place of solitude. "This is Millie's Butterfly Garden."

"Another wish child?" Celia gathered.

"No. Millie was a worker for one of our sponsors, but she passed away at a young age."

Celia gave the garden a quick scan, further amazed at the number of lives that had touched the Village and sure this particular area would definitely be a point of interest for her during the week.

"This is the Caring Center," Anita continued, pointing to the left. "This is where all our volunteers get their tasks and any pertinent information for the day, and clock in."

"Clock in?" inquired Celia.

"They don't get paid, but we keep up with how many hours are being donated this way. It helps us to see how much money they are saving us each year, and it gives them a tax deduction."

"I see."

"Along with the staff, the volunteers try to be a team for the families. We have a wonderful success rate with that here at the village. And there's not a lot of turn-over. People who come here to help find they never want to leave. It becomes a part of their regular routine in life."

Anita smiled back at Isaac as she opened the door of a building on her right. "And this is our Ice Cream Palace."

"Wow!" he yelled.

"And you can have anything you want, anytime you

want. They're open all day up until 9:00 at night. Our motto around here is, 'One can never eat too much ice cream.'" She turned to Celia. "This place seems to be a family favorite."

"No wonder."

"And you'll eat your lunch here if you're on the grounds in the middle of the day. The restaurant only serves breakfast and dinner."

While Isaac took a minute to check out the Ice Cream Palace, Anita added, "Everything served in this building – the ice cream and the sandwiches – is donated by Friendly's. We're very blessed to have them as a sponsor.

"Now *this* is the building you'll especially love," the guide directed to Isaac as they kept walking. "This is the Castle of Miracles. It snows here in front of the castle every Thursday evening. The first snowfall is at 6:45 and the second one is at 8:00. Santa and Mrs. Claus will be in the Grand Hall of the Castle with presents for each child. And you can sit on Santa's lap and tell him what you want for Christmas."

Isaac looked at Celia.

She could see that this was something foreign to him. "We'll talk about this some more later," she whispered.

"Would you like to go inside?"

"Yes," Isaac answered excitedly.

"This is our Fe-Fi-Fo-Fum Room."

There was a giant and an overgrown beanstalk painted on the walls. The entire room was full of child-sized tables covered in building blocks, books, games and crayons.

"That's Franko. He's a friendly giant who watches over the game room." Anita walked to the back of the room. "See this chest?" She opened the lid of the box. "There are all kinds of clothes in here for you to play dress-up."

The tour guide led them into another room. "This is Jolly Hollow. See the lighted footprints on the slide?"

Isaac climbed the lighted steps and came down the slide. "Who did all of this, Celi?"

"Angels," she replied simply. *And literally it was all the angel contributors listed on the pavers.* "Let's see what's in the next room."

"Whoa!" he shouted as he looked up at the stars covering the ceiling and all the beams and rafters. "Look at all the stars!"

"This is where all our children come and make a wish on their star. See the tiny writing on them?"

The child gazed up at the ceiling, trying his best to make out the letters on the stars.

"Here's the bucket where you place your star after you've written your wish on it. You bring it here and make your wish before you put it in the bucket. Then that night, this star fairy," she explained, pointing to the fairy painted on the wall, "becomes life-size and places the stars on the ceiling. Right now, we're at just over 40,000 stars."

Celia gulped. *40,000 stars? That's 40,000 children with life-threatening illnesses.* She began to wonder how many had survived. Without thinking, she began to pray for all the children and their families, her heart hurting for each one of them.

Anita handed Isaac a coin from a small bowl. "See this wishing well?" She pointed to a round faux-stone well in the middle of the room. "Throw your coin into it."

"Boing…oing…oing . . ." the coin echoed.

Isaac laughed.

"Here, try another one," she urged, handing him a second "magical" coin.

This time the coin sounded like it spun around in the bottom of the well.

"It makes different noises as you throw coins into it. And look at this chest behind you."

Following her lead, Isaac jerked open the doors of the dresser and the drawers of the chest to hear all sorts of various animated sounds.

"I love this place!" he shrieked, bursting into laughter.

Celia delighted at the joy she saw written on his face and in his actions. For the first time, she wished that Brad were here to see him. *I'll have to call him later. No, we'll call him later. I wouldn't want him to think he's on my mind.*

Anita walked diagonally to a small vanity in front of a mirror. "This is our Magic Mirror. It tells us who is the king or queen of the castle."

"Oooh," Isaac sighed, looking at Celia.

"Why don't you go over there and stand in front of the mirror and see what happens?" Anita invited.

Isaac looked at the woman and then peered at Celia rather precariously.

"It's okay. Go ahead," his guardian encouraged.

"Be sure to say, 'Mirror, mirror, on the wall, who's the fairest of them all?'" instructed Anita.

The child stepped up to the mirror, still not sure what to expect. Suddenly, trumpet fanfares flared throughout the room and Isaac's appearance transformed in the mirror, a crown on his head and a cloak around his shoulders.

"Celi, Celi! Look! It really happened. I'm a king!"

"I asked if you were ready to be treated like a king."

"I know, but I thought you were kidding."

Celia mockingly bowed down in front of the child, waving her arms up and down. "Your wish is my command, Your Majesty."

Isaac squealed with delight. "This is the most fun I've ever had in my whole life!"

"That's the same thing many of our visitors say when they come into the Castle. There are a couple of other things in here to see before we go back outside."

They walked back through the Grand Hall. "That's Tom Foolery up there," Anita stated as she looked up on the wall opposite the King and Queen thrones where Santa and Mrs. Claus sat each Thursday evening. "He tells jokes and talks to the children." She took a few more steps. "And this is Father Time," she smiled as she peered at the oversized Grand-father Clock. "He tells stories. You'll have to come back later and hear them."

"I will," Isaac assured her.

Once they were back outside, Anita led the pair to the right of the Castle. "The tree there is Old Elmer. Everybody loves to sit and rest under Old Elmer. He's such a pleasant creature. Those benches under his branches are the perfect place for parents to sit and watch their children while they're on the carousel."

"Have you ever ridden one of those, Isaac?" Celia asked.

"No. It looks like fun."

"It is. It's my favorite ride. Everyone loves to ride the carousel. We'll come back here later this afternoon."

"You can eat breakfast or dinner here at our Ginger-bread House. Perkins' donates everything for this restaurant. It's the only place in the village that isn't run by volunteers. Although we have over three thousand volunteers, we also have ninety paid staff members, including the Perkins' employees who take care of this for us.

"The restaurant's closed right now, but you can eat here anytime that you're on the grounds for those meals. You'll see over a thousand dolls and action figures that children have left here when they've visited. The dolls come from all over the world."

"I have an action figure of Dale Jarrett," Isaac proudly informed Anita, holding it in the air.

It was then that the tour guide realized Isaac's background. "I saw your picture in the paper with Mr. Jarrett."

"You did?"

"Yes, you're a very fortunate young man. From what I understand, Mr. Jarrett is a fine person."

"He's the greatest!" exclaimed Isaac.

Anita chuckled as they walked toward the staff offices. "This is my favorite place in the village." They continued up a small path past the offices and entered a building that faced diagonally from the sidewalk. "This is our chapel. I come here first thing every morning and read the notes in the books from the day before." She held the door open for the guests to peek inside. "It makes my job doubly rewarding."

Celia looked at the altar and saw a journal and a box of tissues placed on a table at each end. She could hardly take her eyes off the stained-glass windows.

"This is how we have the four seasons in Florida. Those windows represent each of the seasons. You must come back and see all the beauty and feel the comfort inside this room.

Even the altar is kid-sized."

They continued past the chapel to the pool. Isaac ran ahead of them and knelt down to splash water with his hands. Celia wondered if he'd ever seen a real swimming pool before. *Or even a picture of one.*

Anita took Celia's hand. "Let's walk over here for a moment. There's something I think you'd like to see, given your occupation." She led the visitor to a plaque that was on the walkway leading to the pool from the outside gate – the gate where people entered from their villas.

Celia read the plaque's words aloud, "We make a living by what we get. But we make a life by what we give. ~ ~ Winston Churchill" She looked at Anita before reading the words again. "What a profound statement."

"Yes, it is. We have this here for the volunteers, but also for the parents or guardians. It helps them to keep their child's situation in focus as they realize that their children are giving to the world, too. It's sometimes hard for the caretakers of the children to recognize that in their everyday lives', but here, they can see the impact their child has on everyone. And more importantly, the way the children connect and give to each other through relationships of being with others like themselves."

Celia closed her eyes briefly. *Dear God, thank you for bringing me here with Isaac. I am seeing more and more that my time with him is for me more than it is for him. Thank you for a safe arrival, and may every day of this trip be as rewarding as this one already has.*

"Oh, look who's here!" Anita announced, concluding the guest's silent prayer. "It's Mayor Clayton."

As he turned to see, Isaac's eyes grew in amazement at the six-foot bunny that stood beside Anita and Celia.

"Isaac, would you like to have your picture made with Mayor Clayton beside the pool?"

The child ran and grabbed Celia's hand. "Where's the camera?"

"Right here in my purse," she assured him. *There's not one ounce of fear in this child.* She wondered how many of the students at Tillman Academy would have been so eager to run up to a furry six-foot stranger.

Celia snapped the picture of Isaac holding the Mayor's hand, making sure she got the "Claytonburg's Park of Dreams" sign in the background. Then she stood beside the pair so that Anita could get a photo of her with them, too.

"Do you see the stable back there?" Anita asked, pointing to the back of the village.

Isaac shook his head. "No," he responded, not wanting to admit the only stable he'd ever seen was the one at Tillman Academy's live nativity the year before.

"Look back there at the wooden building. That's Clayton's Saddle Club. You'll have to visit there one afternoon and go horseback riding."

The child's eyes got so bright that it appeared someone had turned on a light switch inside him. "Oh, boy! A *real* horse?"

"A real live horse," she emphasized.

Mayor Clayton waved good-bye as he walked through the village and greeted the newcomers.

"He has to go feed and water the horses every morning," Anita explained. "Well, I think that's about it for all the places you'll need to see here. Now you've got all week to explore and visit each one of them. And there are only two things you need to remember here," she said to Isaac, squatting beside him and taking his hand. "You must have fun and there's always plenty to eat. Are you ready to start having fun?"

"I already started!" he pealed.

She gave him a big hug then stood to shake hands with Celia. "You can go out through this gate and your car's right over there." Anita pointed back to the parking lot in front of the House of Hearts. "You just continue down this drive and you'll find your villa." She looked back at Isaac. "Don't forget to go back to the House of Hearts and tell them what night you want Mayor Clayton to come over in his bright-yellow jalopy and tuck you in. And you'd better be ready for bed, because he'll be in his pajamas, too."

"Okay!"

Anita turned to Celia one last time. "Go and come as you please, and if you need anything - whether medical, spiritual or something in your villa - let us know. We're here for you at all times. We ask that you be observant of the child's tolerance of energy in planning your visits to the nearby amusement parks. Make sure you allow for his rest time."

Celia nodded. "Thank you. Thank you for everything. I so appreciate you giving of your time for us."

"Hey, it's my job." Anita pointed to the plaque at the pool. "It's my life."

"Don't you think it's about time to find our villa?" Celia questioned Isaac, opening the gate and heading for their car. "I understand there are lots of cokes and candy and presents waiting for us."

CHAPTER 27

There had been days when Celia felt she should throw her arms in the air and give up, fearing the world around her was caving in and that evil had taken such a strong hold on society that she was fighting a losing battle in trying to help others. But as she sat at the pool and watched the children, some in wheelchairs, laugh and enjoy the water, squealing with delight each time the water splashed in their faces, her eyes were opened. Opened with a vision as bright and hopeful as Isaac's.

Brad was right, she admitted shamefully.

She saw that it was possible for one being to make a difference, to truly change lives forever, to make the world a better place. And although she did not have the resources to impact the world in the same way as Henri Landwirth did with his vision and building of Give Kids the World, she had the ability to reach out to those who lived around her, who came in contact with her in their daily lives, and who experienced the warmth and the love of her spirit. That world that seemed so impossible to change suddenly seemed like a promising venture as she envisioned every person on the face of the earth *giving* instead of expecting to receive so much.

Celia wasn't blind enough to be fooled into thinking that all humankind was going to do their part to help others, but she became acutely aware that there were millions throughout the world – some celebrities or wealthy individuals with seemingly endless resources, and some with very little – who were willing to engage in social welfare.

Or social warfare, as the case may be.

In the short time she'd been at the Village, she had met families from three foreign countries and seventeen different states. The books of letters in the chapel indicated that there were not only children, but also volunteers, from numerous states and countries who ventured here to fulfill their dream, either as a participant or a giver.

The fact that every family member who graced these acres received a blessing – not just the child who had been selected by a wish-granting agency – overwhelmed Celia. Her mind began to calculate how many people had been touched by the generosity of this one philanthropist, and all the benefactors who made his charitable dream possible. From the individuals who had left a piece of themselves at the Village by a two-hundred-dollar donation for a paver, to the huge corporations who donated large amounts each year, to the many persons who gave the gift of time, vast numbers of people made this place - this dream world - a reality.

In her earlier years of playing in a Jewish temple, Celia had heard countless horror stories of Holocaust survivors. She recounted how they had come to this country with nothing and become extremely successful. Looking back on those persons, she was sure that was what made Henri the giver he was. He had experienced a life without hope, without a dream. But he had been multi-faceted enough to build a dream, to see a vision of what could be.

Her thoughts turned back to Isaac and how coming here with him had given her as much as it had him. *What an invaluable lesson. Will this child never cease to show me direction?*

She looked at him. He was in the pool beside a boy, who resembled the starved children of the third world, whose stomach appeared terribly swollen. The newly-acquired playmate's wheelchair had been pushed in the pool by an older brother who was joining in their game of volleyball.

They're playing like there's absolutely nothing wrong with either of them. They are living life with such a vivaciousness that it seems there's no tomorrow.

Celia forced her thoughts to stop.

There is *no tomorrow for Isaac,* she feared, her mind telling her there was still one last thought, the one she had not wanted to face.

The threats of a morning shower emptied the pool. Isaac helped push his new friend's wheelchair up the handicapped-accessible ramp.

"Can we go to the gazebo and see the fish?" Isaac asked, still not ready to go inside.

"I think it would be okay for you to try to count them. I don't think we should go fishing right now, though."

"Okay." He took off without her to begin his count.

By the time she reached the gazebo, built over the edge of the small lake, the drops of rain had begun to fall. *Thank you, God,* she prayed, glad for the chance to release the tears that had been building. No one could tell they weren't the raindrops falling on her face.

♪ ♪ ♪ ♪

"How about a trip to the Ice Cream Palace?" Celia suggested. "I think I'm wet enough for one day."

"Yeah!" agreed Isaac.

They ran as fast as they could back to the main path through the village. Celia noticed that the boy did not move as fast as he had earlier in the spring. *Dear God, help me not to dwell on this now. Help me to focus on all the new adventures for Isaac and be glad that he's getting this opportunity.*

She jerked the door open and they both darted into the "palace."

"What can I have?" Isaac asked, his question directed to both Celia and the woman behind the counter.

"Anything you want," Celia spoke first.

"You can have a cone, or a sundae or a banana split," added the volunteer.

The chaperone wondered if the boy had any idea what a sundae or a banana split even was. Before she had time to ask or explain, he handled the situation.

"What flavors do you have?"

Celia found it hard to believe this child, who had been exposed to so little in the line of social graces, had such an ability to communicate, especially in areas where she knew he had no experience. She loved the look of intensity she saw on his face as he tried to decide which flavor he wanted.

Then she thought of Isaac's numerous trips to Cabarrus Creamery on Concord's Union Street with Brad. *On second thought*, she smirked, *he's very well prepared for this place.*

"May I have two scoops of Watermelon Smash?"

"That's up to your mom," the lady answered.

Celia wondered what Isaac's next response would be and hoped those words would not stir up a negative feeling to his otherwise festive day.

"Momma said I could have all the ice cream I wanted," he boasted proudly.

"Is that right?" the volunteered chuckled, glancing at Celia for her approval.

Celia had no idea of what to do except nod. She watched as the kind woman behind the glass case piled two scoops in a cup and covered them with whipped cream.

"There are the toppings," she added, pointing to the counter while handing the child the cup filled to the rim with ice cream.

Isaac began to pile sprinkles and candies on top of the heap as Celia breathed a sigh, glad she had overcome her first hurdle of being mistaken for the boy's mother. She had not mentioned her concern about that to anyone and had been apprehensive about how she, and more especially, how Isaac would handle that subject when it arose. But as they sat in the Ice Cream Palace, it quickly became obvious that many of the children here were with adopted parents.

It wasn't until later that one of the volunteers explained to her that many children who were disabled from birth were given up for adoption because the biological parents felt they had neither the desire or means to care for the handicapped babies. That fact broke Celia's heart even more than Isaac's situation, for he at least had one parent until recently. From birth, he was a wanted child. There had never been any doubt of that in his young mind.

Perhaps that's why it's so easy for him to deal with this now, she reasoned. Suddenly, the similarity of her own childhood tugged at her – being unwanted by a father who went out of his way to ignore her, and wanted by a mother who spent her life protecting the unwanted daughter from the father.

Lord, no wonder you brought us together. Celia thought how much easier she felt it was for Isaac not to have had that man in his life at all. *Especially knowing what he passed on to the child.* Her heart began to crumble as she wondered why the father could not have passed on a wonderful heritage to this impressionable boy, whose eyes spoke of love from the moment one met him.

Celia, this is not for you to know any more than it was for you to know "the whys" about your own father, or the situation between he and your sister, she reminded herself.

Her mind turned back to the children, from all corners of the globe, who were lining up for their frozen requests. Many of them were accompanied by a mother *and* a father, and some had younger or older siblings.

Most of the boys and girls had obviously been the part, as well as was allowable by their medical limitations, of a normal home. That thought came to a halt as she took a closer look at the children. *No, there's not a child here that has been a part of a normal home or a normal family. Their various health problems have not allowed that.*

Suddenly it dawned on her that every child here had been the recipient of something horrible that no child should have to endure. Isaac may have been homeless; he may not have had a roof over his head on many nights. *But how many children here have had President's Pie? How many children here can call a world-known sports figure their best friend? How many children have had a mother that knelt over them every night and kissed them goodnight? Or whispered a prayer?*

Celia discovered that Isaac had been a most blessed child in more ways than she could have imagined. Thanks to his mother, this child had received more love than some children would in an entire lifetime. And he had lived a very normal life. There were routine events, such as checking out the world events in the newspapers, learning to write and spell in the dirt, and learning Bible verses from memory. *Learning about Jesus. Learning that Jesus loves him. Learning that when this life is over, Jesus will be waiting for him, ready to hold his hand and take him to his mother.*

"Can we go in the chapel, Celi?"

She looked down to see that his cup was empty. "Sure we can. I think I'd like that about now myself."

As they walked through the door, Celia was amazed at the transformation that took place within her. She wondered what Isaac was thinking and feeling, or whether he noticed the change.

Anita's words from their welcome tour rang in the air. *"This is our chapel. It was requested by our families. It is the only place in the village where people go to be silent, to meditate."*

Now she understood exactly what Anita had meant. There were beautiful orchestral and harp arrangements of the classics playing inside. The rhythmic music that danced over the grounds outside was inaudible from here.

Isaac took her hand and pulled her from one stained-glass window to the next, talking about the different scenes of the seasons. Then he stopped in front of the one of winter and stared in silence.

She sat and read the comments in the books placed on either side of the altar. All of the remarks pointed to one thing. *"Once inside these walls, nothing was insurmountable."*

Celia was amazed at how such a small chapel, in comparison to the rest of the grounds, could make one forget the petty things that were otherwise considered big deals. She thanked God that He had sent a retired minister to the village to pray with families and meet with those who needed consolation and comfort. And then she thought about the term "retired." *This is probably the most difficult job of his entire ministry.*

They exited the chapel, hand in hand, neither of them saying a word. It was the first time since Celia had met Isaac that she noticed a tear in his eye. He didn't wipe it away, but simply walked outside, ready to again face the world.

A world that has been very cruel to him, yet a world that has been an absolute delight. She felt the warm little hand in hers. *Is that world any different than it is for any of us?*

Isaac ran and squatted beside the painted fire hydrant. "Look, Celi, he has big eyes, too. Momma always told me I had big eyes. She said that's why she named me Isaac."

"Your mother was right. You have very beautiful, big eyes."

"She said they were the eyes of my father."

Celia stopped in her tracks and stared at the boy. That was the first time she had ever heard him mention his father. But as she looked into his rounded eyes, she knew exactly what his mother had meant. Isaac saw the world through God's eyes. He loved everyone, seeing only their insides, not their outsides.

Oh, how I wish I had known this boy's mother. She had to be a wonderfully wise woman. Celia gulped. *And oh, how I wish that she could be here to see him this week . . . this week and every week.*

Isaac was off again, this time chasing one of the tiny lizards that roamed the village. "Can we take one home with us?"

"Don't you think they would rather stay here with their families?"

"Yeah, I guess you're right."

He chased the tiny creatures from the sidewalks to the landscaping until he became exhausted and found shelter on a bench beneath the Old Elmer Tree.

"I just love Old Elmer," Isaac said, patting the tree.

"So do I," Celia replied. She stared up at the wise, pleasant face and the understanding eyes painted onto the tree. *It's like having a grandfather right here on the premises. Old Elmer possesses something that every child needs.*

It wasn't long before Isaac was ready to move again, having drawn strength and energy from resting underneath Old Elmer's branches.

"Can I run back inside the Ice Cream Palace and get some napkins?" he asked.

"Why do you need napkins? I have some tissues here." Celia reached in her pocket and pulled out the ones she had taken from the box in the chapel – the ones she had feared she would need later.

"The paper goblin is hungry. Listen, he's asking for something to eat."

She laughed as she gladly offered the tissues. *No wonder this place is so immaculately clean. The kids are all scrambling to pick up the trash and feed the Paper Goblins* – the name the village had given to the garbage cans that begged to be fed.

"Can't we go and bring him some napkins? He's still hungry."

How could any mother ever say "No" to those eyes? As she stared at Isaac for a moment, she realized that he truly *did* possess the most cherubic face she had ever seen on a child. She had felt that before, but dismissed it as the closeness of the bond that had developed between them. But now, she stood gazing down at him, his forehead, his cheeks, the shape of his mouth and nose, and those dazzling blue-violet eyes. He looked like an angel.

I guess every mother thinks that about her child, she reasoned. *Or is it the spirit of this place? Does it give this appearance to all the children who visit here?*

Celia glanced at her watch. "I have an idea. Why don't we grab a sandwich for lunch at the Ice Cream Palace? That way, we can go to Disney World for the rest of the day and see the fireworks tonight. And if you promise you'll sleep in the car on the way there, we'll hurry up and go."

"Oh, boy! *And* we can get some napkins. I'll race you." He tore off toward the Ice Cream Palace, yelling over his shoulder, "Celi, you're the greatest!"

"No, Isaac, you are," she managed to say before turning to wipe the tears that had come. And in the back of her mind she heard a tiny voice, *"Wouldn't Brad be so proud of me?"*

Celia held Isaac's hand as they strolled through the amusement park. One of the songs she had used in her classroom over the years, *When You Wish Upon a Star*, played from the loud speakers.

"I love that song, Celi. Will you teach it to me?"

"Don't you know it?" She immediately wished she could open her mouth like the big whale in the Pinocchio story and swallow those words. *Where would Isaac have gotten an opportunity to see the movie and learn the song?*

The young boy's eyes showed no sadness, looking, in fact, like they knew the thought inside Celia's head. His expression said he needed neither sympathy nor an apology.

"I saw a shooting star once. It was the night that Momma died."

Celia was greatly impressed by the bravery in the child's voice as he uttered those words. He said them with a sense of pride, as if God had paid a great tribute to his mother by taking her as one of His own private angels. Her heart wanted to bleed, and her eyes wanted to unleash the tears, yet how could she show such emotion when this orphan could speak so openly about his loss?

She thought back to the night of the nativity when she first saw Isaac and his mother. He had taught her, and every other person at the scene, a lesson then, too. It was a lesson of immense love – the same lesson he was teaching her now.

Her steps froze as she turned toward the boy and laid her hands on top of his head as she stared into his face, those huge eyes gleaming. It was not an act of laying on of hands, as she had experienced at her baptism or confirmation, but an act of wanting to feel the blessedness that flowed inside this child, this "Angel of the Lord." As she looked far inside those eyes, Celia saw that here stood a boy who was truly chosen by God.

She wanted to ask whether he had been baptized as a child, but decided against that, not knowing the denominational background of Maureen. It struck Celia that she had no idea as to the father's origin and background, whether he really *was* dead or alive, and whether he even knew he had a son. Since no mention had been made of a father, *at least an earthly one*, she saw it best to leave it that way. However, a thread of curiosity ran through her as she speculated about whether Maureen had ever once mentioned the father to Isaac.

Getting back to the conversation of the shooting star, she asked, "Did you make a wish?"

"I sure did. But Mama told me once that if I told my wish, it wouldn't come true. So I didn't tell. I hope you don't get mad, Celi, but I'm not going to tell you, either."

"Of course, I'm not going to get mad. Maybe one day your wish *will* come true."

"I hope so," Isaac replied, his eyes smiling as much as his lips. "It may have already come true."

His words made her wonder whether his wish had to do with his mother. Celia thought back to the evening in December that she and Brad had spent pouring out their pasts. She wondered if things would have been different for either of them had they possessed this child's spirit.

"Can we ride the tea cups, Celi?"

"We sure can."

She marveled at the exhilaration she saw in the boy's face as he took in the rides and showed no fear of any of them, especially the roller coasters – much to her dismay. Again she thought back to her childhood. Even in her childlike innocence, she had a fear of roller coasters and fast rides. But this child showed no fear of anything. Celia wondered how much of his strength and trust came from his lack of a permanent shelter, or guaranteed food or clothing.

♪ ♪ ♪ ♪

As they slowly made their way back down Highway 192 toward the Village, fireworks went off, lighting up the entire sky.

"Celi!" The child was so thrilled that he couldn't even speak.

She put the top down on the convertible so that he

could get an unobstructed view of the sky show. "Those fire-works are just for you, Isaac."

"Really?" His eyes never strayed from gawking at all the sparkling colors cascading as far as he could see.

"Absolutely." Celia smiled. She hadn't lied, for as far as she was concerned, this moment of this night in this con-vertible was no accident.

CHAPTER 28

"What's that building say?" Isaac pointed to a large building that resembled a warehouse in the distance.

"Santa's Workshop," she answered, remembering her promise to talk to him about Santa after the tour through the Castle of Miracles.

"Santa? I got a present from Santa before. He left some things for all of us homeless children at the shelter each year." Isaac looked at Celia with a pained expression. "Do we have to go to the Castle on Thursday night?"

"Of course we do! Why wouldn't you want to go to the castle?" she asked, startled at his inquiry.

"The snow. I don't want to be outside in the snow. It was always so cold in the snow. Sometimes the shelters were full and we had to build a fire and get close to all the other people under the bridge. Some people built fires in their tents and one night a man caught on fire in his tent." He stared at her, his eyes still full of pain. "Do we have to go?"

"Oh, Isaac," she comforted, hugging him with all her might. "It isn't real snow. It's only make-believe. And it isn't cold. In fact, it isn't anything. It's kind of like cotton candy in tiny pieces that comes out of a machine and blows around from a fan."

"It is?" His eyes lit up again.

"Yes, but don't tell anybody. You'll spoil Santa's surprise."

"I won't, Celi. I promise."

"Does that mean you want to go to the Castle on Thursday night now?"

"Yeah!" he grinned. "I wonder what kind of present I'll get."

She smiled at his tender innocence. "Let's go and sit in Millie's Butterfly Garden for a few minutes and see how many butterflies there are."

"Do you think there'll be any lizards?"

"I think there might be."

"Okay." Isaac grabbed Celia's hand and looked up at her. "I love you, Celi. You make things sound nice just like Momma did."

"Oh, Isaac. I love you, too. You're the nicest thing that ever happened to me."

"Yeah, me and Brad." A smile spread all the way across his face as he swung her arm back and forth as far as he could, just like Brad did with him at home.

As Isaac chased the lizards, trying to catch one of the babies, Celia found refuge on one of the mosaic benches and listened to the garden's small waterfall running over flat rocks. There were several brilliantly-colored butterflies showing off their wings and flitting about from shrub to shrub, much like the children who were guests running from activity to activity.

He sat on the bench beside her, delighting in the butterflies. "What makes them come to this garden?"

"I think it has something to do with the plants and shrubs. And these long slender houses are called butterfly houses."

"Do you think they can read the sign that says, 'Butterfly Garden?'"

Celia laughed. "I don't think so. Not unless they've got some really smart butterflies in Florida!"

Isaac joined her laughter.

She looked down at the sidewalk to see butterflies etched in the concrete. *No detail left out.*

Then Celia focused on the child who was seeing the things of life in a way that he'd never had the opportunity to do before. She reflected on all the things that DJ had provided for Isaac and how he had helped the doctors and Give Kids the World Village to actually make this dream possible. *No detail left out.*

CHAPTER 29

"Your limo's here, Miss Brinkley."

"What?" Celia stared at the phone as if it, instead of the voice on the other end, had recited those shocking words.

"Your limo. It's here to take you out for Parent's Night."

"You must have the wrong room. I didn't order a limo."

She heard the man on the phone briefly speaking with another man in the background before he came back on the line.

"This is your limo, alright, Miss Brinkley. The driver says they've been booked for two weeks. He has papers here with all the instructions for your evening and it's all been paid."

"Are you sure this isn't for another child's parents?"

"Unless there's another Celia Brinkley here with a boy named Isaac, which I don't see on our registration, it would be you. And since limos aren't part of the package for parents, this is no mistake. Someone's sent you a special present. Shall I send the chauffeur to your villa or would you prefer to come to the registration desk?"

"Uh . . . uh," Celia stammered, still in a wave of surprise, "I guess I can come to the desk. I wouldn't want the other families to think there's any special treatment for us."

If indeed the limo was for her, the astute musician had an idea of what was going on. She was sure that DJ was behind this surprise as a way of saying "Thanks!" for her part in making Isaac's wish come true.

Although Celia deemed the gesture of the event as most

significant, she had planned to stay in and read a good book or write notes of thanks to everyone who had helped with Isaac's wish. *I don't need the time alone. I have enough of that at home, and there'll be plenty more when . . ."*

She wasn't able to finish that sentence, knowing the time to deal with that situation would come early enough, as well.

"What's going on, Celi?"

She grabbed Isaac and hugged him, clinging him close to her body. "Well, it seems that someone has rented a limousine for my evening out."

"Oh, boy. Can I ride in it, too?"

Celia hated to disappoint the child, who had expectation written all over his face. "I'm afraid you have to stay here with the other children tonight. This is sort of like a night for the parents to have their wishes come true."

"Did you wish for a limousine?"

"No," she chuckled, "as a matter of fact, I didn't." Celia quickly changed clothes, grabbed a silk shawl from the closet and wrapped it around her shoulders. "I'll tell you what. Why don't you walk with me to the registration desk and see the limo? Then I'll walk you back to the theater or wherever it is that the children are supposed to meet . . . for their special night *without* adults," she added quickly, trying to dissuade any lingering disappointment from the child.

Isaac escorted his "special lady," their arms entwined, to the registration desk, each speculating about all the fun that the forthcoming evening would hold.

"Are you ready for your night out, Miss Brinkley?" asked the receptionist.

"Almost. I'd like for Isaac to see my carriage first," she grinned.

"Boy, that car's big enough to hold every kid in this place," Isaac blurted, his eyes larger than usual.

Celia agreed with him, thinking what a waste it was for her to spend the evening in the limo alone. As the chauffeur opened the door for her, she realized this was her first ride in a limousine. Suddenly she felt like Cinderella, sensing a taste of how this week must be for Isaac.

"Why don't you go ahead and I'll take Isaac back to the theater for you?" suggested the receptionist.

The child's small hands waved profusely as he watched the elongated "white pumpkin" drive off through the gate.

Celia had no idea what to expect as the limousine pulled into the valet parking area for Universal Studios.

"I'll be waiting for you when you've finished your dinner at Emeril's," instructed the chauffeur.

"Emeril's?" she asked, nearly as shocked as she had been when she received the call about the limousine. *DJ spared no expense, did he? How will I ever thank him for this?*

"Celia Brinkley. I believe I have a reservation."

"Ah, yes, Miss Brinkley. We've been expecting you."

Funny how everyone's been expecting this except me, she perceived, trying to eye the entire place without looking like a tourist. She followed the host to her table by the corner window. On the middle of the table sat a vase with a dozen red roses.

"Your server will be right with you."

Celia glanced around at the tables near her to see that there were no roses on them. *Boy, he really did go all out. No wonder so many women think he's the ideal man!*

"Good evening, Miss Brinkley. My name is Mauricio. I will be your server for the evening." He handed her an envelope. "I was told to give this to you upon your arrival. Now may I bring you something to drink while you look over the menu?"

"Water with lime, please," she muttered, staring at the envelope.

The curiosity was more than she could stand. Celia ripped open the envelope before looking at the menu.

Dear Celi,

I figured that planning this special evening would allow you to see once and for all that I am not the dumb jock you always suspected me to be. I'd love to see the expression on your face while you're reading this card, for I'm sure you never thought of me being the villain behind this surprise.

You have given so much of yourself for Isaac's sake, and I wanted to do some small thing to show you that you're appreciated. It's not only DJ and I that admire you, but everyone who sees you with that child. God gave you each other, and I feel very privileged to be a part of that unity.

Now enjoy your "Night Out," and know that you are doing exactly what you would be doing if I were there with you this evening. Give Isaac a good-night hug for me.

Missing you both,
Brad

Mauricio returned with the water. "I take it you're not ready to order yet," he noticed, seeing the card still in her hand.

"No, I'm sorry."

"It's quite alright. We had a note that came with the card that informed us to make sure you didn't suffer from cardiac arrest when you read it."

"My friend has an enormous sense of humor."

"From the looks of it, I'd say your friend has a lady friend, too!" Mauricio grinned. "Now there's only one small thing. I'm to take a picture of you for your friend." He took a disposable camera from his pocket and took Celia's picture. "I have instructions to send this home with you," he stated, handing her the camera.

"Wow, I really *do* feel like Cinderella," she softly

mumbled, unconsciously thinking aloud.

"Huh?" asked Mauricio.

"I was simply wondering what was the most delectable item on the menu," she answered, searching for an entrée that was accompanied by Peruvian blue potatoes.

CHAPTER 30

Red twisted ropes swung from shiny brass poles indicating the line for children to see Santa, just like in the big department stores from years past. A giant Christmas quilt hung majestically against a side wall. Celia examined every stitch on it, feeling certain that it had a story behind it – one that dealt with a former visitor of Give Kids the World Village.

"Look at the sky, Isaac."

"Whoa!" he exclaimed, gazing up at the ceiling that twinkled like a starlit night.

"Did you know that an astronomer volunteered his time and came here to do this for the village when he heard about this place?"

Isaac and Celia both turned to hear the explanation of a father behind them.

"He researched what a sky would look like on December 15th, and put the stars in their places accordingly, wanting to make sure the sky matched this Christmas event for the children."

Celia surveyed the ceiling again, noting the many constellations, as the indoor stars twinkled. She was amazed at the many areas of need, all with people who had stepped forth to fill them. *All for children from around the world to know one week of joy and peace.*

"It's my turn next, Celi. I'm going to see Santa."

His eyes took the place of the stars. She glanced at the other children to see that same expression on all their faces.

She couldn't help but wonder how many of these other boys and girls had never sat in Santa's lap.

Isaac reached up and whispered in Santa's ear as Celia played the role of the "Photo Mom."

"You be a good boy, Isaac. I'm going to be watching you."

"Are you really Santa?" Isaac asked softly, but audibly enough that Celia heard his question. She peeked around to make sure no other children were listening.

"You want underwear for Christmas?" the jolly fat man said, a tremendous jovial smile still stretching across his rosy red cheeks.

"Okay, Santa, I believe."

Even homeless children don't want underwear for Christmas, Celia laughed.

"C'mon, Celi. Come get your picture made with me and Santa."

She snapped a couple of shots of Isaac and the man in the red suit.

"C'mon, Celi," Isaac repeated.

"I haven't had my picture made with Santa in years," she blushed.

"You heard what the little guy wants. Here, I'll snap the picture." And with that, the father in line behind Celia grabbed her camera and gave her a slight nudge toward Santa's platform.

She sat on the opposite knee from Isaac and gave a big smile, reminding herself that this trip was not about her and it *was* "what the little guy wants."

"When you go over and make your cookie after this, you've got to make one extra. Don't forget now!" Santa lifted the child so that he could run to Celia, who had gone to retrieve her camera.

Isaac proceeded with an elf to a table filled with gifts that had been donated from various industries for the children. On it sat a small, decorated tree and on the floor all around it were baskets, also filled with surprises from Santa's Workshop. Anita had told her that many businesses donated

"Christmas" gifts throughout the year and that they were stored in that warehouse for each Thursday's celebration.

"Everyone gets a present," declared the elf with the child in front of Isaac. "Even your baby brother and your parents."

"Did you hear that, Celi? You get a present, too. Come pick out something."

She watched as Isaac scanned all the items on the table – an assortment from toys to stuffed animals to books to videos to novelty T-shirts.

"This is what I want," Isaac indicated to the elf with him. He pointed to a stack of Beanie Babies.

"Pick out the one you want," she told him.

He stuck his hand down into the stack as far as it would go, looking like someone going fishing.

When his hand came back with a multi-colored plush animal, the elf offered, "Let me see what it says on the label." She called out the name of the Beanie Baby before reading its birth date. "Born on August 27th."

Isaac began to grin and jump up and down while clapping his hands. "That's *my* birthday! That's *my* birthday!"

Hearing all the commotion, Santa called over to him. "That means you're going to have a great big birthday party this year. Ho, Ho, Ho!"

Thanks a lot, Santa! You're a big help, thought Celia. But already, her mind was racing to come up with just the right party for the child.

Racing! That's it. Maybe DJ can help me come up with something involving little race cars.

"What are you going to get, Celi?" Isaac called. The child was just as excited to see her choose a present as he was to get his own.

"Let's see what this is." She walked over to the table and saw a stack of shirts with race cars printed on them. "This looks good. We'll see if they have one in my size." Celia already knew that after a couple of wears, she would give the shirt to Isaac for a sleep shirt. *On second thought, I'll never get him out of his DJ shirt that he wears every night.* With that thought, she dug through the pile to find an oversized one that would last for a while.

She took Isaac into the adjoining room where he made a Christmas card. "This one's for you, Celi," he beamed. "Don't peek!"

Celia laughed. "I won't."

Her focus turned back to Santa and the attention he gave each child, mindful of every illness or situation. She watched as the elves maneuvered each wheelchair or helped the children make the few steps to Santa's lap. Although there were plenty of tears on the faces of accompanying family members, there was nothing but smiles and laughs on the faces of the children.

There were so many cameras going off that it looked that the painted stars on the ceiling twinkling off the walls.

"Can I make another one?" Isaac asked when he finished the first card.

Celia was so caught up in watching the faces of everyone who came through the line that his question startled her, causing her to look back at him.

"Sure you can," encouraged the elf. "You can make one for every person in your family if you want."

That could take all night! Celia mused, beginning to count all the people who had become like Isaac's family to the both of them.

Before she could come up with a mental count, he began to name them off. "Let's see, there's Brad and Uncle Cory and Mama Jean and Papa Randy and Jan and Tami and Jenn and Cookie and . . . *Dale Jarrett,*" he screamed.

"You know Dale Jarrett?" asked the elf, with the eyes and ears of everyone else in the room looking and listening for the child's answer.

"Uh-huh. He's my daddy," proclaimed Isaac proudly.

Glares came flying at Celia as she began to slouch in her chair.

"He *is?*" questioned the bewildered elf.

"Well, not really," confessed the child. "I don't have a *real* daddy. But DJ became my daddy when my momma went to be with Jesus."

Whispers started rustling through the crowd to replace the glares. Many of the Americans had seen or heard the well-publicized story of Isaac.

One of the fathers in the room came over and knelt beside Isaac. "Are you the little boy who was saved by Dale Jarrett last February on his way to Daytona?"

"Yes," admitted Isaac, busily coloring on Brad's card like his relationship with the racer was an everyday affair.

The man looked at Celia then back at Isaac. "I was at that race when Jarrett won. I saw him thank you for being his inspiration to win that race. There wasn't a person at the track who wasn't glad he won after they found out what had happened on his way to the track."

Celia smiled. She appreciated the man's interest in the child, but she hoped he didn't ask too many questions, putting Isaac in a bad situation. *Relax, Celia. Have you ever seen Isaac in a situation in which he couldn't take care of himself? After all, the kid is street smart!*

"So have you gotten to see Dale Jarrett anymore?" the man inquired.

"Uh-huh," Isaac answered, coloring another card and never raising his eyes.

"What, Isaac?" Celia corrected, insisting on his use of polite manners.

"Yes, sir." The boy stopped just long enough to glance up at the guy, and then went right back to work. "This card is for him."

Celia and the man both looked down to see a picture of an oval with several cars at various places on it, and one brown truck.

"Hey, have you got him driving the truck?"

"Yes, sir," the child replied, smiling at Celia to let her know he remembered his manners. Isaac went on to explain, "But it's only to make him laugh. Everyone knows DJ doesn't drive the truck."

She gave Isaac a quick wink to say, "Good job!"

"Cool card, kid. I'd like to be there when you deliver

that one." The guy watched Isaac writing his name on the inside of the card. "Hey, will you actually get to give this to him yourself?"

Isaac nodded proudly. "I'm going to ask him to take me for a ride in the big brown truck for Christmas if I'm not at my momma's house."

Both Celia's eyes and ears caught the last comment. *Oh, boy. How am I going to explain this one to him?* She decided that somewhere on the long way home would be a good time to broach that subject. For now, they needed to forget all thoughts of his mother's fate and her "new home," as Isaac called it.

They went outside just in time to enjoy the second snowfall of the evening. As the children ran and played, an older child approached Celia.

"Is Father Christmas still here?" he asked in a strongly punctuated accent.

"Yes, he's right inside," she answered. "Are you just getting here?"

"Yes'm. I came from South Africa."

"Why don't you enjoy the snow first? You'll still have time to see San . . . , I mean Father Christmas."

"It's fun," invited Isaac, handing Celia his cards, then chasing the flakes and trying to share them with the boy.

The new arrival joined Isaac in running around the trees and shrubs to catch the flakes. They instantly made a game of seeing who could dump the most snow on the other's head.

Celia noticed a blind girl who had also exited the castle after visiting Santa. Besides having the beautiful face of an angel, she held a hula-hoop in her hand, her "Christmas" gift. Once she had gotten a good distance from the door and out of the path of the snowfall, one of the volunteers helped her get the hoop around her. The girl let go of the sides and began to rotate her hips, keeping the circular object from falling. Other children ran into the castle to get hula-hoops.

The music teacher laughed. "*And suddenly there was with the 'angel' a multitude*" . . . *doing the hula-hoop and laughing and clapping*. She was not surprised when the blind girl outlasted everyone, adults and volunteers included, with the hoop.

"My son is not expected to live until Christmas. That's why he so badly wanted to see Father Christmas."

Celia spun around. The mother of the South African boy, with the same punctuated accent, was speaking to her.

"He wants to ask for presents for his brothers and sisters because he will not be here with them," the woman concluded.

Oh my gosh! Quick! Think of something appropriate to say. But Celia simply stood there. She could think of no words to share with the hurting mother that would sufficiently express her concern.

"Will you pray for him?" the mother asked.

"Absolutely," assured Celia. *What a simple request.* "And I'll add your son and your family to a list for prayer when I get home.

She hugged the woman, who gave a light whimper. *I'll have a mile-long list to hand to the Prayer Pigs when I get back to Concord.*

"I don't want my son to see my tears," the mother sobbed quietly.

"I understand. I have to hide the tears myself."

"I'm so glad your son asked my boy to play. Is he going to get better?"

"No," Celia answered, hanging her head. "I'm afraid he's not."

"My pastor told me that getting better for my boy meant going to live with Jesus."

A winsome smile came over Celia's face as she looked at the woman and took her hands. "Then both our boys are going to get better."

The mother nodded her head in understanding.

Celia called to Isaac. "Why don't we beat the rush to make your cookie? Your friend here needs to see Father Christmas."

"See you later," Isaac yelled, grabbing her hand and running to the Ice Cream Palace. "I'm going to go have some hot chocolate and get warm."

She chuckled at his holiday spirit, enhanced by the snow.

Then he turned to Celia. "Who's Father Christmas?"

Before she had time to answer, Isaac caught a glimpse of some of the children's cookies through the palace window.

"Look at those!" He pulled her with all the strength he had to get inside and make his own creation.

Children were putting designs of all kinds on their cookies, some piled high with icings and toppings. There was an entire table full of sprinkles and candies, not to mention a wide variety of colors of icings.

Isaac found an empty table, took a cookie from a tray and busily went to work.

One of the volunteers, a man whom Celia had seen walking around the grounds attending to various duties, entered the Ice Cream Palace. As he was coming in, an older child was exiting. "Are you keeping my secret?" the volunteer asked in a low tone.

"I sure am," the boy replied, noticeably proud that the man remembered him.

"That's my boy!"

Celia had noticed earlier how this man interacted with each child he met. She watched as he moved from child to child, making comments about their cookie creations or ice cream selections.

"How about a cup of hot chocolate?" he asked one girl. "It gets pretty cold out there in the snow."

"Is that *real* snow?" the girl asked, skeptically.

"About as real as it gets in Florida in July," he confided. The volunteer went to the counter and returned with two cups of hot chocolate – one for the girl and one for her mother.

He glanced at another table where a family sat in silence. It was obvious from the expression on his face that he inherently understood what was going on.

Or not *going on,* Celia thought as she watched him inch toward that group.

"Have you tried one of our cookies yet?" he asked the afflicted boy.

There was no answer.

"We've got lots of colors . . . even purple."

Still no movement.

As another volunteer walked by with a tray full of cookies, the man reached out, took two cookies and squatted beside the boy. "You want to do a cookie with me?"

A natural born teacher, Celia observed.

While the eyes of the child's family members ogled the man, he handed a tube of icing to the boy. The boy watched the man squeezing orange-colored confection onto the cookie. After a few minutes of seeing how much fun the man was having, the child squeezed some blue icing onto the cookie from the tube in his hand. Then he reached for another tube and added some purple. It wasn't long before the child had added every color and every topping possible to the cookie and then piled another cookie on top of the tall creation.

"I'm done," the boy announced, holding up his sweet treat.

"We've got a belly buster over here," the volunteer exclaimed to the mother of the child who at first had shied from making a cookie.

The boy leapt from the table and ran outside yelling "Bye" to everyone he saw coming in the door. He was waving his double-decker creation in the air as he went.

"Look, Daddy," he squealed to his father, who had gone to sit underneath one of the trees on the sidewalk.

Heads turned to see the reaction of the man. The father, who had given up on his son doing anything interactive with the other children, beamed and looked inside the window at his wife.

At another table, an older girl took a bite out of her cookie, then turned and handed it to her sister. "Here, this is for you."

"Look! It's Santa," called a boy who was seated by the window. He darted out the door with his cookie to offer it to the man who had listened to ninety-six wishes that night.

The other children went flying out the door behind him, each one waving a personally decorated cookie.

Isaac looked at Celia. "Why are all the children taking Santa a cookie?"

"Because children always leave," came the natural reaction. She caught herself before the next three words flew from her mouth. "Love to share their cookies with Santa."

That was all Isaac needed to run out the door, also bearing a cookie for the man who was now surrounded by children.

Many of the parents sat in the air-conditioned comfort of the Ice Cream Palace where they could watch their youngsters from the window-covered facade while others ran out waving cameras, looking like their children with the cookies.

Celia invited the volunteer to sit with her. "Aren't you going to have an ice cream?"

"No. If I eat one, a child may have to go without. You see, I come every Thursday to set up for the Christmas celebration, so that's fifty-two children who could be served over the course of a year."

Wow! That's what I call putting things in perspective, Celia thought, still more impressed with this individual. "I noticed that you certainly have a way with children. Are you a teacher?"

"No, but let's say I've been taught a very important lesson." He saw the look of confusion on Celia's face. "Two years ago I was struck by cancer. It hit me suddenly and after chemo, it started up again. I had to go through the treatments all over, and was out of work for a long time. But after the second round of treatments, it appeared that the cancer was gone.

"I was one of those people who prayed, 'Lord, if you'll let me live, if you'll let me stay to see my children grow up, I'll do anything for you.' That was not an empty promise just for the moment. The Lord saw fit to heal me, and I kept my word.

"When I finally got out of the hospital, I wanted to do something for all the people who had helped me through that difficult time. I tried to volunteer at the hospital where I had stayed for so long, but they had plenty of volunteers already. One of the hospital staff asked, 'Why not go to Give Kids the World Village?'

"I work for a place that sells building materials and was sending things out here. That's how I had first found out about the children. So after the hospital's recommendation, I came here and checked into the place. They told me that the Christmas volunteers had the hardest work, so that's the job I wanted."

He looked out the window at all the children circling Santa. "Ever since then, I've been here every Thursday except two, coming straight from work, setting up and decorating. It has been a fantastic therapy for me. I never feel bad or worry about myself, for I'm always concerned with others – the ones I meet here."

Celia sat spellbound by the man's story. She felt she had given of herself to help others through the academy's outreach programs, but this man made her sacrifices seem terribly insignificant.

"This disease picked the wrong person. I was meant to stay here and make a difference in the lives of others."

The listener could find no words to express her thoughts or feelings. Luckily, Isaac had his usual impeccable timing.

"Did you give Santa a cookie?" asked the volunteer.

"Yes, sir," he answered, pounding out both words.

The child's brief intervention gave his guardian the necessary time to express herself. "I'm sorry I didn't introduce myself earlier. My name is Celia Brinkley. I'm a music teacher at a private school in Concord, North Carolina, but I'm also their Director of Outreach. You could not have shared your story with anyone who would have enjoyed it more."

He extended his hand. "And I'm Jeff Frank. It's a pleasure to meet you." The volunteer looked at the boy. "And you must be Isaac."

"Yes, sir. You read my badge, didn't you?"

"Now whatever made you think that?"

"I saw your eyes. My momma taught me to watch

peoples' eyes. She said you could tell a whole lot about them by watching their eyes."

"Your momma must be a very smart lady." He smiled at Celia.

"She was," agreed the child as he tore off to get another cookie.

"Isaac was actually homeless. His mother was killed in an accident last February and his life was spared. Or so we thought before we found out about his illness. I'm only his guardian."

"Don't feel bad. A good percentage of the children who come here are adopted. One family who came here had seven or eight foster children."

Celia watched Isaac sit down at the table with another little boy. "Do you see that child beside Isaac?" she asked Jeff.

He nodded.

"We were with him and his mother in the castle. He threw a penny into the well and when it made a sound, he just stood there. Isaac went over to him and handed him another penny. Isaac threw one in first and began to imitate the "boing" he heard at the bottom of the well. That little boy threw in his other coin and listened. When the well made a completely different sound, he laughed and joined Isaac in trying to mimic the sound.

"They took off running through the castle, stopping in each room to play, starting first with the dress-up room. His mother told me that was the first time her child had laughed in two years. Two years," emphasized Celia.

"That's the thing about this place. Once you start coming, you don't want to quit. Every week, you meet *so* many wonderful families and hear such heart-warming stories. Some times there are those children who come out and grab you, just as that boy over there."

Celia looked back at Isaac and the other child. "What I especially love about this place is the way it provides such a wealth of support and strength – not only for the recipients, but for their families. Look at those two. It amazes me how those two children are drawing healing from each other.

"And that boy's mother is literally beside herself with joy. She confided in me earlier today that they almost didn't make the trip. Her husband's vacation was rejected at the last minute and they were all going to stay home. A neighbor heard about what happened, and came to help with the other children in the family so that the little boy could have his wish."

She looked back at Jeff with a tear in her eye. "Children really *are* the best teachers for each other."

"I know," he said simply. "Did you see the tall girl who was the elf at the gift table?"

"Yes. She helped Isaac choose a gift."

"That's my daughter. She's sixteen-years-old now, but when she started coming, she was just thirteen. It was only a couple of weeks after I began to volunteer. She'd heard me coming home and telling my wife about all that happened here. I was so excited that she begged to come with me. My wife and I agreed to let her come the next week and observe and do a few things with the children.

"She announced on the way home that she wanted to help every week. I told her that she couldn't because she was too young. I felt like the strain of seeing kids her age like this would be too hard on her. I was only trying to protect her.

"But she went home and told her mother, complaining, 'It isn't fair, Mom. It just isn't fair.'

"'We need to take a ride somewhere and talk about this,' I suggested. We got back in the car and drove around for a few miles while I tried to explain my point of view and the rationality of my decision. Then I let her know that, ultimately, it *was* my decision and that there was nothing else she could do about it.

"'I don't like your decision!' she balked. I was surprised by her lack of respect and her attitude. Then, before I had a chance to make a response, she added, 'What are you going to do the next time I tell you that you can't do that because of your illness? What if God took that attitude with you?'

"Her words really hit home. I knew that she was right. She was intelligent, she was mature for her age and she had watched me battle a terminal illness. She was right. There was no reason that she couldn't come. I drove her home and discussed it with my wife, whose response was, 'I thought you'd see it that way, too.'"

Jeff laughed. "That was the best decision I ever made." A massive grin covered his face. "Next to coming here to volunteer. She has a certain kind of magnetism, some sort of inborn skill or knack, with the children. She's like a small Pied Piper with them. Even the most timid of the children will go up to her. It's funny, she offers them a safety and a security that we adults can't. So she's even given the rest of the volunteers a lesson into the realistic view of life from the eyes of some of the recipients.

"And now, my nine-year-old comes once a month and helps. She's acquired pen pals from all over the world and has even gone out to dinner with some of the children her age."

"Wow! That's incredible," Celia replied. "Now I feel bad that I can't stay here and help myself."

"There's always tomorrow," Jeff encouraged.

"Yes, there is," she smiled, knowing there would come a day when she *would* have the opportunity to come back here.

Isaac came running up to the table with two cookies. "Here, Celi. I made a cookie for you."

She looked at his self-portrait on the cookie and burst into laughter. "This is great, Isaac. It's too cute to eat."

"Ah, go ahead. I can always make you another one." He handed the other cookie to Jeff. "And here, Mister. This one's for you. Brad and DJ will be glad to know you're taking good care of Celi for me."

"Who are Brad and DJ?" he asked warmly.

"Brad is mine and Celi's best friend, and DJ is the race car driver."

"You mean, as in Dale Jarrett?"

"Uh-huh . . . I mean, yes, sir."

Isaac hugged Celia then went back to sit with his new friend.

"Is that the boy that was rescued by Dale Jarrett?"

"Yes, it is," Celia answered, looking back over her

shoulder at the two boys at play.

"I'm sorry I didn't make the connection earlier when you told me he was homeless. I remember reading that story, and hearing the interview about the child after Jarrett won the Bud Shoot-Out."

"You're the second person I've met that said that this evening. One of the dads here was at the race."

"Well, I've run into a lot of exciting characters here, but I've never met a celebrity."

Celia laughed. "Isaac is no celebrity. He's a normal, little boy like," Her words stopped. She took another glance over her shoulder then looked back at Jeff. "It's so hard to realize that there *is* a problem with him and that he won't be around forever."

Then she thought of Frank's earlier words, *'There is always tomorrow'* and the fact that she knew she would one day be alone again. "I really do hope I get to come back here and share with others what people have given him."

"You know, you hear about all the bad things in the world, and how horrible the young people are in today's society. But you want to know what's really great? Here, you may see the kids who come battling with illnesses and how hard life is for them. But on the other hand, you see great people coming from all over the world.

"Last week there was a group of Girl Scouts who came from Georgia, and a group of college kids who came from Purdue University. My favorite was the group who came from Ireland – half Catholic and half Protestant, and they worked side-by-side with the kids. It was wonderful. And they all had a blast doing something positive for their country."

Jeff gave her a gentle smile. "It makes you take a different view of the world when you see all the great churches, college kids and families out there." He started to stand. "Well, I guess it's about time for me to be cleaning up the place."

Celia glanced at the clock on the wall. It was nearly nine. She had been so engrossed in listening to Jeff's story and watching Isaac with his new little playmate that she'd lost all track of time.

"What happens on Thanksgiving?" she asked, her curiosity mounting.

"Christmas is Thursday, regardless. You have them both on the same night. I've rushed straight from the holiday table to get here. I've even had Halloween to fall on the same night here as Christmas. That's really strange. You should try to get used to saying 'Merry Halloween' to the children."

"Do they dress up in costumes?"

"Absolutely. To the hilt. There are stands set up in front of the villas for the kids. It's great. And sometimes we'll have Christmas and New Year's on the same night. But every year, I get to have Thanksgiving and Christmas dinners on the same night. Now how many people get to do that?"

Jeff walked over to Isaac and his friend. "It's been a pleasure having you guys. Did you enjoy the cookies?"

"We sure did," exclaimed Isaac.

"We've made one for every volunteer who came tonight," boasted the other boy.

"Ooh, we may not let you two go home," Jeff playfully threatened.

"Oh, boy!" Isaac and his friend chimed in unison.

"Hey," the volunteer said to the boys as he squatted and placed a hand on the shoulder of each of them. "Did you know that Give Kids the World has a picture drawn by one of the children each year displayed on a race car? This year's car is going to be at Darlington in August."

Isaac's eyes lit up. "What kind of picture? Can I draw one?"

"You most certainly can. This year's picture has five ribbons on it, as I understand, to represent that this is the fifth year we've been doing this. One of the drivers and his team allows us to put it on his car for that race."

Celia could see that Isaac was already drawing his picture in his head.

"Talk to Anita about it. She can give you all the information. Also, if you like to draw, as it looks like the two of you do from seeing these cookies, there's a Give Kids the World Calendar done each year with a picture by a different child for each month. They're for sale on the village's Web site."

"Can we buy one?" Isaac asked Celia.

"Oh, I think we can," she smiled.

Once Jeff left, all the stragglers in the Ice Cream Palace wandered outside, the boys making plans to see each other the next day.

The two female volunteers turned out the lights and closed up the building. "Good-bye, all," they called.

"Good-bye," waved the boys.

As Celia and Isaac walked toward their villa, a boy came running as hard as he could toward the Ice Cream Palace. "Ice cream, ice cream," he screamed, terribly excited, in an accent that the teacher recognized as Hispanic.

"I'm sorry, the Ice Cream Palace just closed," she consoled.

The child kept trying, to no avail, to get the front door of the building open.

Celia walked over to him to try to explain that the palace would reopen the next morning, her heart breaking. *An ice cream shop where a kid can eat as much ice cream as he wants all day long, and he has to get here five minutes late.*

"He just flew in from Colombia."

Celia heard the female's Hispanic voice from behind her. She turned to see the child's mother. Now she hurt even more to think how this child had looked so forward to his trip, only to have just missed Christmas and ice cream.

Jeff walked by, having removed all the Christmas decorations and organizing things for his return the following week.

She ran to catch him, explaining the situation and trying to see if there was not something that could be done.

"I'm sorry," he said, also obviously torn that the child's timing had caused him to miss the evening. Then he smiled. "But if I were you, I wouldn't worry about it too much."

Celia turned to see that Isaac and his new friend from the Ice Cream Palace had greeted the new arrival and were blowing and chasing bubbles taken from the evening's gift table.

"See what I mean about them learning from each other?" Jeff asked. "They can't even speak the same language, but words are unnecessary. They understand playing and laughter."

"I hope I get to see you again someday," Celia smiled. "No wonder the children enjoy Christmas here so much. Thanks again for making it happen for them."

"I'll be looking for you to help me down here sometime when you can get away."

"You can count on it," accepted Celia, giving the man a hug. "And Isaac and I will say a prayer for you." She saw a tear form in Jeff's eye as he turned and walked toward the gate where his daughter was waiting for him.

CHAPTER 31

Has it been a week already? Celia asked herself. *Time certainly flies when Isaac is having fun!*

She packed the last of his clothes into the suitcase and double-checked to make sure she had left none of the souvenirs the child had bought for all his friends and "family" back in Concord.

As she looked at the six shopping bags full of presents, it was hard to imagine that they came from a little boy who had been homeless until five months ago. Celia took a quick inventory to make sure he hadn't forgotten anyone on his list. *Funny, there's not one thing here for Isaac. It's all for someone else.*

All accounted for. She thought about the fact that he had even given away many of the items he had brought. *It's like he knows he won't need them later.*

Celia went to look in on Isaac, who was still asleep. *I wonder if he knows . . .*

As she watched his small chest moving up and down, and stared at the cherubic expression on his face, she was sure that he did. *Yet he's not once mentioned it. He doesn't appear to be alarmed about it.*

She pictured Brad standing behind her with his hand on her shoulder. *"Celi Brinkley, you are trying to read things into the situation that aren't there. Quit trying to play God."*

As badly as she hated to admit it, she knew that those were exactly the words the coach would have used had he been there. And not only that, she knew he would have been right in his assessment.

She continued to watch the child, so pure and innocent yet so full of wisdom, and thought of the world of miracles – *literally miracles from all over the world* – that were congregated here. Celia suddenly realized what a small piece of the world she actually was.

What a base for a support group, she mused, thinking of Jeff's words and her earlier observations. She had watched as families compared notes, swapped e-mail addresses, and commiserated and counseled each other.

Instead of the blind leading the blind, it's the life-threatening illnesses leading the life-threatening illnesses. What a genius Mr. Landwirth really is! This place is much more than a facility to bring children a week of happiness.

♪ ♪ ♪ ♪

"Let's walk past the pool one last time," suggested Celia. "Maybe if we're lucky, we'll find Mayor Clayton walking around the village and be able to tell him bye." *Besides, it seems most appropriate to end our visit at Claytonburg's Park of Dreams.*

Isaac took her hand and slowly walked the grounds with her. When they came to the pool's entrance, Celia stood inside the gate and silently read the words of Winston Churchill again. *"We make a living by what we get. But we make a life by what we give."*

Those were the first words she had seen upon her entry into the village. And now they simply would not leave her. She read them several times over until she was unconsciously saying them aloud.

"Huh?" Isaac asked, trying to make out the words on the plaque himself.

"That's something for all the adults who come here," she explained. "You kids get all the good stuff and have lots of wonderful memories. These words are the good stuff and wonderful memory for the parents and volunteers."

"Okay," he replied, his face still showing confusion,

but his mind satisfied that she'd answered his question.

Celia knew this was not the last time she would read these words on this plaque, but she knew the next time, Isaac would not be beside her, holding her hand.

"I want to go to the Gingerbread House, Celi. I'm hungry."

She glanced at her watch. "They're still open for breakfast. Let's go."

They took their food and sat down at one of the "peppermint" tables. Anita had told her that the volunteers had placed more than 26,000 peppermints in the tables' tops, giving them a most colorful and delightful appearance. Celia stared at the shelves lining all the walls. They were all covered in dolls, dolls from all over the world that had been left by the children who came.

"There's over a thousand dolls," stated the waitress, noticing Celia's interest.

She continued to look around the walls, trying to picture a child to go with each doll.

"Aren't they pretty?" Isaac, too, was examining the dolls.

How odd that a little boy would see the beauty in these. She glanced at his face and realized that what he saw went much deeper than the surface of the dolls. He had a connection with each doll. He had a connection with each child who had ever visited the village.

"I'll be right back." He scooted out of his chair, his DJ action figure in hand.

Celia watched as he ran to the front of the restaurant and said something to the hostess. She saw the woman call a tall man from the kitchen. The man bent down and talked to Isaac. After seeing them exchange dialogue for a couple of minutes, she saw Isaac reach up and hand the man his racing character.

Tears filled her eyes as she watched the man take the doll and place it on a shelf right at the front of the food line. *"But we make a life by what we give."*

Twice now she had seen this little boy give his most

prized possession so that another child might find happiness. Celia bit her lip as the child hopped back in his seat, undaunted by what he had just done.

"Are you ready to go home now?" she asked as he took his last bite.

"Almost. I want to write something in the book at the chapel."

Celia followed the young child from the Gingerbread House to the place that had become home to him while at the village. She knelt beside him on the altar while listening to the reflective music of a harp soaring and ebbing, capturing the emotions of the crescendos and decrescendos of real life. *This is so symbolic of what must be going on within the heart and soul of every parent who comes here with a child.*

She stared at the windows while Isaac bowed his small head.

When he finished his prayer, he looked longingly at each window while still kneeling. "Celi, do you think Momma sees all these things in heaven?"

"Oh, I think she does. I think she sees all these and a whole lot more. The scenes in these windows, although extremely beautiful, are nowhere as beautiful as where she lives."

"Do you see that stairway to heaven?"

Celia looked at the window in front of the altar. "Yes. It's magnificent, isn't it?"

"Uh-huh," the child replied simply. "That's the same thing I saw the night Jesus took Momma to heaven. Momma had to go up the stairway, but I'm going to have stepping stones like those."

She looked at the window to see the stones that made a path up beside the stairway. "How do you know that?" she questioned.

"I saw the light, just like that one," he pointed, "when the angels opened the door for her at the top of the stairs."

Celia stared at Isaac in disbelief. Had this child had a dream about his mother after seeing this window earlier in the week, based on some ideology she had passed on to him about the pleasantries of the hereafter? Or had this child, who truly *did* seem to possess an unnatural understanding of God really get a glimpse of heaven when his mother died? Had he been close enough to death himself to have a vision of what was to come?

No wonder he thought Dale Jarrett was an angel. Celia began to wonder about all the things Isaac had told her and the many ways she had seen him touch the lives of others. *Dale Jarrett truly was an angel . . . an angel who rescued another angel.*

"Look at all the flowers in the window. Momma loved flowers. And they're my favorite color – Carolina blue."

Celia thought back to the evening of the live nativity and Isaac's blanket dotted with holes from use. It had been Carolina blue. *No wonder it's his favorite color.*

She inspected the window more closely. The path of stones was lighted in contrast to the brown earth covered with the blue flowers. Celia turned her body enough that she could see every detail of the other windows from her knelt position and read the caption of each window. "Love – Summer, Faith – Fall, Peace – Winter, Hope – Spring."

Her head bowed as she prayed that she had given - *No, helped to develop* – the fruits of the Spirit that this child's mother had planted in him.

As she listened to another short prayer that Isaac offered, an ocean of tears billowed down her face. Her heart was crushing and it felt as if someone were squeezing every breath from her lungs. Celia looked down at the floor as she tried to wipe her eyes. *This altar and all the pews in this place may be kid-sized, but the prayers are surely not!*

She listened as he prayed for God "to take good care of Momma and Dawn." *It's a good thing that someone had the foresight to leave the tissue boxes.* Celia grabbed a handful of tissues.

When Isaac finally said "Amen," he stood and walked over to the table beside the altar. "Will you write for me and let me sign my name?"

Celia picked up the pen and another handful of tissues, and began to take his dictation.

"I love this place. It was lots of fun and it let me see

that Momma is doing just fine." He paused for a minute and smiled at Celia. "And Dawn, too."

The child reached up and signed his name. Then he took Celia's hand and walked out the door.

This place has prepared both of us for the days to come. She looked down at the child, whose eyes and smile were the same as they always were. *Full of love.*

"How about one last game in Amberville before we leave?" she invited.

"Can we drive the boats and race the cars? I'll bet I can beat ya!"

"I'll race you there and we'll see!"

The pair took off down the sidewalk to the entrance of the game room.

Most of the games were designed for two players, so they went around the room playing every game. Celia laughed aloud. She had never played a video game before in her life until they came here.

Then she looked down at Isaac. *Imagine that! He had done something I hadn't.* She envisioned the lifestyle he had experienced before the death of his mother. *I suspect he's done a lot of things that I haven't.*

Her heart still carrying the wrenching pain from earlier, Celia went to the game where she hit the balls with the mallet. "What a great stress reliever," she mumbled, getting a perfect score as she pounded out her frustration. She played the game over and over until she realized that Isaac had curled up on one of the oversized plush animals piled in the corner and was taking a nap.

Celia stood staring at him for quite a while, wishing she could make a wish on a star and have a star fairy place it on the ceiling. There were so many thoughts going through her head at the moment, but all of them revolved around the little boy who lay curled up in front of her.

All of this time, she had hated that his mother could not be here with him. But as she reflected on the words of his prayer from the chapel, Celia realized that Maureen *was* here. *At least in her son's mind.*

She reached over and picked him up. "Don't you think it's time to go home, little fellow?"

"Uh-huh," he mumbled, still half asleep, as he clung his arms around her neck.

And in my mind, too.

As she buckled Isaac in the passenger seat, Celia thought of the words she had heard from another wish child's parent. *"Give Kids the World Village offers its recipients the opportunity to live the life of a normal child, and a week for the family to be away from the stresses of home and the illness.*

Celia drove out the gate, catching a last glimpse of Mayor Clayton's picture on the sign in her rear-view mirror. *This is what vacation is meant to be for* every *child.*

She listened to the hum of the motor in the T-Bird. *We truly* were *treated like royalty the entire time we were here,* she realized. *From start to finish,* Celia grinned, tapping the pearly-white knob of the gearshift.

CHAPTER 32

"I heard there was a party going on here. I decided I'd better come over and make sure no one has too much fun!"

"Braaaad!" Isaac yelled as he ran across Celia's back yard and jumped into the man's arms.

"Do you think you could teach Celi to do that?" he jeered toward the hostess.

"Uh!" was the only response Brad got as she hurried past him.

The young boys, all from the academy, clustered around the coach. Each one was anxious to tell about his summer activities.

"Why don't you guys find a seat?" Celia called. "We'll be having cake and ice cream soon, but first we're going to have some special entertainment."

"I'll bet it's a clown," guessed one child.

"I think it's a magician. That's what we had at my party," bragged another.

"Brad, would you do the honors of introducing our entertainment?" Celia asked, a twinkle in her eye.

"I'd be honored," he answered. "Okay, guys. This afternoon we've invited someone very special to come and entertain you. But I'm not going to tell you this person's name because, well, just because I think you'll all recognize this guest."

The boys looked at each other in excited curiosity.

"I know," volunteered another boy. "It's going to be Dr. Lacey all dressed up or something."

"Okay, gentlemen, let 'er roll," yelled Brad.

A soft buzz began around the side of the house and then grew louder so that it sounded like the roar of small engines. Heads were spinning in anticipation of what was coming around the corner of the house. All of a sudden, a remote control car came spinning around the sidewalk followed by another one, and then another.

The boys all began to squeal excitedly while straining their necks to see the movements of the cars. Suddenly they recognized Dale Jarrett, followed by several of his racer friends, all dressed in their racing uniforms, each one holding a controller and steering their cars to the delight of the audience.

Larry McReynolds followed them and in his typical Hollywood Hotel fashion, announced the antics of the cars.

The boys all began to yell and cheer for the drivers and the cars. Brad winked at Celia, whose laughter was so great that it was overpowering the tears of joy at seeing these grown men giving of their time and energy to make a small boy very happy. *And in the midst of it, they're all having so much fun themselves!* she observed.

It was then she noticed that the miniatures all had the same paint schemes and logos as the drivers' real cars. She listened to the boys' shouts, noticing that they were so caught up in the actions of the cars and who was in the lead that they were totally unaware that they were standing within feet of some of the world's best-known athletes.

Little boys, she chuckled. *All still little boys.*

Celia's eyes turned to Brad, on whom they became glued. She couldn't help but notice the love and compassion he had, not only for Isaac, but also for all of the students. And he was just as excited about all the goings-on as the youngsters. *"All" still little boys,* she reiterated in her mind.

Brad caught her eyes watching him. He winked at her, mouthing, "Great job! This was most definitely a hit," and then nodded toward Isaac, who was running on the grass alongside the cars on the sidewalk.

Her attention turned to the fact that she was supposed to be the photographer of this grand event. She grabbed her camera from the picnic table and began snapping shots as fast as the film would advance.

Brad inconspicuously made his way beside her. "How did you ever pull this off without the media hounding the place?" he marveled.

"It helps to know people in high places," she grinned, proud that he was impressed with her plan.

"Well, all I can say is that you've pulled off a birthday party that none of these guys will ever forget. This one included," he added, kissing her cheek.

Celia hurriedly glanced around to make sure no one had seen Brad's action.

"Relax. All I wanted to do was say, 'Thank you.' This was really something else."

She smiled, still watching to make sure that no one had noticed them. "Do you think anyone will be interested in cake and ice cream after this?"

After nearly thirty minutes of "wild and *literally* neck-to-neck racing," Brad helped Celia herd the crowd into her sunroom for refreshments.

"We need something after all that," joked one of the drivers. "That was more work than being behind the wheel."

"Yeah, and we'll see who wins tomorrow at Bristol!" prodded the driver who had come in last place.

It was no surprise to anyone, given the afternoon's entertainment, that the cake would be in the shape of Jarrett's car with his number 88 and logo done in appropriately-colored icing.

The drivers wolfed down cake and ice cream like all the other males at the table. Then they sat with the young guys and signed autographs.

When it was Isaac's turn for autographs, Jarrett announced, "And for you, Mr. Birthday, I hope you don't mind if we leave all these cars so you can race with your friends when they come over." The racer took off his cap and put it on the head of the boy who had come to look upon this man as both his dad and his angel.

"Thanks, DJ!" Isaac screamed as he jumped into the

lap of the driver. "And thanks to all you guys for coming, too. Come back and play anytime."

"I see he gets his manners from you, Jarrett," scoffed one of the other drivers.

Celia could see that the remark was to cover up ensuing tears of the grown men.

"Yes, thank you," offered Celia. "And yes, Mr. Jarrett, Isaac truly *does* have wonderful manners just like you."

She couldn't help but think what exemplary role models these men were for the impressionable young minds seated with them. Celia had prayed many times over the years to leave her students with valuable lessons. *And now, thanks to this beautiful child having the birthday, my students have received not one, but two, valuable lessons,* she mused, thinking of his visit to the academy's live nativity the year before.

The drivers shook hands with each of the boys and then took off, leaving all the boys "oohing" and "aahing" over what had just happened.

"Man, that was like the coolest birthday party ever," announced one of the children.

All of the boys joined in agreement.

"Thanks for inviting us, Isaac!" blasted another.

"Yeah, wait 'til I tell my dad who I ate beside," bragged one.

"Wait 'til *I* tell my *mom*! She thinks Dale Jarrett's got the most gorgeous eyes in the world!" blurted another.

"She and how many other million women?" laughed Celia, realizing that she had been the only female at the party with all those men, all of whom were heartthrobs for the thirty-million female NASCAR fans.

"And wait 'til I see his mom. She'll never live that one down," Brad whispered to Celia.

The remark cost him a sharp punch in the ribs. "You guys!" she scorned, shaking her head.

As parents began to arrive, the boys all rushed to be the first to tell about the afternoon's activities.

"Thanks for a great time," called a child from the back seat of his dad's car.

"Can we come over again next Saturday and race the cars?" yelled one.

"Can I come with him?" asked another's dad.

"Only if I can come," added the mom.

After the last boy had left, Isaac grabbed Celia and hugged her with all his might, which she could tell was very little after all the energy he had exerted during the course of the afternoon.

"Would you like to take a nap?" she questioned, squatting to be on his level.

"No way!" he boldly answered. "There's too many toys to play with. Hey, Brad, wanna race?" the child called, running to grab Jarrett's remote car.

"Only if you let me win!" laughed the coach, running behind the boy.

Celia watched the two of them at play for a few minutes before beginning the chore of clearing the wrapping paper and trash from the back yard.

"Don't worry with that stuff! There's plenty of time for that later," Brad ordered.

The weary hostess smiled at him appreciatively and sat down to watch the rest of the backyard race.

It wasn't long before Brad announced, "I guess you're the winner." He could see that the little fellow was nearly out of steam. In a playful manner, he picked up the child, still clutching the remote control and the car, and carried him to his bedroom.

The child's eyes were closed and he was already asleep by the time his body hit the bed.

Celia followed and pulled a lightweight wrap over the child. "Should I put the car on the dresser in case he rolls over?"

"Absolutely not. He'll probably not let go of that car for days." Brad looked at the child and gave an audible smirk, "I know I wouldn't have when I was his age." He gave another smirk. "In fact, I've been eyeing one of those cars pretty hard myself."

"Uh!" sighed Celia, playfully dismissing him as earlier and walking out the door.

"That was a most impressive party," he complimented when they were back outside.

"It was something, wasn't it? I hope I didn't tire Isaac out too much or that it didn't take too much of a toll on him."

"Are you kidding? This was probably the greatest day of his life. He'll never forget this as long as he . . ." Suddenly the words stopped as he saw the look of dismay appear on Celia's face. "I'm sorry . . . I didn't mean . . ."

Celia reached over and took his hand. "It's okay . . . really. I know what you meant . . . or didn't mean." She tried to force a smile, but instead tears streamed down her face.

Brad took her in his arms. "Let it out. If you're going to be that boy's strength and caretaker, you're going to have to unleash all this pain."

Knowing he was right, Celia let the tears flow freely. "It's so hard to think about the future."

"That's exactly why we're *not* supposed to think of the future," he comforted.

"Thank you for being here. I really needed this time to regroup."

"You're welcome. And I hope you know, Celi, that I'll be here anytime you need me. You or Isaac."

"I know. I appreciate that. Sometimes I feel like I can't carry it alone."

"You don't have to and I had better not ever see you trying."

She gave a light smile.

"And neither had DJ," Brad added.

Celia nodded. "Thanks for the warning," she acknowledged, the shakiness from moments before leaving her voice.

"I still want to know one thing, though," he coaxed, picking up all the debris from the gifts. "How *did* you manage to keep away all the reporters and photographers?"

"Simple. I didn't invite them," she boasted, walking toward the garbage can with an armload of wrapping paper.

CHAPTER 33

"Are we gonna take the truck around, DJ?" came the voice weak from exhaustion.

"We sure are."

The driver and the child began to walk toward UPS Trackside Services, hand in hand. Celia knew that Isaac had run out of fuel when she saw the tall statue-of-a-man bend down and take the child in his arms. Even in the boy's tiring moment, you could tell from the joyful expressions on his face that he and the racer were engaged in an exciting conversation – *at least from the standpoint of a seven-year-old.*

Celia instantly realized that was what made Dale stand apart from all the other drivers. He was in an intensely stressful profession, yet he could change gears with his thoughts and emotions - given the situation - as quickly as he could change gears in the "88" car.

"How did Isaac ever pull that one off?" one of the nearby spectators asked.

Celia grinned, glancing over at one of the guys in DJ's pit crew, who was returning her smile. *And* waiting to see what explanation she would come up with for this one.

"People love the truck. People love the kid. It's a winning combination."

Suddenly, a horde of reporters came out of the pits - the proverbial woodwork - at the very instant Celia made her comment. Pens were flying and cameras were flashing toward the driver and child, who were climbing into the passenger side of the truck.

"What a great addition to our logo. We ought'a put you on the payroll," one of the UPS spokesmen joked.

"Hey, I'm always looking for a better job," she kidded back.

"Miss Brinkley, you couldn't *have* a better job than the one you've got now," the man said, entirely changing the mood.

She looked at him as her smile turned into a gentle, radiant glow. "You're right. Two years ago I was in the tumultuous throes of burn-out, praying for a way out that would allow me to touch lives in an extraordinary way and still use my musical skills. And now, here I am, in a totally new venue, a strangely new environment, and I get to use all my talents and fulfill all my needs – all at the same time."

♪ ♪ ♪ ♪

"Crank her up!" Jarrett said, as he sat in the "big brown truck," securing Isaac on his lap.

"Say what?" asked the UPS driver, shuffling his newspaper and pulling down his foot that was propped on the dash.

"Crank her up!" repeated the racer.

"Are we taking this truck around the track?" came another question with the turn of the ignition.

"Not if you don't step on it," smiled Dale.

"Oh, wow! Wait 'til I tell my wife!" laughed the driver. "This is the best load of cargo I've ever had," he smiled, glancing at the child.

♪ ♪ ♪ ♪

Crowds were jumping up and down and cheering loudly as the truck rounded the fourth turn.

"Woo-hoo," came the yells of onlookers as the cameras and pens took a second wave of action.

Celia could tell from the way DJ carried the child from

the truck that Isaac was suffering severely from his illness. Yet, his adrenalin was making up for any loss of energy caused by the debilitating virus.

"How was it?" called the crewman.

"It was great!" yelled Isaac, an abnormal weariness evident in his enthusiastic voice.

Jarrett didn't even attempt to put Isaac on the ground as he neared his pit. Rather, he handed the child to Celia and called for one of the many golf carts running through the pit area to come and take the pair to their car.

No words were spoken, but the racer and the teacher exchanged glances of appreciation for each other. The joyful spectators did not notice the look of impending fear that also exchanged between the two.

CHAPTER 34

Isaac had become a mascot for the racing world. Fans had seen his face splashed on the front pages of sports sections, in sports magazines and news broadcasts as he had been portrayed as adopted by the NASCAR drivers.

Celia's favorite shot, yet the one she also hated the most, was one snapped two days earlier at the Talledega track where Jarrett had taken the small child's hand, which had become terribly frail, and was walking him toward the "big, brown truck." The following frame showed Dale having to pick the child up because he was too weak to take any more steps. Every time she looked at that article, she couldn't help but wonder how many tears had been shed thanks to that one photographer.

Thinking of that picture now, she said a special prayer of thanks to the Almighty that He had seen fit to let this young child be full of life, his blue-violet eyes beaming, for this day as he actually got to share in the excitement of a real race. Her thoughts were cut short as he yanked on her hand and said, "C'mon, Celi, the man's motioning for us."

Isaac stepped up to the platform, causing an instant hush to come over the entire racing arena.

Celia, who was walking close behind him, moved over to the piano that had been placed on the stage. She sat down, found her spot of perfect balance and extended her long, slender fingers over the keys. *My eighty-eight. May that be a lucky number today.* From the first note, she knew that she had complete control over the instrument. She also knew Who had complete control over her. And a quick glance at Isaac told her who had complete control over the crowd.

Her eyes and throat hinted that there was a mass of tears and lumps looking for a place to hide. But her tranquil pride in Isaac and Dale Jarrett, and his friends and associates who had been a part of this extraordinary happening, forced the tears and lumps away, promising them their own turn for attention at a later date. Celia knew that Isaac's battle could not last much longer, and there would be plenty of time for her internal feelings to take their own private course of grieving and healing.

Not wanting to miss a moment of the glory that came with her privileged honor, she forgot all thoughts but those of feeling the music with her entire body. She could sense Brad's eyes on her and his spirit meeting hers somewhere out in the air over the crowd, even through the airwaves from Concord. And she could feel the heart and soul of every person who had met Isaac straining to watch his every move on the big screens at the track, and in family rooms and sports cafes around the nation.

At the very moment that she hit the last note of *The Star-Spangled Banner*, Isaac took three steps closer to the microphone.

"Gentlemen . . ." There was a long pause as the child looked out over the crowd and flashed an enormous smile, the largest Celia had ever seen on him. It matched his huge blue-violet eyes, as big as saucers for the whole world to see, full of a perfect and pure love that only a child could know. He rested his eyes on Celia for a second, blew her a kiss, and turned back to the microphone. With all the voice and strength he could muster, he yelled, "May the best man win. Star . . . ar . . . art your engines!"

The crowd's laughter and thunderous applause did not take a back seat to the roar of the engines. Celia knew that in addition to the sparks that had been ignited under the hoods were the ones that matched them in the hearts and soul of every driver on the field and every fan in the stands.

There was no doubt in her mind about who would

win this race. And she suspected that there was no doubt in the minds of the spectators or the drivers, either, for Isaac had just ordained the winner in his simple voice and his young mind. *No matter who crosses the finish line first.*

Once again, this child had become a messenger as the Holy Father chose to publicly smile down on one of His children who had given the gift of love and generosity many times over.

♪ ♪ ♪ ♪

Isaac's small head rested against Celia's arm. His short-lived burst of adrenaline ran out about the same time as the first caution flag at lap 22. The race became inconsequential as her thoughts were filled with prayers rather than speeding cars.

"Dale Jarrett . . ."

Isaac's arm raised as he waved his DJ pennant every time he heard the racer's name over the speaker system, which was barely audible over the combined roar of the cars and the crowd. "Go DJ," he would call out, a tiny voice protruding in spite of the closed eyes. His action figure of the racer was tightly clasped in the other hand.

Celia wanted to blame the lackadaisical state on the euphoria that came from worshipping with all the drivers and their families earlier that morning, and meeting Miss America and several pro football and basketball players. But she knew those were the things that were probably keeping him alert at all for the time being.

She knew that a trip to NorthEast Medical Center was eminent once they returned to Concord, but she didn't want to face that for the moment. DJ and Isaac were both basking in the glory of the day, even though the child could barely hold his head up, and the racer was not in the lead.

"Looks like your little fellow's tuckered out," noticed the woman behind Isaac.

"Yes, it's been a long weekend," Celia responded.

"Do you know what I'd give to get as close to Dale Jarrett as that little boy? He's the best thing on two feet," grinned the woman seated next to the first woman who spoke.

Celia smiled. She'd heard of all the female race fans and Jarrett admirers, but this was the first time she'd actually been approached by one.

"We're both members of DJ's fan club," announced the first woman.

"Yeah, we stand in line for autographs and pictures, and both have DJ "everything" on our cars and in our houses," confessed the second.

"DJ's the greatest!" exclaimed Isaac with what voice he had left as he held up a skinny finger and motioned the driver around the track, falling back against Celia.

"You said it!" both women agreed in unison.

♪ ♪ ♪ ♪

Isaac was barely able to open his eyes to see DJ cross the finish line. "Can we go now, Celi? I'm tired."

With the help of the two female fans behind her, Celia managed to get Isaac to the ground level of the Moss Thornton Tower, where she then called to a passing NASCAR worker in a golf cart for aid in getting the child to the parking lot.

Celia was able to beat most of the race traffic as she hurriedly made her way east on Speedway Boulevard toward I-20. She noticed that Isaac's coloring was extremely pale as he lay asleep against the seat.

The sky was unfolding into the most spectacular sunset she had ever seen as they neared Atlanta. Skyscrapers, resting against the backdrop of deep-orange and pink glowing colors, took on a golden hue as they reflected the last of the day's bright rays.

"Momma!" Isaac sat straight up in the seat as he called the name.

Celia turned to see him gazing into the sky.

"Can you see it, Celi?"

"See what?" she asked, startled.

"It looks just like the stained-glass window in front of the altar at the Give Kids the World Village."

He's right, she realized, staring into the clouds. The colors of the clouds, combined with the glow of the steel buildings of the Atlanta skyline looked like an iridescent city of gold. A shiny yellowish-white cloud began to open so that it looked like a donut, possessing a hole in the middle that looked like an entranceway into the heavens.

Celia panicked. *It's exactly like how he described what it looked like on the night his mother died.* She pulled the car over to the emergency lane so that she could get a better look. *Perhaps I'm imagining things, or letting fear get the best of me.* But as she stopped the car and looked at the sky, her eyes confirmed that what she saw was real.

Had it not been for Isaac's yell, she'd have been raving over the magnificent evening sky as she headed toward Atlanta. But as it was, she knew this was her cue to immediately get the child to the hospital.

She'd heard tales of people, who were nearing the end of life, seeing or hearing deceased loved ones. Celia wondered whether that had been the case with Isaac since he had been asleep until his sudden outburst. Given the sky's unusual appearance, she found anything believable.

Grabbing her cell phone, she dialed the number she had committed to memory in case of an emergency.

"Hello."

"DJ! I'm so glad you were able to answer. Are you in Hickory?"

"Yes, we just landed and we're on our way to the car. Is everything okay?"

"I don't think so. In fact, I think something's very wrong. Isaac needs to get to the hospital."

"Where are you?"

"Still on I-20."

"How soon can you be to Atlanta?"

"I can see the skyline now, so it shouldn't take long."

"Get to the airport. I'll bring someone to drive your

car home and we'll get Isaac back in my jet. Can you alert Dr. Teague that we're on our way and have Brad meet us at the Concord Regional Airport?"

"Yes."

"Let me say bye to my family and I'll be on my way. Drive safely and call me back if there's a problem."

Celia, while calling Brad and asking him to call Dr. Teague, hastily headed toward the airstrip that drivers used for the Atlanta races. She looked at Isaac, who was already back asleep.

Dear God, please let it have been a dream. She wanted to wish it were a bad dream, but if he had actually seen a vision of his mother, she hoped it was a good dream.

CHAPTER 35

"What happened here?" Dr. Teague asked, seeing that the patient looked considerably better than he expected.

"Isaac missed all his friends at NEMC," boasted Cookie. "Isn't that right, Isaac?"

The boy nodded.

"So that's it? Isaac was simply having Cookie withdrawals," smiled the doctor, glad that the immediate scare was stabilized, thanks to the blood transfusions.

"Yeah! I need a cookie, I need a cookie," the patient sang. "She's bringing me something special for supper tonight."

"She is? Well, I'll bring you something for supper if you promise me there will be no more tricks to get into the hospital," joked the doctor. "I need you to take care of Cookie while I talk to Celia for a minute. Can you do that for me?"

"Yes," grinned Isaac, his eyes and color beginning to resemble their usual appearance.

Dr. Teague motioned Celia into the hallway. "We've been able to hopefully keep the illness at bay for a little longer with the blood transfusions. However, I'm not sure how much longer Isaac's body can resist the increasing infections, even with the cocktail drugs. He's become so extremely anemic that it's going to be very difficult for the rest of the time."

"Are you trying to say that the time is growing shorter?"

"It's been growing shorter since the day he first came here. For him and for all of us. That's part of nature. What I'm saying is that I think we must try to keep his schedule as structured as possible in regards to school and activities. Although it will exhaust his energy, it's that interaction that will boost him."

The doctor led Celia to the consultation room and sat her on the loveseat that had first served as her "hot seat." "We're getting close to what I call the 'give them their cigarettes and their Jack Daniels' stage."

"What?" she scowled in total confusion.

"It's like the 'have your cake and eat it, too' principle. Except in this case, nearly everything he has will be bad for him instead of good for him. If he's on his way out, let him enjoy it."

"Sort of like the treatment the children receive at Give Kids the World?"

"Precisely," answered the doctor. "Let him play when he wants, eat what he wants. If he tries to sneak outside on the hospital playground, let him. Bring him food from wherever he wants. He pretty much rules his own situation from now on."

Celia heaved a long sigh as she took a deep breath. "How much longer are we talking about?"

"It's hard to say. But I'd take each day as a blessing if I were you." Dr. Teague reached for a tissue box and handed it to Celia. "Would you like to call Mr. Jarrett or shall I?"

"I think I'd prefer you do it."

"I understand. Why don't you call Brad and ask him to come over after school?"

"That's probably unnecessary. I'm sure he'll come straight here."

"I suggest you let him take you out to dinner. It's going to get extremely strenuous in the days to come. For now, Isaac has wonderful supervision and care. You need the same."

As badly as Celia wanted to insist on being with the child every waking minute, she knew the doctor was right. "Okay, it's a deal." Tears filled her eyes. "Thank you, Dr. Teague. You've been so very wonderful with Isaac."

"Isaac's been so very wonderful with all of us," he

smiled. "Go outside and have a good cry. I'll watch for you to come back in before I finish checking on him."

She nodded as she took the tissue box and disappeared around the corner.

♪ ♪ ♪ ♪

"Has Cookie been taking good care of you while we were gone?" questioned Dr. Teague.

"Yeah! She got Consella to play CANDY LAND with me."

"Consella Costa is one of the volunteers who works with our Child Life Specialist at NEMC," explained Cookie. "She comes in during the week to read and play games with the children."

"I'm winning!" added the boy.

"You'd better win fast!" announced the pediatrician, winking at the guardian. "Celia just informed me that she's going to the Red Pig for lunch."

"Oh, boy!"

"What would you like, Isaac?" the guardian asked while grabbing her purse.

"Is this Monday?"

"Yes."

"This is Mama Jean's meat loaf day. I love meat loaf," blasted the child who looked totally opposite from the little boy who had been transported here the night before.

"I should have guessed," sneered Celia.

"And next time you want to see Cookie, just call the hospital. You don't have to give us all a scare like you did last night," joked Dr. Teague, exiting the room.

♪ ♪ ♪ ♪

"Knock-knock," came a soft voice that accompanied the rap on the door.

"Come in," invited Celia. She turned to see Donnie and Anna Little at the door with Bobby.

"Isaac," she said. "Look who's here."

A smile flashed across the child's face as Isaac swallowed his last bite of meat loaf. "It's Mary and Joseph."

Celia realized that the child had never been introduced to the Little family. He had only seen the academy's custodian and his wife with their baby one time. And that was during the live nativity at the academy the prior Christmas when the three had portrayed the Holy Family.

As she introduced the visitors to Isaac, she noticed that Bobby was clutching the blue blanket that had been given to him on that eventful evening back in December.

"Does he like my blanket?" asked Isaac.

"He certainly does," assured Anna. "Bobby likes it so much that he wanted to bring it back to you. He thought that you might need it yourself right now since it's getting colder again."

The young mother reached to the bed and helped Bobby to let go of the blanket.

Celia had to turn away and catch a breath, wiping away the tears that came with it.

"Are you sure he'll be warm enough without it?" Isaac questioned apprehensively.

"Oh, yes," answered Donnie. "Thanks to Celia and the academy, we've been able to have all the lights and heat that we need." The man took a step closer to the bed and placed his hand on the child's. "And thanks to you, Bobby stayed warm all last winter."

Isaac jerked back the covers, revealing his Dale Jarrett hospital gown that had been made especially for him, and grabbed the blue blanket.

Donnie helped spread it over the child.

"When I gave your baby my blanket, Momma told me I would get it back ten times over. I wasn't sure what she meant when she said that, but I guess this is the first time," he declared, his normal huge grin spread across his face and the blue-violet of his eyes sparkling as brightly as ever.

Celia found herself thankful when Anna announced that they had to leave, saying that they would be back to check on Isaac. "I'll follow them to the elevator to make sure they don't get lost," she volunteered, glad for the opportunity to lose the tremor in her voice.

"We wanted to come sooner, but we were afraid that Isaac would think we were ungrateful for his gift."

"This was perfect timing."

"I hear tidbits at school, but it sounds like he's getting much weaker," said Donnie.

"I'm afraid those tidbits are correct."

She hugged both Donnie and Anna, thanking them for their visit. Then Celia reached down and kissed Bobby on the forehead, the same gesture she had caught herself doing to the original giver of the blanket ten months ago. The lump in her throat would not be swallowed.

CHAPTER 36

$\mathcal{O}$ctober 31st had traditionally marked All Hallowed's Eve for Celia. But she was not sure how to approach the significance of that celebration with Isaac, so she opted to keep the day to herself. For him, he would see the day as did most other children throughout the country. A day to dress up and get treats. *And in today's society, sadly, from people they know and trust.* She opened the front door of the cafe. *Thus a visit to the Red Pig.*

Isaac walked into the restaurant in his specially made bright-red pig costume. Jean peeked out the window to see him coming in the door, his black sun visor with red letters on the front proudly bearing the name of the establishment. "Trick or treat," he yelled when he saw her.

Jean came out and hugged the child. "Well, well, well, if we don't have our very little piglet. You're starting a little early, aren't you? It's only time for breakfast."

"I know, but I couldn't wait until tonight," he admitted, his eyes full of excitement.

Until that moment, it had not struck Celia that this was probably the very first time the child had ever gone door-to-door in search of treats. She dared not ask.

Jean turned and nodded at Cory through the kitchen's window.

He appeared at the table with a whole coconut cream pie. "Here you go, Little Man. But you've got to promise you won't eat it all at one time, and you have to eat your breakfast first."

"Oh, boy," squealed the child. "Is that for me? I don't have to share it with anybody?"

"Not a soul," came the answer from Jean and Cory at the same time.

"Where's your cell phone, Celi? Can we call Brad and tell him what I got?"

"No need for that," Cory volunteered. "I just saw him pulling into the parking lot."

Cory sat down and spoke to Brad and the boy briefly while Celia moved to another table with Jean.

"How's he doing?" Jean quietly inquired.

"I'm so glad Halloween fell on a Saturday. He'll be exhausted by lunch. He tries to stay at school half days, but we're decreasing that next week. I'm not sure he'll even be able to handle that much."

"Are you sure he should still be going to school?"

"The doctors and I all feel that it's best to keep his schedule as normal as possible for as long as we can. We want to keep him busy and interactive with the other children."

Jean nodded her understanding. "If you need a night off, let me know. I'll be glad to help."

"Thanks. I appreciate the offer, but Brad likes to come and visit and I enjoy watching the two of them play. Lately, though, Isaac has simply slept in Brad's arms while the TV is going."

"I've got to get back to the kitchen. Saturday's are always busy." The woman whom the child affectionately called "Mama" patted Celia's arm. "Just know I'm here for you." Her eyes averted to the child. "And him."

Celia nodded, moving back to the table with Brad and Isaac. Jean and Cory each gave the child a hug then headed for the kitchen.

"I'm having an omelet. Uncle Cory said he was going to throw in everything except Mama Jean's kitchen sink."

"Oh, my," chuckled Celia. "We'll be here all day if you eat that much."

Isaac laughed, his eyes dancing as they had that first night she saw him at the live nativity.

Through the eyes of a child . . . She looked at Brad, darted her eyes toward the child, then looked back to the man and pointed to her own eye, hoping he would get the message.

A nod told her he had seen the sparkling eyes, too.

Dear God, please don't let his eyes lose that heavenly glow. I don't think I could bear it if that ever-present glimmer of hope disappeared from his face.

The arrival of their food signaled her *"Amen"* so that Isaac could say the blessing.

CHAPTER 37

"Good morning and Happy *almost* Thanksgiving!" announced Dorothy Lee as she peeked in the hospital door on the day before the renowned turkey day.

"How nice to see you," exclaimed Celia, glad for the company of a cohort from the academy.

"Did you bring me something?" Isaac asked merrily.

"I certainly did," Mrs. Lee answered. "Some of the middle school students wanted to send you some holiday stories and pictures." She held up a large manila envelope full of stories written by some of the students. "And a few of the elementary students drew some pictures for you."

Isaac flashed his customary grin while reaching out for the envelope.

"There's only one thing. In return for all these pictures and stories, the teachers sent you paper, colored pencils and crayons. All of the students want you to design the Christmas card for the academy this year. There's traditionally an annual contest, but this year, the students rallied and made an executive decision to have you do it. So why don't you come up with something for the card?"

The excited child beamed as he looked at Celia.

"Did you hear that, Celi?"

"I sure did," she smiled back, patting him on the shoulder.

"What should I draw?" he asked, looking from one teacher to the other.

"Whatever you'd like," answered both teachers at the

same time.

The gears in Isaac's head were practically visible, he was thinking so hard. "I know!" he screamed. "I know what I'll draw."

"What's all this fuss about?" Cookie asked, rolling in the machine to take the patient's vitals.

"I'm going to get to draw the picture for the school's Christmas card this year," Isaac shared. "Mrs. Lee said so."

"Do tell! Now what do you think of that?" The nurse laid her hands on top of the child's head. "Oh, no," she said, her voice full of concern.

"What's the matter?" asked Isaac.

"If his head gets any bigger, we're going to have a problem," Cookie stated, directing her words to the women rather than the child.

Both teachers chuckled.

"It's a good thing you taught me to write my letters so well, Mrs. Lee. Or I wouldn't be able to write anything on the card."

Dorothy loved Isaac's enthusiasm and appreciation. It reminded her of why she loved her job so much. "Glad I could be of help." She gave Celia a hug. "I'd better be on my way. My Christmas shopping isn't going to happen by itself."

"Thanks so much for stopping by. And please tell the teachers and students how much I appreciate them taking the time to do this."

"You know that my class has the children's area of the hospital for their outreach project," Mrs. Lee whispered as Cookie spoke with the patient. "Being able to send things to Isaac makes it even more rewarding for them." She waved at the boy and left.

Celia understood that. Being here with him had given her an added appreciation of her job as Director of Outreach for Tillman Academy.

Cookie jotted down all the numbers from the vitals and headed for the door. "I'll be checking on that drawing now. You do something real good, and maybe we'll use it here at the hospital, too."

"It'll be good. Just you wait and see. Momma loved for me to draw her pictures. I'm going to draw this one for her."

Celia glanced at Cookie, whose eyes met hers. She pressed her lips together to hold back the tears.

Isaac tore into the envelope and pulled out all the contents. He handed the stories to Celia and flipped through the pictures, taking time to describe each one aloud. The child had nearly gone through the entire stack when he stopped talking and stared down at one of the drawings.

"Look at this, Celi."

She leaned over the bed and examined the picture.

"There's shooting stars in this one!" he proclaimed. "And a church with a purple steeple." He glared at the artwork a few more seconds then said, "See the music notes in the sky?"

Celia nodded.

"It looks like Momma is singing with the angels up in heaven and the notes are falling down to earth."

His guardian pressed her lips together a little harder.

"Why don't you read me a story while I color?" Isaac suggested.

Celia glared at the child for a moment before leafing through the stories. *How far beyond his tender years this young boy is. It's hard to believe that he was homeless for so long.* She briefly observed his fascination with the paper and crayons. *And that he went through his life without the simple pleasures of most children.*

The Director of Outreach watched as he began to make shapes on the paper. *No, he understood the simple pleasures of life that most other children didn't. His images of life weren't scarred by countless toys and clothes and unnecessary items to take away from the true "priceless" luxury of life – the love of a mother.*

Celia scanned the words of the stories. One caught her eye as she saw the title, *Coming Home for Christmas.* She began to read the words silently.

As Jackie started walking across the snow-covered street she heard her mom call her name. Then her world went black. The last thing she heard was screeching tires against the slick icy road.

Jackie was soon in the hospital. All was silent except for her family's cries and the machines keeping her alive.

As Christmas inched closer and closer, her family prayed for her to recover. That was all they wanted for Christmas. After many doctors said that she would not recover that soon, her family imagined Christmas without her. They continued to visit her everyday, hoping that she would become well again.

A few weeks later, three days before Christmas, Jackie saw light for the first time in weeks. The prayers had been answered.

Although Christmas Eve came and Jackie was not yet home from the hospital, all that mattered was that Jackie was coming around. Her family stayed the night at the hospital and celebrated Christmas with her the next day.

As the years passed and Jackie had now been home for many more Christmases, her family realized that the Christmas Jackie was in the hospital was their best one yet because the greatest gift of life is family.

Celia stood speechless. All she could imagine was Isaac's mother spending Christmas without him. And worse than that, Isaac spending the holiday without her. Her heart tore in two. She had become so engrossed in the story that she failed to hear the footsteps in the room behind her.

"I forgot to tell you," spoke Mrs. Lee lightly, "that I thought you'd be intrigued by some of the stories. No one told the students what to write, but it seems they all wrote stories that reminded them of Isaac's situation. I really think that most of the stories are more for you than him." She smiled that gentle smile that was her trademark at the school.

"I agree," Celia said, holding out the story she had just read.

"I didn't mean to startle you, but I wanted to share that with you."

"Thank you. And thank the students. I can already see that this is going to be an eye-opening realization for me."

"Remember Celia, that school is full of love for both you and Isaac. They all care about what is happening, and they really are here in spirit with you, as you'll see from the many heartfelt stories."

Celia nodded her head, unable to speak for fear of escaping tears.

"Is anything wrong?" asked Isaac.

"No, no, dear," answered Mrs. Lee. "I wanted to make sure that Miss Brinkley realized that some of the stories were for her."

"Are they bad?" he questioned further, seeing the expression on Celia's face.

"Oh, no," replied his guardian, struggling to quickly catch her composure. "They're so good that they brought a tear to my eye."

"Read one to me," he begged.

Mrs. Lee walked over to the bed and gave Isaac a hug. "Keep up the writing and call me when the card's done."

"I will," Isaac promised.

As Mrs. Lee exited the room, Celia found a fun story. "How's this one? It's called *An Elf's Christmas.*"

"Okay," he smiled, sitting up in the bed. "I'll pretend that I'm one of Santa's elves while you read and I draw."

"What do you know about Santa and his elves, Isaac?" Celia proceeded with caution, wondering if the child's past, prior to Give Kids The World, included any of the traditional stories of "the jolly fat man in the red suit and white beard."

"Momma told me about Santa. She said that he always saved the best until last, and every Christmas, we'd get to go to the Salvation Army and have a huge feast. Then Santa and one of his elves would show up and bring presents for all the kids."

"Did you ever sit on his lap or send him a letter before we visited Florida?"

"No. I just prayed that there would be something for Momma each Christmas, and if there was anything left, that I'd get something."

The tears were fighting to come back and before Celia could ask any more questions, Isaac continued.

"We got a bag filled with apples and oranges every year. Momma and I would hide them in our clothes so the people under the bridge wouldn't steal them. Sometimes we'd share them with the older people who couldn't get out for the Christmas party. And Momma would get something real pretty and I'd get a toy. We always got small things that we could carry with us."

He colored a little more then looked at her. "Read me *An Elf's Christmas*. Let's see if they're like the elves in Florida."

Celia sat on the side of the bed and let the child see the words and the pictures as she read the story, thinking of Jeff Frank and his daughter.

"Did Santa have to choose the North Pole?" complained James. "I mean, why couldn't he choose Jamaica or Hawaii?" (James is an elf who works for Santa. He only has two friends, Peter and Ralf, because nobody else can put up with all of his complaining. One time Peter and Ralf got so annoyed that they tried to send him away in a box, but Santa caught them just in time.)

Isaac was already laughing as he imagined that picture in his mind.

"James, will you just put the toys where they belong?" questioned Peter.

"But that takes out all of the fun in work!"

"Oh, get over it! If you ever want to be promoted, you're not going to get it by complaining and distracting your friend."

"Why do you want to be promoted?" asked James.

"Hmmm," Peter said in mock thought, "let's see. Maybe because I want to be with my other friend and work with the deer."

"But why can't we work and talk at the same time? Oh, what's it called, uhhhh . . ."

"Multi-tasking? Is it honestly that hard or are you . . .?"

"What are you two fighting about now?" asked Santa Claus.

"We were, ummm. . ." stalled Peter.

"Just commenting on the uhhhh . . . wonderful weather we're having," finished James.

Santa looked doubtfully at the two elves, then added, "Peter, if you want that promotion this year before Christmas, you only have twelve days. James, you need to make sure you don't doze off again."

"Yes, sir," answered the elves in unison.

Santa Claus turned and made his way back to the house to eat more cookies.

"Yep," Isaac interrupted. "Just like the Santa at Give Kids the World. Always wanting more cookies."

Celia smiled and kept reading. *"I can't believe there's only twelve days until Christmas. We'll probably wind up having to do this again next year. How did Ralf get promoted so easily?" asked Peter.*

"Maybe because he didn't goof off like we always do," James commented.

"Yeah. Well if we want that promotion, we aren't gonna get it by standing here reflecting on how we're gonna get promoted. Let's start sorting!"

So the two elves worked five hours straight. When they finished sorting the toys, they both collapsed on the soft snow and drifted off to sleep. They were awakened when somebody accidentally tripped over them.

"Why can't elves ever pick up after themselves?" another elf asked in disgust.

The two sleeping elves sat upright.

The elf that tripped then gasped and said, "James! Peter! Santa sent me to tell you that you only have to do one more pile of toys and then you'll be promoted!"

"So, eh, what's your name?" asked James.

"James, don't you remember me?" asked the elf.

"Uhhh, give me a hint."

"Hey, intelligent one, it's Ralf," blurted Peter.

"It is? It doesn't look like Ralf."

"That would be because you're looking at Comet," laughed Ralf, standing beside the reindeer.

James took a closer look at the elf and exclaimed, "It is you, Ralf! You don't look much different."

"And you don't act much different, either!" added Ralf with a joking smile before turning back to Peter. "So, how've you been, Petie?"

Peter glared at Ralf before replying, "Not bad, Raphikii. How about you?"

"Just peachy. And Jamie, how've you been?" asked Ralf.

James, remembering their old nicknames, replied, "Okay. So all we have to do is sort one more pile of toys and then we can join you and take care of the reindeer, Raphikii?"

"Yep. In fact, the pile's coming now. Look!"

They all stared at the pile of toys being pulled from the workshop in disbelief.

"That must be as tall as Mount Everest!" exclaimed James.

"Nah, not quite. Look, I'm sorry guys," apologized Ralf. "I'd help if I could but Santa Claus said if I do, he'll get rid of me permanently."

"It's okay," replied Peter, still staring at the mountain of toys as Ralf slowly led Comet away.

James and Peter began sorting the toys. After nine hours of tiring work, they finished and fell back into the snow. Peter could hear James' snores and then he heard the crunching of snow under someone's feet. He looked up and saw Santa walking towards him eating a cookie.

When Santa saw the toys all sorted, he exclaimed, "Well done, elves! You two have earned your promotion."

At the word "promotion," James suddenly sat up and looked at Santa.

"We will be having supper in ten minutes," announced Santa Claus. "I'd like you two to be there so your promotion can be announced and you can start working with Ralf immediately."

"Thank you, sir," replied James and Peter in unison.

Santa walked back to his house humming "Jingle Bells."

"I can't believe we're really going to be promoted!" exclaimed James.

"Yeah," agreed Peter. "We should probably go now to get there in time."

James and Peter walked off together. When they reached the Dining Hall, Mrs. Claus greeted them. She led them to their seats, where they waited for a few minutes before the other elves came pouring in.

After all the elves were seated, Santa stood up and exclaimed, "This evening, two wonderful elves will be promoted. James, Peter, please come forward."

He said a few more words before all the other elves began to *clap. James and Peter were then excused.*

They rushed outside to find Ralf, who was busily feeding the reindeer.

"Congratulations, guys! We only have four days to tend to these guys and then we can do whatever we please for a few days."

On Christmas Eve, James, Peter and Ralf stood and watched Santa and the reindeer disappear into the night.

"Well, now that the reindeer are gone, what do you two want to do?" asked Ralf.

James and Peter glared at each other and Peter nodded his head slightly. The next thing Ralf knew, he was being pelted with snowballs.

"This is the best Christmas Eve ever!" thought Ralf as he dodged another snowball. "I can't wait till next year!"

"I wish we could have snow," Isaac confessed. "I'd like to throw snowballs at Brad."

Celia noted how different this was from his attitude about snow in Florida. "Maybe if we're lucky, we'll get a few flakes before Christmas," she said, hopeful. *I'd love to see the two of them playing in the snow. Isaac would make a perfect snow angel.*

"Momma always said that if we were *unlucky*, it would snow."

Celia thought back to how difficult it must have been for Isaac's mother to try to provide for him. *And to think she never knew anything was wrong with her child.* The caretaker couldn't help but wonder if Maureen suspected the child was sick. *She was obviously a very bright woman to have taught her son as much as she did with what they had.* Then she looked into the boy's eyes. *Or what they* didn't *have!*

"Can you read me another story?"

Glad for the distraction, Celia reached for the next story in the pile.

"Can I try to read some of the words?"

"Sure you can," Celia agreed.

She handed him the paper and was shocked when he said, "What Does Christmas Mean, Mommy?" in slow and distinct syllables.

He stopped.

Now it was her turn to wonder if anything was wrong.

"Celi, do you mind if I sit in your lap while you read this story to me?"

"Of course not."

She carefully helped him out of the bed and into her lap as she sat in the spacious rocker, making sure all of the I-V lines stayed intact.

"I remember asking Momma what Christmas meant once," he confessed.

"What did she tell you?" Celia asked warily.

"She pulled me into her lap and told me about Jesus' birthday."

No wonder he wanted to climb into my lap. "Would you like to try to read some other words of the story?"

"No. I think I'd like to listen to you read it to me now." And with that reply, Isaac leaned back into Celia's shoulder and nestled himself into a comfortable position.

Celia repeated the title, *"What Does Christmas Mean, Mommy?"*

One Christmas, in the cold countryside of Paulding, Ohio, there lived a little girl who was at the age of six.

"That's how old I was, Celi," interrupted Isaac.

"Yes, it was," Celia nodded with a smile.

"Do you think she had snow in the cold countryside of Paulding, Ohio?"

"That's very possible."

"Maybe we can go *there* and throw snowballs at Brad."

"What's that about throwing snowballs at Brad?" came a voice from the doorway.

"Brad!" exclaimed the child with eyes that instantly lit up the room.

"Throwing snowballs, huh?" Brad glared at Celia and sneered. "And just who has been filling your head with that idea?"

"It wasn't Celi, honest! Some of the students from school sent me some stories. We just read one about elves pelting snowballs."

"Okay. If you say so." Brad tousled the boy's hair and then reached down and hugged him. "And how is Isaac today?"

"I'm fine." The child hesitated for a moment. "Aren't you going to ask Celi how she is?"

Still bent over the child, Brad looked directly into the woman's eyes. "I can see how she is."

"She's beautiful, isn't she?" asked Isaac boldly. "Just like Momma when I sat in her lap and she read to me."

"We're reading a story," explained Celia. "You're welcome to sit and join us if you'd like."

"Thank you. But only if there are no snowballs." Brad took a seat on the edge of the bed.

Isaac laughed heartily, at which Celia and Brad joined him.

"Back to the story," continued Celia, with a joyful pep to her voice.

One Christmas, in the cold countryside of Paulding, Ohio, there lived a little girl who was at the age of six. Her name was Hannah. She liked the little things, like watching her brother sleep, seeing Daddy come through the door from work, and Mommy making her favorite dinner (which was beef and noodles).

Celia wondered whether or not she should continue. She feared the picture of a loving and caring family would be too painful for the child.

"Keep reading, Celi. You haven't gotten to the good part yet," urged Isaac.

She caught Brad's eyes, full of encouragement and strength.

She had already missed a week of kindergarten because of all the ice and snow on the road.

"They *do* have snow, Celi, they *do* have snow!" Isaac chirped with glee.

"Uh, uh, uh," shot Brad, wagging his finger at the boy. "I told you there'd be no snowball fights."

"That's enough, you two," reprimanded Celia. "Listen to the story."

She was sitting by the fireplace, all wrapped up in a blanket with some hot chocolate. She was thinking about all of the Christmas presents that she was going to get this year. She was also thinking about her brother's presents.

Celia stopped long enough to glance at Brad.

"Go on," his eyes silently coaxed.

Her mommy and daddy always let her help him open his since he was too small to open them by himself. Then she started to wonder, "What does Christmas really mean? I know that it can't all be about presents. There is something more, but what?"

Celia's eyes caught Brad's again, only this time there was a look of relief in hers.

"Now we're getting to the good part," proclaimed Isaac.

Brad's approving nod convinced Celia that she could make it through the rest of the story.

Hannah walked into the kitchen, and looking at her mother, she asked, "What does Christmas mean, Mommy?"

Her mother stopped what she was doing and looked at her daughter with an understanding eye. "Let's go sit down."

They walked into the living room and sat down on the couch together. Hannah looked at the beautiful Christmas tree in the corner, and then at her beautiful mother.

The mother looked into the eyes of her little girl and said, "Christmas is a time of love and praying to the Lord." Then she reached for the Bible that was sitting on the table next to the couch. She opened it to the book of Matthew. "There once was a young woman named Mary that lived in the town of Nazareth. One day an angel of the Lord appeared to her and said, 'Do not be afraid, I bring you good news and great joy. You will have a son that you shall call Jesus. He will be the king of all and the Son of God.'

Mary replied, 'Let it be.'

When it came time to have the baby Jesus, Mary and her husband, Joseph, traveled to Bethlehem. There they hoped to find an inn to stay where Mary could have her son, but all of the inns were full. One innkeeper offered his stable to them, so that is where Jesus was born. They dressed him in swaddling clothes and laid him in a manger.

"That is what Christmas is about," announced the mother.

The little girl was so happy that she called her daddy at work to tell him what Christmas meant.

Now that little girl is all grown up and has a family of her own. She has two little boys and a little girl.

Celia felt Isaac's head fall over on her shoulder. She glanced at Brad who indicated the child was dozing off.

This Christmas, Hannah's little girl is at the age of six. One cold winter, on an early Sunday morning, Hannah was making an apple pie for her Christmas party. Her daughter, all wrapped up in a blanket, walked into the kitchen.

"Can I have some more hot chocolate, Mama?" the little girl asked.

"Sure, sweet pea," replied her mother.

Then the little girl asked . . .

Before Celia could complete the sentence, Isaac said in a drowsy voice, "What does Christmas mean, Momma?" His head dipped even lower into his guardian's shoulder.

The End, concluded Celia.

"Should we try to put him back in his bed?" Brad asked.

"He's fine right here for a while. I think he's missing his mother, and perhaps sitting in a woman's lap is helping him to cope with that loneliness."

Celia laid the story on the bedside table and brushed the child's hair gently as she rocked the chair.

"You look completely natural holding him," observed Brad.

"Thanks." She paused a second. "I think. At least I hope that was a compliment."

"It was an observation." He looked straight into her eyes. "Celia, have you ever given any thought to having children of your own? Holding Isaac, reading to him and rocking him becomes you."

She gave a deep sigh. "I think there's a step that comes before having children. That's the one I've never given much thought."

Brad saw that he was treading into uncomfortable territory, so he changed the conversation.

"Everyone at school sends their love."

"Thanks for relaying the message. They certainly have been most supportive of Isaac."

"They're merely following their leader. You exhibit a fine example of caring for those less fortunate than ourselves."

"How could you *not* exemplify that with Isaac?"

"Is he really any different from any other homeless person?" Brad gave Celia a brief second to think about the question. "At least, in your eyes?" He saw the gears in her head turning. "That's the whole point, Celia. You're doing what you do best here. Caring for another."

She opened her mouth, but Brad cut her short.

"I've been watching you and I realize that there's more to life for me."

"What are you getting at?" Celia voiced the question, but in her mind, she had a suspicion of the coming words.

"I told you how I almost became a minister. As I've watched you in your role as Director of Outreach for the academy, I've realized that I'm not following the calling that God has given me."

"And are you sure about that calling?"

"Yes." His grave expression matched his words. "I am."

Brad reached out and placed his hand on Celia's arm. "You'll never believe what I want to do."

Before Celia had time to question him, he continued, "I want to work with the children who come to the race tracks with their parents. Children of the fans who may need a positive role model in their lives. Children who may not hear the good news and great joy that the angels expressed. Children who may have fathers like I did."

"Or like Isaac did," Celia inserted, able to picture Brad in that role. After a few moments of silent thought, she continued, "Why don't you talk to DJ the next time he comes to visit Isaac?"

"I've already done that. In fact, this was gnawing at me so badly that I called him yesterday. He gave me the name of someone to call who works with Motor Racing Outreach, a ministry for NASCAR. I'm thinking of going to the next race just to meet with the man."

"MRO has an office at Lowe's Motor Speedway. Why don't you call there?"

"DJ mentioned that. Maybe that's what I should do." He looked at her with thankful eyes. "Are you sure I can't help get Isaac back in bed before I leave? The soccer team has a game this afternoon or I'd stay."

"I'm positive. I think I'll sit here and think about things myself for a while."

After he left, Celia wondered what it would be like to hold a child of her own. Then she wondered how any mother could deal with losing a child of her own.

For the first time, she was actually glad that Isaac's mother was not here to suffer with this little boy in his illness. *At least God spared her that.* Then the question he had asked his mother resounded. *"What does Christmas mean, Momma?"*

She could imagine a sweet feminine voice answering, *"Christmas is a time of love."*

The closing words of the first story rang in her ears. *"The greatest gift of life is family."*

Celia slowly began to understand how God had taken care of things in His own way. Isaac's mother was carrying the HIV virus, but she didn't know it. Isaac's illness would have hit and he would have gotten no medical attention. His mother had been spared his drawn-out illness and had gone to a place to await her son's arrival. Isaac had received the gift of a happy time of having a family. A family of friends who cared about him and would have spared no expenses or energies to see that he was given a fair and just chance at life.

Cookie peeked in the doorway.

"Oh, Cookie," called Celia, her voice shaking. "Could you help me get Isaac back in bed?"

The nursing assistant eagerly obliged the request. "He looks like he's going to be out for a while. Why don't you take a break for a few minutes?"

"Precisely what I had in mind."

Cookie walked to the elevator with the young woman. "You've finally figured it out, haven't you?" she asked.

Celia stared blankly at the nurse for a moment, then nodded.

The veteran caretaker reached into her pocket and took out a small plastic pouch of tissues. "Go and have a good one," she urged. "It'll help you make it to the end."

Reaching out to take the tissues, Celia nodded again, her eyes already filling with tears. She quickly got on one of the elevator cars and pushed the button to close the doors.

CHAPTER 38

"Celi, do you remember at the beach in Florida when I told you about me seeing that shooting star with Momma?"

"Yes."

"I want to tell you what I wished for that night before Momma died."

She felt the impending tears, for she suspected if Isaac wanted to share his secret, he knew his end was near. *Oh God, please give me the same courage you have given this child. Let me be a pillar of strength for him.* Celia wished she could recall some verse of scripture on that subject. But her mind drew a blank as she stood beside the bed and ran her fingers through the child's limp hair.

When the nurse came in to do the routine vitals check, she glanced over at Celia. Those eyes told the dedicated chaperone all she needed to know.

"Can you stay here for a couple of minutes? I need to get something out of my car." She hated to fib, but she needed an excuse to get out of the room. *I'll rush to the car and grab something so this won't be a lie.*

"I'll be glad to. As long as this little fellow promises to behave himself," the nurse teased.

"You can count on that," Celia answered for the child, winking at him.

As she literally ran down the hall, she fought back tears with every breath. *There'll be plenty of time for that later*, she tried to convince herself. *Right now there are more important things on your agenda.*

She dialed the number she had on that night home from Talledega. When she heard the male voice on the other end, Celia suddenly felt like she had been given access to the Hot Line.

"Mr. Jarrett? Sorry, Dale? I mean, DJ?" Her voice was trembling. She struggled to find words, much the same as he had done on that first night when he called her from this same hospital.

"Yes?"

"This is,"

"Hi, Celia, I thought that sounded like you. What's going on?"

"If you can manage to get away, I think you might want to come to the hospital. Things are beginning to happen here."

"How's Isaac?" came the words of concern.

"He's his usual exuberant self. I expect there'll be no change in that. I'm the one I'm more worried about in that sense."

"I understand."

As Celia stood holding the receiver, she was sure that this man, full of genuine compassion, *did* understand.

"I'll be down in the helicopter shortly," he informed her. "Can you have Brad meet me at the Concord Regional Airport in an hour?"

"He'll be there," she volunteered, thankful that race season was over and that DJ wasn't on the other side of the country. *Like it would have mattered. But at least this way, it won't take long for him to fly here.*

Sprinting to the car, she found herself grateful for an excuse to call Brad. She didn't want to feel like she needed him, and even more, she didn't want him to suspect that. *But then, Isaac is his friend, too. They've become great buddies.*

Celia grabbed a file folder from the back seat of her car. She had no clue what was in the folder and she didn't even bother to look at the label. All that mattered was that she had actually retrieved something from the car. *I'll buzz Brad when I get back to Isaac's room and see if he'd like to visit for a few minutes. Then I'll alert him to DJ's arrival at the airport.*

"That was a long couple of minutes," Isaac smiled weakly. "Maybe we'd better call Brad and tell him that you need some pointers in track."

Ah, a perfect excuse! "Why don't *you* call Brad? I'm sure he'd rather hear your voice than mine." Celia dialed the number of Brad's cell phone and handed the receiver to Isaac.

"Brad? Celia needs you over here." His voice was weak and slow, but he was still able to make jokes.

Great! That's all I didn't *need him to say,* chagrin written all over her face at thinking of Brad's face.

"She's a little slow and I thought you could give her some tips on running faster."

Celia could hear the roar of laughter coming through the receiver.

"I'll be over in a few minutes," Brad responded.

Isaac handed the receiver back to Celia with a grin on his face that told her he knew exactly what he'd done. Even in his weakened condition, it seemed he was still calling the shots. Had this been under any other circumstance, she would have gently and jokingly scolded him, but this was not the time.

Instead, she reached down and kissed the cheek of the child, whose eyes were showing the same lack of energy as was apparent in his voice. "Now about that star?"

"Oh, yeah."

The fact that he had forgotten told Celia that everything about him was slowing greatly. It was rare for any child, much less Isaac, to forget something that important to him.

"There was a shooting star the night my mother died."

"I remember. I saw a shooting star that evening, too."

"Did you make a wish?" the child asked, his already soft voice diminishing.

"Yes, as a matter of fact, I did."

"Did it come true?"

Celia hesitated. She remembered that evening so well. It was shortly after she had begun her position as the Director of Outreach for the academy. When she had seen the star flying across the sky, she immediately made a wish that she could make a difference in the life of at least one person during the next year. Therefore, when she received Dale Jarrett's call, she had taken no time to even think before she responded to his request for help with Isaac. "Yes, it did come true."

"My wish came true, too. I wished that Momma and me would get a big beautiful home to live in. A home where we could be warm and not be hungry anymore."

"What a beautiful wish." Again, she was amazed at the wisdom and the ability to handle situations of this child. She had heard the saying, "God never gives anyone more than they can handle." Isaac had proven the truth of that statement to her.

"I want to go home to Momma. She's got everything ready and is waiting for me."

Celia had known those words were coming. She sensed it when he wanted to disclose the wish. And she wished she had some words to say. Some profound or prophetic words that would make this easier. *Easier for myself. Isaac is handling it just fine.* All she could do was force a strained voice, "I'm sure your new home is very beautiful. And I'm sure your momma is going to be so very happy to be with you again."

"Uh-huh. She told me so last night."

The guardian stared at the child. She had heard of these kinds of things happening. Cookie had warned her about them. *No wonder there was such a noticeable change in him this morning. He's ready to go.*

Every ounce of energy and self-control in Celia's body went into action to stop the flood of tears. *Dear God, please help me not to break down in front of this child. I should be happy for him. I know the grief I'm feeling here is my own, so please . . . please help me. For Isaac's sake,"*

Her prayer was cut short by his voice that was now barely audible. "There's one other thing, Celi."

"What's that, Isaac?"

"That star they gave us at the Village. We wrote my name on it and the date we were there.

"Yes, I remember."

"You know I made a wish with that star, too?"

"Of course I do. We went back to see your star on the ceiling before we left."

"Uh-huh. I hope I didn't do something bad."

"How could you have possibly done something bad?"

"I wished that you and Brad would get married and have a little boy named Isaac."

Celia glared at the child in disbelief. Her stomach landed in her throat in that sudden instant, causing her to gulp loudly. She wanted to scream, "How could you do that?" But she knew that would be terribly inappropriate. The child had meant no harm. *I guess he didn't realize how perfectly happy I am in my private life of singleness.*

Isaac caught the look of dismay on her face.

"Don't you *want* to marry Brad, Celi?"

She paused, having no idea how to answer the boy. All he wanted was happiness for two people he had come to love. What he did not understand was their relationship.

As Celia's stomach returned to its proper location, she tried to think through this newly-declared wish combined with the words, "Celi needs you," that Isaac had relayed to Brad on the phone. The voice she heard in her head was not her own as the words seemed to come from nowhere. *Perhaps it's the two of you that do not understand your relationship.*

A shiver ran up Celia's spine. She suddenly wished that she were not here. And Isaac's comment to Brad about teaching her to run faster seemed totally out of context, for at the moment, she felt she could run faster than anyone to get out of this predicament. She thought of having Cookie to sit with Isaac for a few minutes while she took a break.

As Celia wrestled with her need to escape versus the child's deteriorating condition, she heard a faint knock at the door. She turned to see Brad standing there. His eyes, full of concern for both the child and her, brought her own thoughts back to why she was standing in this room. *And it's not about you, Celia Brinkley.*

Brad took her hand as he walked over to the bed.

"How'd you get here so fast?" Celia mouthed.

"I was already on my way here." Brad smiled. "I had a

hunch that one of you might need me."

He looked down at Isaac, whose eyes had closed.

"I guess he's exerted his quota of energy for the morning," Celia explained with a whisper.

She scorned herself for being so wrapped up in her own situation that she had missed the child slipping back into the world of a deep dark sleep. *I will be here until the end. I will take care of this precious child.* Celia felt needed strength in the grasp of the hand holding hers. *And then I will take care of myself in all the aftermath.*

Brad put his arm around Celia and led her into the hallway where their voices could not be heard. "What's going on?"

"Isaac's fading more and more into an unconscious state. His vital signs are decreasing. I've called DJ and he's on his way here. He'll need you to pick him up in about thirty minutes at the airport."

"Why didn't you call me earlier?"

Celia looked at the eyes staring into hers. "I don't know." But subconsciously, she did know. She was frightened. Not by the child's condition, or that his end was approaching, but frightened by her own feelings. Feelings for the man standing in front of her. Feelings that she did not want to accept.

Brad placed his hand on the back of her hair and pulled her head into his shoulders.

The tears streamed down Celia's face. She knew that the erupting flood came from many sources, yet she was not willing to share that information with this man who had become more a part of her thoughts than she wanted to admit.

Celia pulled her head back and wiped her face. "I don't want Isaac to see me this way."

"Why don't you go and splash your face and take a short walk outside? The weather's not too cold today. I'm sure Cookie can sit with Isaac until you get back. From the looks of it, he's going to be asleep for a while."

She nodded and started to pull away.

Brad pulled her back and kissed her lightly on the forehead. "That's from Isaac."

Celia swallowed hard and said, "Thank you," in a voice that still trembled.

He kissed her again, this time placing his hand under her chin and lifting her face so that his lips met hers. "And that's from me. Thank you for the love you've shown that little fellow."

She wrapped her arms around Brad and again allowed the tears to flow.

"Hey now, I didn't mean to upset you. It's just that you've been a real trooper and I simply wanted to show my appreciation for all you've done. Your love and spirit has touched everyone who has seen you and Isaac."

"You didn't upset me. It's . . . it's . . ."

Brad reached down and kissed Celia again on the lips. "And that's from me." He grinned. "Because it didn't upset you. Now go and get cleaned up and take that walk. We'll work on the running exercises later." He whirled her around and gave her a gentle shove down the hallway toward the nurse's station.

Celia smiled back over her shoulder as she watched him leave for the airport.

CHAPTER 39

"And how are things on this end of the hall this morning?" Cookie's smile was larger than usual. That told Celia that this woman had already seen the morning's report.

"Celi needed a little help this morning. I had to call Brad to come and be with her."

Cookie stared over at Celia and Brad who both seemed to look fine, given the fact that they were about to lose someone they dearly loved. Someone who had forced them to honestly examine their feelings about each other.

"Are you okay?" This time the question was directed to Celia.

"I'm fine," she offered. "Isaac just wanted to see Brad and he used me as an excuse."

"She really *did* want to see him. She was just too chicken to call."

Brad stifled a chuckle, but he still made an audible sound that said he was enjoying this grilling session immensely. His eyes grinned at Cookie as he gave a "Gotcha" wink to Celia.

"Thank you, bud. What would I ever do without you?" Brad squeezed Isaac on the kneecap as he questioned the child.

Cookie continued to eye Brad and Celia. She wondered if they had any idea how hard the upcoming hours were going to be on them, especially this woman who had taken over as Isaac's primary caregiver.

A reach into her smock pocket produced a small box of juice. "Thought you might like to have this," she added, passing the gift to the child.

"Thank you." Isaac's weak little arms were unable to grasp the box.

Brad reached over and took the juice, placing it on the bed tray. It was at that moment that he, too, realized how near the end was. "Would you like for me to open it?"

"Yes."

The child took a couple of sips, visibly a struggle, before he fell back on the pillow and went to sleep.

"You hit that buzzer anytime you need something. Anything," Cookie demanded. "If I'm not here, someone else will come straight to this room. Everyone has been alerted to watch for his every need."

"Thank you, Cookie." Celia fondly recalled the first day that the care partner came into Isaac's room. Her habit of being present whenever he needed something or someone had never failed. It was a habit that the teacher suspected never would.

♪ ♪ ♪ ♪

Consella peeked in Isaac's room on her rounds of reading to children.

"How are you doing, my dear?" she asked Celia.

The child's guardian stepped into the hall to speak with the volunteer for a moment. She recalled the stories, some of which she shared with Consella, of the volunteers at Give Kids The World Village. Celia then told her about Jeff Frank and his miracle of life.

"I, too, robbed death of its opportunity to take me away from life," the NEMC volunteer proudly admitted.

"Maybe there's still a chance for Isaac," Celia longed.

Consella took Celia's arm and walked her down the hall away from the child's room. "My dear, life is a precious thing. But in Isaac's condition, what a miracle it would be to join his mother for Christmas. What more blessed gift could there be? Who of us would rob him of that opportunity?"

Celia looked at the wise woman. "Thank you, Consella. I needed you this morning worse than your other patients. Thank you for sharing your time. And thank you for all the volunteer work you do at the hospital."

"It's a healing for me, too, dear." Consella squeezed Celia's arm and moved down the hall with her cart of books and games.

CHAPTER 40

"I'll bet you're a great daddy, aren't you?"

The racer took the child's small hand, a hand that had been bruised from I-V's, between his. The needles were gone and all that was left were the traces of the insertion points.

The observant teacher, who had made reading people a specialty of hers, saw the hesitation on Jarrett's face. She knew it didn't come from a lack of the right words, but rather the emotional strain of the answer.

"DJ won an award for being such a great father. I saw it on the internet," she informed Isaac.

A slight blush helped bring a smile to the driver's face. He turned toward Celia with eyes that spoke an appreciative "thank you" for getting him past a difficult moment.

"Is that right, DJ? Did you get a trophy or a hat or something?"

Looking back at the child, he snickered. "No, nothing like that. All I got was recognition for doing with my family what any other loving father would have done." Still holding the child's hand with one of his, Dale scooted a chair up so that he could sit beside the boy's bed, then again clasped both hands around the child's. "Isaac, you have a Heavenly Father who loves you more than any man, any father, here on earth could love you. He loves my children more than I could love them. He loves me more than my father, Ned, loves me."

"Momma told me about Him," shared Isaac. "And she said it didn't matter that I didn't have a daddy, because my Heavenly Father loved me more than any man on earth could love me. But how does He know my name?" The child's words dwindled off as he fell into a world of sleep, unable to stay awake now for more than a few minutes at a time.

Jarrett held Isaac's hand for a few more minutes before letting it go. As he turned to walk into the hallway, Celia noticed a tear that matched the voice. At this point, she felt more sorrow for the big man than she did for the small child. For he, like herself, was hurting more than this young creature they both held so dear.

CHAPTER 41

It was a long night. There had been very little happening, indicating that the end was near. Celia sat in the recliner, with Brad and DJ on either side of her in straight-back chairs. They had taken turns drifting into fitful sleep during the evening hours until Cookie tiptoed into the room.

"You're early," managed Celia.

"I couldn't sleep, either," she confessed. In her hands she carried a bag full of country ham biscuits for the watchful guards. "I figured you could all use these about now. I'll run back down the hall and bring you some fresh coffee."

"What, no chocolate chip cookies?" asked Brad, trying to break the dreadful solemnity in the air.

The nurse's assistant reached into her pocket and pulled out three plastic storage bags, each filled with a cookie. "Just for you!" she grinned. "I knew you'd be here, so I was expecting that."

"What would we have ever done without you, Cookie?" questioned Celia.

"What would we have ever done without Isaac?" she answered.

DJ stood and took the nurse by the hand. "Cookie, I want to thank you for all that you've done for Isaac, but also for Celia and Brad. You've been family to them."

"I'm family to everybody, Mr. Jarrett. But this boy," Her voice quivered as she stopped and looked at the patient who lay in the coma. "This boy was *special* family. Everybody that he met was family."

The racer hugged the woman. "We'll never forget the impact that you've had on this child or us."

"Nor shall I forget you every Sunday when I hear the race. You've made me a real fan, you know."

"Good! I'll remember that with every lap."

"I'd better go and take care of a few other patients. But I'm here. You call me."

"We will," assured Brad.

They ate their hand-delivered breakfast in silence after DJ offered a blessing. Although they were not particularly hungry, they knew they'd need the added strength before the day was over.

Dr. Teague came into the room earlier than usual. "Any change?"

"The breathing is getting more and more shallow," Celia offered.

The pediatrician listened to the boy's chest and quietly put away the stethoscope. "Are you all going to be here today?"

"Yes," came the unison answer.

"Good. I'll be checking in from time to time. Please have the nurse page me if there's any change at all."

DJ stood and shook hands with Dr. Teague. "On the night I first met you here, I asked that you would make sure this boy got everything possible for his healing. You've done that to the highest level, and I want you to know that you have my utmost thanks and respect."

"And you, mine, Mr. Jarrett. I've never had much exposure to NASCAR, but if you're any indication of the rest of the organization, that's one fine group." Dr. Teague gave a congenial smile. "And I must admit that I find myself catching the race on the radio if I'm driving, or turning to the sports section on Monday to see how you did. You've gained a lot of new fans around this place."

"Thank you. Thank you very much. However, I feel I must credit Isaac for that," acknowledged the racer.

♪ ♪ ♪ ♪

It seemed that the trio of visitors could watch Isaac's breaths literally get weaker with the passing hours.

"Shall I run downstairs and get some lunch?" offered Brad.

"No need for that," came a familiar voice at the door.

The team of guardians turned to see Mama Jean, Papa Randy, Uncle Cory, Jan and Tami at the door, each bearing a handful of carry-out boxes and sacks.

"Who's minding the store?" asked Brad.

Mama Jean set her stack on the bedside table. "Jennifer and a couple of the other waitresses are there for a few minutes."

"The Breakfast Club came in and said they'd hold the fort long enough for us to come down here," added Uncle Cory. Marijke and Ike are leading them in Christmas carols until we get back."

"With Jennifer leading all the customers through the restaurant doing the train, I'm sure," joked Celia, with as much enthusiasm as she could muster.

"We've brought all of your favorites," offered Papa Randy.

Cookie brought in a folding table and set it up as Jan and Tami went about setting out real plates and silverware for the trio.

Jean pulled out a coconut cream pie and a pan of bread pudding while Randy brought out the squash casserole and mashed potatoes. Cory unpacked a big bowl of country style steak while Jan and Tami poured glasses of tea.

"Didn't you forget anything?" asked Brad, watching the display of food set before them.

"The kitchen sink," smiled Cory.

"We'll bring it next time," laughed Jan.

Tami took servings of desserts to the nurses in the pediatric unit while Jan waited on Isaac's visitors.

No one asked about the child's condition, but rather, each made his or her own individual assessments. The gloom, although masked, was extremely evident in the room.

Jean took Celia's hand. "Is there anything else we can

do for you, dear?"

Celia swallowed hard as Brad placed his hand on her shoulder. "Pray for him. Pray that," Her sentence was cut short by DJ's elbow.

She looked at the racer and saw him staring at Isaac. The child's eyes were blinking as if he were trying to open them. Everyone in the room froze as Celia pressed the buzzer for the nurse.

Both Cookie and Dr. Teague came running down the hallway, followed by the nurse on duty.

"It's President's Pie!" exclaimed Isaac, as clearly as if he had just awakened from a normal night's sleep. He peeked around the room to see his entire family assembled around him. "Are we having a party?" he asked.

"Yes. For you," answered the pediatrician, the only one in the room who could find his voice.

Jan pulled herself together enough to hand Isaac a slice of pie while Tami and Jean placed their arms around Celia.

The child's hands were too weak to hold the plate. Celia stepped forward, took the plate and spooned a tiny bit of the cream filling into his mouth. His eyes met hers with the same joyful expression they had possessed at their first encounter the previous December.

She spooned another small bite into his mouth, and then reached down and kissed him on the forehead.

"I love you, Isaac," she whispered.

"I love you, too, Celi," he managed with a smile. Then Isaac's gaze turned Brad. "You always told me to take care of Celi when you weren't here. Are you going to take care of her when I go see Momma?"

"You bet I am, sport," bolted the coach, trying to mask his emotion.

DJ reached down and hugged the child.

"I knew you'd be here when Jesus came for me, just like you were for Momma." Isaac's eyes slowly circled the room, giving each person who had become his "family" a smile. His eyes stopped when he came to Dr. Teague and then Cookie.

They each bent down and gave the child a hug.

"Thanks for the pie, Mama Jean," he said, looking back at her, his eyes fighting to stay focused.

Isaac looked back to Celia and tried to reach his arms to her.

She grabbed him and hugged as tightly as she dared. "Be sure and throw a snowball at Brad for me," he grinned, looking toward the window.

To the amazement of the roomful of visitors, they followed Isaac's eyes to the window to see huge flakes of snow falling from the sky.

As Celia reached down and kissed the child's cheek one last time, she felt his tiny body go limp.

♪ ♪ ♪ ♪

Celia, Brad and DJ were left in the room with Dr. Teague. The setting was the same as it had been on the evening Isaac had first come to the hospital.

"Do you know what day it is?" the pediatrician asked.

"Tuesday," volunteered Celia.

Dr. Teague said nothing, but shifted his eyes to Brad.

"December 21st," offered Brad.

Still the doctor made no comment, but looked at the racer.

"It's Winter Solstice," stated Dale.

"That's right," said Dr. Teague. "Isn't it most appropriate that Isaac chose today to leave this earth?"

"Winter Solstice," recalled Celia. "The shortest day of the year. The day that they say the sun stands still as it passes over the tropic of Capricorn."

"Because the sun is the farthest distance away from the equator, the highest point or culmination," added Dr. Teague.

"So you're saying that today was the highest point in Isaac's life although it marks his death," reasoned Brad.

"Bravo!" heralded the pediatrician.

"You're right," agreed Dale. "This is a remarkable day . . . for *many* reasons."

CHAPTER 42

Celia requested a few minutes alone while she packed her belongings. Brad told her he would wait downstairs for her while DJ made the trip back to Hickory.

Cookie came into the room and put her hands on the teacher's shoulders. "I brought you a little something. I thought you might like to have it beside your front door or somewhere visible." She reached into her jacket pocket and retrieved a gray object.

The woman in mourning looked down to see a jagged, flat stone with a saying carved into it. "Those we have held in our arms for a little while, we hold in our hearts forever."

Tears rushed down her cheeks as she threw her arms around the nurse's assistant that had become an integral part of Isaac's life. "Oh, Cookie, how can you stand to lose one of these precious little children after you've spent so much time with them? After you've held them in your arms and looked down into their empty eyes?"

"Baby, baby." She pulled herself back from Celia just enough to look into the young woman's eyes. "In Isaac's case, it was easy." Cookie reached up and wiped the tears from the cheeks of the woman clinging to her. "You see, Isaac had someone waiting for him at Home to wrap her arms around him. I was only babysitting him for a short while. Some of the children who wind up in the hospital like him have no one who loves them. No one who has cared for them during their early years. Those are the ones it's hard to give up."

She took a strand of Celia's shoulder-length brunette hair and placed it behind the listener's ear. "I could see Isaac's mother in his eyes from the very beginning. He was not afraid, for he knew she was going to be there to meet him with her arms wide open."

"He felt like my own child to me. I shouldn't have let myself become so close to him."

"No, no. Don't you ever feel that way. That bond was exactly what that little fellow needed from you. He had no one else when his mother was killed. You filled the void in Isaac's life until it was time for him to be reunited with his biological mother. For him, you were a mother, too."

Celia loosened her arms from around the appropriately-named care partner. "Cookie, from the first time I saw you walk in Isaac's room, I thought you were an angel sent straight down from heaven. Now I'm sure of that."

"Oh, child. You're the angel. For me, this is my job. Sure, I love every minute of it – even when I have to let them go. But for you, this was no job."

"I thought it was my job at first. When I was given the position as the school's Director of Outreach, I never knew what a stretch that would be."

"Honey, when I walked in Isaac's room the first time and saw the way the two of you looked at each other, it was clear to me and everyone else that saw you that God had placed you in that little boy's life. You don't think it was an accident that you met him last Christmas, do you?

"That child and his mother were sent to that nativity setting. I can't tell you how they found out. Think about it. They were homeless. Where'd they find out about what was going on at the school? And how long did it take them to get there?"

Cookie leaned closer to Celia and took her hand. "Think about it. God planted you there. He planted Isaac and his mother there." She patted the hand in hers. "You did a most wonderful thing for Donnie and Anna Little, and their baby, Bobby." The nurse looked straight into Celia's eyes and slowly spoke her last words. "But the *real* miracle of last Christmas came when a woman named Celia met a little boy named Isaac."

"Oh, Cookie, dear Cookie. You truly are an angel. How else would you have known all of that?"

"And Celia, dear Celia. This is a hospital. Next to the beauty shop, we know more that goes on in town than any other place."

Celia smiled and kissed Cookie on the cheek. "Well, whether you were an angel or not, Isaac and I were both blessed to have you for a little while."

The woman who had gone from being a music teacher to an outreach director to a guardian of a child took a deep breath as Cookie walked away. Then Celia began to pack up the few things she had left in the room. As she placed the crayons and papers in a tote bag, she noticed a story that had gotten laid aside.

"*Aria*," she said, reading the title aloud. *That's a lovely title for a story . . . especially to a musician.* The story had a cover sheet that had been carefully designed by the student. There was a pair of white angel's wings set in a lovely golden shape with intricate edges, which was placed on top of a rectangular paper that was a deep shade of Christmas green.

Interesting, mused Celia, intrigued by the cover and the title. She turned to the first page to discover a story that had been skillfully written by one of the academy's middle-schoolers, complete with chapters.

Chapter 1 – "*Good Night, My Little Princess*"

We finished singing the song over the telephone, the same song – one my father had written – that we'd sung together every night since I could remember.

"*Good night, my little Princess. See you tomorrow night for Christmas Eve dinner," my father whispered.*

"*Good night, Dad," I whispered back.*

~ ~

Ring! Ring!

"*Hello," my mother answered.*

"*Hello, Danielle . . . are you sitting down?" came the voice of my father's best friend over the phone.*

"Yes, why?" she questioned. "What's up, Greg? It's eleven-thirty."

"There's been a terrible accident, Danielle . . ."

"What happened? Is John okay?" my mother asked, jumping from her bed.

"No, Danielle. I'm afraid . . . I'm afraid John is dead. He was hit by a car right after talking to Arianna on the phone."

The phone fell to the floor with a clatter.

Celia'a heart pounded. She wanted to throw the story away . . . yet it called to her to be read. Swallowing hard and taking a deep breath, she sat in the recliner that had become her "second home" for the past few months.

"What is Mom doing up?" I wondered, hearing movement in her room.

I rolled the covers off me and walked to my parents' bedroom where I heard Greg yelling my mom's name.

"Greg? What happened?" I asked after picking up the phone.

My mother sat on the bed, paralyzed from shock and tears in her eyes.

"Arianna, is your mother okay?"

"I don't know . . . what happened, Mom?"

"Arianna, please let me speak to Greg." She held her hand out for the phone.

"Greg, let me call you back," she requested, and hung up the phone.

"Mom? What's wrong? Why did Greg call? Why are you crying?"

She pulled me onto the bed beside her. "Arianna, your father . . ." she said as tears continued to escape her eyes.

"Yes, Mom?" I reached for her hand.

"Your father . . . is not coming home. He's . . . he's dead."
Mother closed her eyes and squeezed my hand tightly.

"No! No! He can't be! How?"

"He was hit by a car after he called you."

"Mom . . . no . . . he, he . . . no, it can't be!" I cried.

"I know . . . come here." My mother took me in her arms and embraced me. We sat together on her bed and called friends and relatives who came over all during the night to comfort us.

~ ~

"You should go to bed, Arianna. It's nearly five in the morning." My mother's voice was scratchy from crying and greeting the visitors.

Without a word, I got up from the kitchen table and went straight to my bed.

Chapter 2

I woke up at one-thirty the next afternoon and went downstairs to watch TV. I sat there, not moving or saying a word, until finally my mother couldn't take it any longer.

"Arianna, go on a walk with someone," rang my mother's voice at eight o'clock. "Go with Dmitri."

"Do I have to, Mother?" I whined.

"Oh . . . I smell cheese. Would you like some to go with your wine?"

"Mom, I'm depressed. I'm only fourteen, my father's been killed and you want me to go on a walk at eight in the evening?"

"He was my husband! I knew him, too. Now get going or I'll come with you and Dmitri."

"Okay! Let me get my scarf, coat and gloves, and I'll be leaving."

"That's what I thought," she smiled with a mother's love. "The walk will do you good."

~ ~

"Ding-Dong!" went the sound of the doorbell.

"Hey, Dmitri, come and go for a walk with me," I said commandingly as I searched my coat pocket for my glove.

"Where?" he asked.

"On a walk through the forest," I replied.

"Says who?" he questioned, looking at his watch.

"Says me, now go get your coat, and please make it fast! My mother threatens she'll come along!"

Dmitri raced into his kitchen and back out with his coat.

Chapter 3

It was dark and cold, and you could just make out the frost beginning to form on the hard, solid earth. Dmitri and I were walking side-by-side through the "Dark Forest," as we called it. Our breath was transparent as we huffed and puffed.

"Where are we?" asked Dmitri in a voice that said he could better be spending his time.

"Well, umm, hmm . . . " I replied, looking around.

"Well, what?" he snapped.

'Oh man!' I thought. 'I dragged Dmitri out here because of my problem. He, being a friend, reluctantly came, and now I haven't a clue as to where we are! I don't even know which way is home!'

"Ithinkwearelost," I mumbled.

"Wait . . . what? I didn't quite catch that?" tormented Dmitri. "Did you say something?" He had his hand cupped around his ear.

Celia smiled. There has to be a Brad in every bunch! She continued to read.

"I said, 'I think we are lost.'"

"Oh, great!" shouted Dmitri. "Here we are, lost in the middle of a forest!"

"Actually, it's the Dark Forest," I corrected him.

"Who cares what it's called?" snapped Dmitri. "The Black Forest, the Enchanted Forest . . . whatever! How are we going to get out of here?"

Snap!

"What was that?" he whispered.

"I don't know," I murmured.

"You don't reckon?" Dmitri began to question.

Snap!

There it was again.

"You don't really think there . . ."

"Wait, stop!" I whispered. It had just begun to snow. "Did you see that?"

"See what?" His voice was shaking.

I stepped closer to Dmitri.

Snap . . . snap . . . snap!

There it was again, and whatever it was, it was getting closer.

"Dmitri . . ." I squealed.

"What?" he whispered.

"Did you see those yellow glowing eyes?"

"No. Where?" He was craning his head to see through the

snow, which was coming down harder now.

Snap . . . snap . . . snap . . . snap . . .

The sound stopped. I grabbed Dmitri's hand.

"I . . . saw . . . something . . ." he said, pronouncing each word slowly.

"Wh –at?" I said, separating the word for a gasp of air.

"I saw . . . Arianna?" Dmitri turned me so that I faced him. "Arianna, are you okay?"

My face was as white as the snow in my hair and my eyes were wide as I stared into Dmitri's face.

"Arianna? Arianna, what's wrong?"

I closed my eyes, swallowed, and opened my eyes again.

"Dmitri . . . I, I think . . . I'm gonna . . ."

"Arianna!" he shouted while his reflexes caught my fainted fall. Dmitri carefully knelt down and shifted me in his arms. He called again, "Arianna! Wake up, Arianna, please . . . AHHHHH!"

Chapter 4

I woke to see Dmitri's panic-stricken face, then turned and saw the ugliest hairy face I had ever seen. Whatever it was had fangs and yellow eyes, but worst of all, when it would breathe, it would breathe in all the air around it.

"Dmitri . . . what is that?" I asked, trying to focus on the creature and everything around us. "What happened? Why am I lying in your arms on the ground?"

The creature was now drooling.

"I'll explain later. Whatever you do, don't make any sudden movements," Dmitri ordered as the creature growled.

"Okay," I replied while Dmitri slowly got up.

Never taking his eyes off the beast, he helped me also to get up. After standing, everything came back into focus. First I saw the snow falling, and a beast staring at me from about six feet away. Then I felt Dmitri's warm hands settle around my waist, making sure I didn't faint again. He gently lifted my hair from in front of my right ear.

"Are you alright?"

I felt his warm breath on my neck. I nodded, still staring at the creature's ugly face.

"Okay, then . . . on the count of three . . . slowly back away."
I broke my stare and reached my hand out to grab Dmitri's.
"Ready . . . one . . . two . . . three . . ."
We slowly backed away. It seemed we had gone pretty far, but we could still see it's yellow eyes.
Suddenly the beast lunged forward. "Howwwwwwl!"
We turned and sprinted as it shot after us. I ran after Dmitri, dropping his hand.
"Howwwwwwl!" It was gaining.
Then as if the devil himself were there, Dmitri's coat caught a thorn bush.
"Dmitri!" I cried, tugging on him.
The creature was getting closer.
"Pull!" I stammered.
"I am!" he shouted back. He tugged one more time and this time his arm was caught on the thorn bush. "Ahhhh!" Dmitri cried as blood rushed to the spot where he had torn his skin.
"Come on! It's gaining! We have no time," I screamed, trying to pull him to his feet.
He sprang to his feet, grabbed my arm, and we ran till we couldn't run any more.
~ ~
"I . . . think . . . we . . . lost . . . it . . ." I stated between breaths. "What . . . do . . . you . . . think . . . Dmitri?" I turned to see him sitting on an old stump and cradling his arm. "Is it okay?"
"Yeah . . . yeah, it's fine."
"Are you sure?" I unwrapped my scarf from around my neck. "Here . . ."
"No . . . really . . . it's okay," he argued.
"Let me see it," I commanded, sitting next to him with my hands reached out for his arm.
"No! Arianna . . ." he bellowed. "Fine," he consented when he realized he had no choice and that the scarf had already been wrapped around the cut.
"There," I whispered contentedly.
Dmitri got up, wrapped his coat around him as best he could and started pacing. He never once glanced at me.
We stayed silent for a few minutes until I stopped on a tree

---

stump and stared at him. To stop tears from reaching my eyes, I sat down and looked toward the ground.

"Hey . . ." Dmitri had stopped pacing and was now striding toward me. "Hey, it's alright."

"I'm sorry," I sobbed. "It's all my fault we're in here."

"Aria . . ." he said, using my nickname. "It isn't your fault at all." He sat down beside me. Tears fell into my lap.

"Yes it is," I cried.

"No . . . no . . . Aria, it's okay." Dmitri gently tilted my chin up so he could see my tear-drowned face. "Arianna . . ."

"What?" I answered, trying to control myself.

He stood up, pulling me up as well. We stood staring at each other for a long time.

"Aria," Dmitri said, as he stepped closer.

"Yes?" I replied, looking up at familiar eyes.

The snow fell around us.

"I just wanted to say . . ."

"Yes?" I took a step closer to him and those eyes.

"I just wanted to thank you."

"For what?" I asked, backing up again.

"For bringing me with you into the forest. It's been . . ."

"Great," I finished his sentence.

"Yeah . . . great . . ." he answered with a smile.

Chapter 5

He reached for my hand. "What do you say we get out of here?"

"Sure," I smiled. "How?"

"Umm . . . well . . ." Dmitri looked around. "I'm not sure . . ." he finished blankly. Then his gaze fell on me. "Will . . . will you sing for me . . . Aria?" he asked in the whisper of the wind. "After all, Aria means song . . . that's why I call you that."

I was silent as a tear rolled down my cheek. "No one . . . no one," I repeated.

"'No one' what?"

"No one has ever asked me to sing for them. My father was the only one I ever sang for," I finished.

"Arianna, I'm sorry," he consoled.

"No," I interrupted. "It's okay. I have to get over the fact that I will never see him again." A few last tears escaped my eyes.

"Are you sure?" Dmitri questioned.

"Yes," I said, wiping the tears from my eyes. I sat down and gestured for him to sit down next to me. "When I was a little girl, my father wrote me my very own special song. Every night before my father tucked me in, he would sing me the song."

I began to sing the words, barely audible at first, but then they seemed to come from nowhere, with no effort. "I can remember my father's voice, deep and strong. After he sang, I'd sing the song back to him. No matter where we were, we sang. If he were on business, we'd sing over the phone. Every night. We never missed it."

I lowered my head. "He always called me his Little Princess." And I sang the song again.

"That was incredibly amazing! Your voice . . . it's so pure, it's so beautiful!"

"Thanks," I mumbled uncomfortably. But I realized I was no longer frightened. Memories of my mother, my father and I together, walking through these trees flooded my mind. My father and I singing to each other, even over the phone the last night before my life suddenly changed.

"Good night, my little Princess," I heard in my dad's voice.

"Good night, Dad," I whispered.

Those words kept ringing through my ears. Then a clear picture of my father faded away as Dmitri took my hand and pulled me up.

Chapter 6

"Hey, I'm sorry about your father, I really am," Dmitri offered after we had taken several steps in silence.

"I appreciate that." I squeezed his hand. "Hey! I have an idea. Let's get out of here," I exclaimed.

"How? Oh," he smiled as he saw me pointing toward my house.

You could barely make out the Christmas lights on the back porch.

"Thanks for coming on the walk with me."

He nodded and we continued our steps toward the house.

"Arianna," he said, finally breaking the silence, "Merry Christmas, Arianna, Merry Christmas."

I started to cry, so much that Dmitri picked me up and carried me the rest of the way home.

"Thanks again, Dmitri," I said as I opened the front door.

"Any time," he answered.

I stepped into my house and my mom came up behind me. Dmitri watched us hug. He then smiled and started down the street.

"Hey Dmitri!" I shouted from the doorway. "Merry Christmas!" Joyful laughter followed.

I turned to my mother, who gave me a kiss on the cheek and went back to the kitchen. As I turned back to shut the front door, a voice came shouting at me from down the street.

Full of wonder, I stepped back out the door.

"MERRY CHRISTMAS, ARIA, MERRY CHRISTMAS!" a voice shouted. There was no one there.

My hand clamped over my mouth, just as a magnet to a refrigerator, as tears came again to my eyes.

Dmitri wasn't a human . . . he was an angel.

He was my angel.

Celia gazed at the last few lines, reading them over several times. Then she turned to see which student had written the story. To her amazement, it was a seventh grader. Celia wasn't sure which astonished her more - the girl's writing ability, or the way the story found a hiding place until just the right time to be read.

There had been so many angels, *angels in human form*, around her during the past several months. Angels that Celia was sure had been specially sent to watch over both Isaac and her. *Angels that walked with Isaac when he lost his mother. Angels that helped him battle a terrible monster. Angels sent to help him find his way "home."*

She packed the story into the tote bag, making herself a note to write the student and compliment her outstanding work. The rock from Cookie was still on the bedside table. Celia picked it up, read it and closed her eyes for a second.

"Celia?" she heard in a light voice at the door.

She turned to see Dorothy Lee.

"I'm so glad you're still here. We heard the news at school. All the classes stopped for a moment of silence." The veteran teacher hugged her co-worker. "I found something a couple of days ago that I wanted to share with you. About a month ago, the students were assigned to each write a letter to someone for Christmas. When I came to pick up the drawing Isaac had done for the academy's Christmas card, I asked if he'd like to participate. He had me to help him with the spelling, punctuation and grammar. Bless his heart, he said he wanted them to be perfect, and he wrote two. It's hard to believe a child his age could have written them."

Like the seventh grader's work, huh?

"Given his condition, I decided to hold onto them for a while. But, well, after this morning, I thought maybe you needed them now. Dr. Lacey agreed, so he's watching the class so that I could bring these to you."

Celia smiled. "Sounds exactly like him." She took the envelopes from Mrs. Lee to see that one was addressed to Santa Claus and one was addressed to her. She pulled the letter from the first envelope and unfolded it slowly. It was as if she could still feel the warmth of Isaac's small fingers on the page.

Dear Santa,

I hope you remember me from our meeting in Florida. I am praying that you are real and that you can grant my Christmas wish just like DJ and the people at Give Kids the World granted my other wish.

Mrs. Lee placed her hand on Celia's shoulder as the woman continued to read.

What I want most is to spend Christmas with Momma. I know that might be a hard wish for you, and if you can't make it come true, it's alright because I love living with Celia. And Brad is the coolest. And DJ is the most wonderful dad in the whole world. And thanks to the Red Pig,

*I'm never hungry anymore. So I will be happy to stay here
with them if you can't really give me what I want.
And please do not leave me any underwear.*

> *Your friend,*
> *Isaac Fuller*

Cookie had walked into the room unnoticed and now read the note over Celia's shoulder.

*P.S. If you can't make my wish come true, could
you please tell Momma hello for me and say that I miss her?*

Tears poured down Celia's face as she covered her mouth, trying not to lose all sense of composure. She turned to see Cookie.

"Oh, Cookie," she cried, throwing her arms around the care partner's neck.

"It's okay, baby, let it out."

"Oh, Cookie," she mumbled. Celia turned so that her words included both the women. "When I was in Florida with Isaac, I felt so bad because I felt like the child had no tomorrow." She swallowed hard as more tears streamed down her face. "This *is* Isaac's tomorrow, isn't it?"

Neither of the listeners said a word. They simply surrounded Celia in an understanding hug, giving her comfort and strength.

Celia opened the other envelope.

"Do you want me to read it for you?" offered Mrs. Lee.

"No. Thank you, but I need to read it myself."

"That's my girl," encouraged Cookie.

"*Dear Celi,*" she read aloud as she looked at the beautifully shaped letters. Turning to Mrs. Lee, she commented, "You really did a good job helping him with his handwriting."

"His *mother* really did a good job helping him with his handwriting," replied the teacher.

Celia nodded. "And everything else."

She turned back to reading the letter.

Dear Celi,

I hope you're not mad at me for this, but I asked Santa to let me spend Christmas with Momma. I don't know if he's really real, or really able to give boys and girls what they want, but Momma told me to always believe. So I hope he gives me my wish.

Please don't think that I don't like living with you. You're the greatest. Especially when Brad comes over. You two make me laugh. Thank you for taking me to the race-tracks, to London and Paris and to Florida to see Santa.

I like school and the birthday parties and the Red Pig and all the other cool places that you and Brad take me. But I miss Momma, and I want to see the big new mansion that I wished for her to have, and I'd like to have a daddy like the other boys and girls. DJ said that when I go to live with Momma, I'd have a Heavenly Father that would know my name and love me even better than giving me parties and ice cream and President's Pie. I believe him, so I want to go and live with Momma.

I love you.

Your boy,
Isaac Fuller

P.S. You have been a very good mommy, and if you ever have a son, I hope you will name him Isaac.

"That would be the day, huh?" she asked, trying to joke about the postscript.

"Never say never," warned Cookie. "You know what they say about that."

Celia turned to Mrs. Lee. "Thank you so much for bringing these. I really *did* need to see them now." A smile tried to make its way onto her face as she repeated her question from before. "Isaac began his *tomorrow* today, didn't he?"

"He sure did," exclaimed Cookie. "You know that saying about 'today being the first day of the rest of your life?'

Well, honey, today is the first day of the biggest tomorrow that boy will *ever* see!"

Celia laughed aloud, tears pouring down her cheeks as she did. "Oh Cookie, I love you! I told you that you were an angel."

"I think you may be right," agreed Mrs. Lee. "My husband, who works for the hospital, says Cookie's the life and breath of the pediatric floor." She gave Celia a long hug. "I'd better be getting back to my class. Please call the school if we can do anything to help."

Celia nodded. "Would you please mail this for me?" She handed the tutor the note addressed to Santa Claus.

Mrs. Lee took the note. "You really *were* the best mother in the world for Isaac during all of this," she said as she hurried out the door.

Cookie gave her a last hug. "I've got another patient I need to see." And with that, she also exited the room.

The circle of life continues, she mused as she watched the "angel of life" go down the hall.

Celia picked up the stone and read it one last time. Then she placed it and her letter in the tote bag and turned and walked down the hall, now ready to make the necessary preparations.

CHAPTER 43

After the visitation, a "planned" two-hour wake that lasted over four hours, Celia fell on the sofa of the funeral home, exhausted from greeting the steady stream of people. Her mind raced to the year before when the school held the live nativity for the Little family. Cars drove through for hours. *Has it really been a year?* Celia sat focusing on the fact that tomorrow evening would be exactly a year since that night. *That night I first encountered Isaac. That night I saw the effect he had on people. That night God sent a "real" angel into my life. That night . . .*

"Celia," she heard the voice.

"I'm sorry. Have you been calling my name long?" she asked Brad.

"Only a couple of times. Would you like to go somewhere to wind down a little before you go home?" Brad hated to see her stay in an empty house this evening, but he was not about to invite himself. She had done fine the evening before, but Jean, Jan and Tami had stayed with her. This evening she would be on her own, a first in nearly ten months.

♪ ♪ ♪ ♪

When they arrived at the Red Pig, the mugs and saucers of the Breakfast Club were already in place for the next morning. Celia watched as Marijke sat at her place in the corner booth and glanced down at the cheap souvenir mug Isaac had brought her from Florida.

"If you don't mind, I think I'll take this home and put it in my china cabinet. I'd hate for anything to happen to it."

"That's fine," came the response from the kitchen window where Cory had heard her. "I think we can find your old fine china cup and saucer back here somewhere."

He and all the waitresses had voluntarily opened the restaurant for anyone who wanted to come by and have coffee after the visitation. They had anticipated the crowd and emotional drain the evening would have on everybody, especially Celia and Brad. This was their way of showing sympathy for *all* of Isaac's "family."

Celia recalled the afternoon they had all gathered there after Dawn's memorial service. One of the Breakfast Club asked the question, *"What would Dawn have done?"* And Isaac jumped from his seat and yelled, *"I know! I know!"* while grabbing Jennifer's hand and leading everyone through the restaurant and doing 'the train' line dance.

Now all she could think about was *"What would Isaac do?"*

Her thoughts must have been terribly loud for at that moment, Ike called out, "I know what this place needs." He whipped a folded sheet of paper from his inside suit pocket, unfolded it and began to sing some words to the tune of *Winter Wonderland*.

Celia glanced over his shoulder to see in large red letters at the top of the page, *A Red Pig Christmas Carol*. She listened intently as members of the Breakfast Club began to join in as Ike sang.

> *At the Pig, every morning,*
> *Coffee's poured, it's never boring;*
> *We're having a blast, eat'n breakfast,*
> *Meet'n at the Pig Restaurant.*
>
> *In the corner, talk an issue,*
> *And if you're gone, we will miss you;*
> *But when you re-land, have presents in hand,*
> *Meet'n at the Pig Restaurant.*

In the booth we can get a crowd in,
It's very close when others come to sit.
If you're touching thighs it's no sin,
Just be sure to share your egg and grit.

Cut rate ham and free refills,
The last to leave pays the bills;
Eat'n so big at the Red Pig,
Meet'n at the Pig Restaurant.

The musician in her told Celia the lyrics might need a little help, but the Pig lover in her said the song was perfect. She could imagine Isaac sitting there singing, *"Eat'n so big at the Red Pig, Meet'n at the Pig Restaurant."*

Good or bad, she knew there was no way she would ever forget those words, or want to. "Do you have another copy?" she asked.

"I'm sure we could find one," Ike answered proudly.

"Why don't you find several?" Jan suggested. "That made pourin' coffee much easier!" With that comment, she proceeded to spill the liquid caffeine on the table.

"I'd hate to see what it was like before!" laughed another one of the guys in the Breakfast Club.

"Which one of you talented individuals wrote those lyrics?" Celia inquired.

'That would be my husband," laughed Marijke.

"Nobody else'll claim them," another member joked.

"Sing it again!" pleaded Jennifer as she grabbed Brad, who in turn grabbed Celia.

Everyone knew what was in store when the threesome began the train, the Breakfast Club singing as they went.

♪ ♪ ♪ ♪

Jean walked over to Celia and sat down. "You look tired, dear. Why don't you go on home and get some rest?"

"I think I will," she agreed, putting her coat on.

"Would you like for one of us to stay with you?" Marijke offered.

"No, thank you. That won't be necessary."

Jean looked at Brad. "Do you think you could sleep on the sofa?"

Celia was quick to answer. "I'd really rather be alone. I think I need the time to sort through some things before tomorrow morning. Eleven will come early."

Everyone gave Celia a last hug and expression of sympathy before she left.

Randy caught Brad on his way out the door. "Here," he said, offering the coach a drink holder. "There's several cups of hot cocoa. Why don't you share one with her before you leave her house? This should relax her a little."

"Thanks." Brad turned and looked at all the eyes on him. "Thanks to all of you . . . for everything," he added, a tremor in his voice.

"Too bad the two of them young'uns don't get married," exclaimed Ike when they were out of earshot.

"Why would they want to go and do something stupid like that? They've got a perfectly good relationship going," replied one of the men. "There's no point in ruining it."

The rest of the Breakfast Club guffawed at his candor.

"I think little Isaac filled a void for both of them. They're sure going to be lonely now," stated Jan.

All of the patrons were touched by her words, the voice of experience.

♪ ♪ ♪ ♪

Celia stood, lost in thought, on the cafe's sidewalk. "Brad, did you ever see the *Star Wars* movie where the victory celebration is going on at Endor and Luke looks out into the stars and sees the trio of his teacher, his father and the Jedi Master?" Not waiting for an answer, she continued, "That's how I felt this evening. When I sat in that corner booth and stared out the window, I could have sworn I saw images of

Isaac, Maureen and Dawn looking in the window at all of us and smiling."

She looked straight into his eyes. "It was that very same feeling I had last year at the concert. That "strangely warmed" feeling, as John Wesley called it. Like God had reached down and truly become a part of my very being. I threw it off as penned-up emotions on the loose, but after all the other odd things that have happened with that child . . . you know, like all those times when he seemed to know what needed to happen . . . well, I almost wonder . . ."

Brad said nothing. He didn't have an inkling of *what* to say. All he knew is that Celia was going to feel a great loss, just as he would, as well as everyone else who had come in contact with Isaac.

"Celia, you *do* know that you were a mother to that child?" He waited for only a second, and went on, "I know he called Jean 'Mama,' but you were the one he thought of as his 'Momma' after she was gone."

"I'd like to think that's true," she said, her voice and her eyes drifting off into space.

♪ ♪ ♪ ♪

Brad parked the car in the driveway, but Celia made no move toward opening the door. She sat there, gazing at the stars in the sky without saying a word.

Finally she turned to Brad. "You know how Dawn said she thought of Randy as her father? Well, you were the father Isaac never had."

He sighed. "I'd like to think that's true, too, but I think DJ had that honor."

"No, there was a difference," Celia explained. "DJ was an angel to Isaac. He was there for the boy when his mother passed, and he was there for him when Dawn passed. And he was there to make sure that Isaac had everything necessary to provide the best quality of life possible for the months he had left after the accident."

She reached over and took Brad's hand. "But it was *you* who was there on a daily basis to give him that quality of life." Celia's mind rambled back to her own childhood. "You were the 'daddy' that every child wants."

"I certainly hope you're right," he replied solemnly. "Besides," he added with a grin, changing the somber mood, "no one ever accused me of being an angel!"

"You're right," she smiled, also sensing it was time to move on. She started to open the door.

"No, wait. Allow me." Brad jumped from the car and ran around to open her door.

"Wow! I'm impressed. Thank you, sir."

"I just wouldn't want to you go through your life forever thinking that I'm no more than a dumb jock."

Celia laughed. "I truly *am* sorry for that misconception," she apologized, thinking back to when she actually "met" him at last year's committee meeting to discuss the Little's Christmas project. She stood under her front stoop staring into his eyes as she took his hands. "I know we've seen a lot of each other lately. For Isaac's sake," she quickly added, "but please don't become a stranger."

"I don't think you have to worry about that." Brad pulled Celia to him and kissed her. Then he veered his eyes toward the ceiling of the front porch.

Celia looked up to see a ball of mistletoe hanging there. "Where'd that come from?" she asked in astonishment.

"Must have been some angel," he smirked coyly.

"You're not going to get me to call you an angel *that* easily," she jokingly scoffed.

"Okay . . . but you can't blame a guy for trying."

She shook her head from side to side. "Don't tell me we're back to your shenanigans."

"Would you expect any less from a PE coach?" he teased, a grin spreading across his face.

Celia looked into his eyes, now taking on a serious tone both with her glance and her voice. "Brad, have you thought any more about the ministry you once felt called to do?"

The grin left his face, replaced by a tender smile of contentment. "Do you mind if I come in for a minute?" he asked. "I've been wanting to talk to you about that."

She knew it was getting late and that tomorrow would come early, but Celia knew there was no way she would sleep now anyway. And besides, how many nights had this man given up time and energy for Isaac – *and me?*

"Sure, come on in," she invited. "Should I put on some coffee or something?"

"No, we've got hot chocolate in the car from Randy. I'll grab that. Besides, this won't take long. But since you brought up the subject, I really *do* want to tell you what's going on."

♪ ♪ ♪ ♪

They sat on the sofa, the same one where they had sat a year earlier after their first dinner together, on the night when Brad disclosed his initial call from college years to serve in a ministry. "I'm going to be leaving the academy, Celi."

She could feel the stiffening in her back as she sat rigid, waiting for the horrible announcement that he was leaving the town of Concord.

He reached over and took her hand. "I love my job. You understand that . . . so did you."

Celia nodded, dreading the words to come.

"But, like you, I've had the sense for quite a while, especially after being with Isaac and DJ, that there was something more for me out there. You and I discussed this briefly at the hospital."

Here it comes. Celia braced herself.

"I loved all the ministry going on at the race track in October when I went with you and Isaac to Lowe's Motor Speedway. Motor Racing Outreach has a way to get into places that many ministers would never get. They touch millions of lives each year, and they offer worship for the racers and their families every Sabbath that they have to be on the circuit.

"The idea of worship, then running off 'to the races'

bothered me at first, but the more I thought about it, I took an objective look at the lives of the ministers in local churches. They, too, have to work on Sundays, leaving their families to take care of their flocks.

"But what an enriching and rewarding work. Just like you continue to use your music, I can stay involved in sports."

He leaned his face a little closer to hers so that he could look straight into her eyes. "Celi, I can't tell you what I felt when we worshipped with those drivers and their families. But what I can tell you is that it was a call from God. I no longer felt the shame of my father's past. I no longer felt I was unworthy to spread the love of Christ."

A voice of determination took over the conversation. "And what I *did* feel was the knowledge that I had to follow that call. I've contacted the MRO office in Charlotte, as DJ suggested, and already interviewed with them and gone through all the security and background process. I'll be taking a few classes to finish my degree in Divinity, during which time I'll be working with a team at the tracks to get oriented in their ministry and programs.

"Then upon completion of my ordination, I'll tour certain tracks each season, working with the fans and the drivers. And I'll get lots of opportunities to minister to young people."

Celia gave Brad a congratulatory hug to show her support in his acceptance of his calling.

"And the best thing is, I'll be able to keep my home here. I won't have to move . . . at least for now."

Thank God, sighed Celia, glad that he couldn't read her mind.

"For some reason, I want to stay in this area. I've grown accustomed to . . ." The words stopped as he found himself at a place he was not ready to admit.

"*Your face*," sang the musician to herself, borrowing the title from "My Fair Lady." Sensing the tension of the silence, Celia tried to ease the moment. "Brad, I understand completely. I've thought, ever since I met you, that you were not fulfilling the purpose in your life. That same purpose for which

I went searching last year.

"When Isaac and I were at Talledega and attended the service and he played with some of the other children, I could picture you in the position of that minister. At one point, even Isaac asked, 'Isn't that guy just like Brad?'"

Celia moved so that she was seated beside her guest rather than looking at him. "I can't tell you what a difference there's been in my life since I made the decision to follow my heart. And I know Who put me in that place last year at the concert, and the nativity, and with Isaac at the hospital. I would never look back."

Brad placed his arm around Celia. "I knew you'd understand."

"And that feeling of growing accustomed," she added sheepishly, "I've gotten that, too."

His eyes suddenly lit up.

"I was afraid that you were going to tell me you were moving or something," Celia admitted.

Brad hugged her, wishing there was no tomorrow. *In more than one way*, he thought, remembering the service for Isaac. "Should we step out under the mistletoe?" he asked, returning to his playful humor.

"There's some hanging between the kitchen and dining room," she confessed.

"There is, huh? Don't tell me an angel put it there."

"Nope. Isaac insisted on that from the hospital."

"So it was at the hands of an angel?" he joked.

"Nope again," she laughed. "My hands, the angel's idea!"

"I hate to leave, but I think we both need some rest before tomorrow." He stood, pulling Celia up with him, and headed toward the dining room.

"For Isaac," he said, kissing the woman who had shown him a life besides sporting events.

"For Isaac," Celia replied, kissing the man who had expanded her horizons past the arts.

"Shall I pick you up in the morning around shortly before ten?"

"Sure. I don't think I'm up for breakfast tomorrow."

"I understand. I figured you might feel that way. DJ said he'd meet us at the funeral home at ten and that we could ride to the church with him and his family. They're all coming for the service."

She nodded, masking a tear and closing the door slowly behind him.

CHAPTER 44

Dale Jarrett bent down and hugged Celia as she sat stoically under the tent. "Don't hesitate to call me if there's ever *anything* I can do for you. There are going to be some final bills to crop up, I'm sure. Send those straight to me." He smiled with those same eyes she had come to know personally. "You've got my cell phone. Don't be a stranger."

A tear made its way down her face. "I won't."

He shook hands with Brad, who sat beside Celia. "You take care of her. And I'll be looking for *you* trackside."

"Yes, sir. Mr. Jarrett, thanks for everything . . . with Isaac and Celia, and for helping me find my purpose."

"You're welcome, and my name is Dale."

Brad and Celia both smiled as he held onto their shoulders for a few moments. Then he took a last look at the small casket and walked away, escorting his family to their limousine.

Everyone else left the cemetery quietly after speaking to Celia and expressing their condolences. How strange it seemed to her that the people who came to pay their respects to this precious child felt the need to speak to her. *But then I guess I was the closest thing to a living relative that the child had in the world.*

At least that he knew, she concluded, wondering where Isaac's father was and whether he would have even cared. Celia refused to let her mind spend any more time in query, as she rejoiced that the boy had known a wonderful Father.

Officer Britten and Mrs. Schell hung around toward the end of the line with Cookie and Dr. Teague.

"You did a great job with that kid," complimented the police detective.

"Yes. I'm glad things worked out the way they did," consoled the social worker. "I mean, with you getting custody of Isaac."

"Thank you. I know what you meant," replied Celia.

"You *did* do a great job with that child, Celia," stated Dr. Teague. *No one* could have been better for him."

The teacher fell into the doctor's shoulder. "I don't know what I would have done without the two of you. You were my stronghold."

Dr. Teague smiled. "You're a wonderful mother, Celia. If you ever have children of your own, give me a call."

"That'll be the day!" she grinned, wiping away another tear.

"You never know, Miss Celi," warned Cookie. "We may see you back in that hospital yet."

"Don't hold your breath," advised Celia, shaking her head.

Cookie turned to Brad. "And this is for you," she said as she reached into her purse and pulled out a giant chocolate chip cookie.

"You're too much!" laughed Brad.

"I'll bet you say that to all the girls."

Cookie hugged Brad, then Celia, and walked away with Dr. Teague.

Celia stepped toward the place Isaac's young body had been laid to rest beside his mother, an arrangement made by Jarrett after it was discovered there was no family. She stood staring down at the ground, swallowing hard, and thinking how this little boy, who had appeared out of nowhere and shaped her life - and all those with whom he had come in contact - had caught the attention of so many peoples' eyes. Not only the people of Concord, but people throughout the country. And not only the people who went about the routine walks of life, but many world-renowned celebrities.

Celia shivered as the wind picked up.

Brad, who had been standing quietly behind, allowing her the time and privacy to say good-bye to Isaac in her own personal way, took off his jacket and slipped it around her shoulders.

"Thanks," she said blankly as she glanced at him. Her emotions and her words were at a loss for the moment. He put his arm around her and held her close, letting her know he understood her feelings and that he cared. "Reach in the left pocket. There's a present there for you from Isaac."

She glared at him with a questioning look in her eyes, but not at all surprised that this miraculous child that had walked into her life could have pulled off such an act. Her hand felt into the pocket and pulled out a small package. Celia glanced at him hesitantly as she untied the ribbon and flipped up the lid of the box.

"Celia Brinkley, will you marry me?" came the words as the diamond glistened in the sunlight.

"How did you know?" rolled the reaction from her lips.

"I heard him tell you his wish that last morning at the hospital. I was about to burst into the room when I heard him telling you about the shooting star, so I decided it was not a good time to interrupt. It was not my intention to eavesdrop, but I was trying to listen to figure out a good time to make an entrance."

"What made you think I would accept your offer?" she threw at him, her eyes still full of questions.

"It was that pause, that time you had to think of an answer when Isaac asked you if you didn't want to marry me. You took too long to come up with an excuse."

She gazed at him, now the shock of his question fully hitting her.

"Well, I'm waiting." This time he took her right hand, knelt on one knee and looked into her face with eyes full of unashamed love. "Celi, will you marry me?"

A smile that erupted into laughter spread across her face. "Only if we can have a little boy named Isaac."

"It may take several tries, but we'll eventually get there," he grinned, jumping back to his feet and grabbing her off the ground and swinging her around. "I love you, Celia Brinkley."

"I love you, too, Bradley Sells."

He took the ring from the box and placed it on her left hand. Then he carefully placed the box on the top of the small wooden coffin with the white roses that had been left by the pallbearers, all NASCAR drivers. "Thank you, Isaac."

Celia reached up and wiped the tears that were beginning to flow from her eyes.

The sun, that had made its way behind a giant puffy cloud, sent streams of rays down upon the earth, catching both the attention of Brad and Celia.

"He still got the last word," she said, her tears turning back into a smile as she slipped her arm through Brad's and they walked away to begin a life of their own. "Would you like to come over to my place to look at the stars tonight? I'm sure the sky will be full of them."

As Celia tried to force a smile, Brad reached across her into an inside pocket of his suit jacket to pull out another present which he handed to her.

It was only wrapped with a handkerchief around it. Celia pulled back one side of the white piece of cotton to reveal a stone plaque that was covered with raised stars all over the top. Underneath the stars were etched the words, "Perhaps they are not stars in the sky, but rather openings where our loved ones shine down to let us know they are happy." The final letter gracefully wound its way down to form an etched star underneath the words.

Celia read the words aloud before running the index finger of her right hand over the star at the bottom, tracing its points in a slow motion. She gave a long sigh and sang softly, "There's a song in the air! There's a star in the sky! There's a mother's deep prayer and a baby's low cry!" Her voice came to a halt as she stared down at her left hand, her present from both Brad and Isaac.

"I'm sure there will be an opening in tonight's sky,"

he said, taking her left hand in his and looking at the diamond ring that sat perched there.

"Isaac really *did* get the last word, didn't he?"

Brad nodded gently and gave her a reassuring smile. "Yes . . . he did."

He put his arm around Celia and led her toward the car. Then, to his future bride's amazement, Brad began to sing. Not just in a haphazard voice, but in a lovely tenor voice whose notes soared as he sang, "And the star rains its fire while the beautiful sing, for the manger of Bethlehem cradles a King!"

There's a Song in the Air

There's a song in the air! There's a star in the sky!
There's a mother's deep prayer and a baby's low cry!
And the star rains its fire while the beautiful sing,
for the manger of Bethlehem cradles a King!

There's a tumult of joy o'er the wonderful birth,
For the virgin's sweet boy is the Lord of the earth.
Ay! the star rains its fire while the beautiful sing,
for the manger of Bethlehem cradles a King!

In the light of that star lie the ages impearled;
and that song from afar has swept over the world.
Every hearth is aflame, and the beautiful sing
in the homes of the nations that Jesus is King!

We rejoice in the light, and we echo the song
that comes down through the night from the heavenly throng.
Ay! we shout to the lovely evangel they bring,
and we greet in his cradle our Savior and King!

Josiah G. Holland, 1874

Most people experience personal tragedy at some point in life and the characters of *A Song in the Air* - although fictional - are no exception. We can choose, through our struggles and tragedies, to either hold on to our last remaining seeds of hope or turn to a state of hopelessness.

Hope is that which pushes us forward when all else threatens to immobilize our progress and, in the worst of times, drags us backwards. In teaching Bible studies, we often liken hope to hunger pangs; although both are absolutely intangible, you know when you've encountered one of them.

Hope is evidenced in the twinkling eyes of the dying. It's the quickened pace in the step of the weary. And it's the only remedy for despair. There is no more pitiful state than that of hopelessness.

There was One who came to abolish the eternal state of hopelessness and it is the author's sole desire that you found Him in the pages of this book. Catherine Ritch Guess is no stranger to the taunts of despair. We have watched her overcome personal tragedy and been amazed at her resolve to conquer her fears, and the looming despair that accompanies devastating adversity. Catherine's focus on her Father's will for her life is steadfast, and continually leads her in a path of ministry. Her talent and skill for writing and music, combined with her passion for serving others, bears the proof of her calling.

Life's struggles are often worse in our thoughts, due to our personal fear, than they are in real life. For once we reach out, Christ is always there to give us a hand. The study questions that follow are to help direct and focus your thoughts in the areas of trusting God for all our needs, recognizing those around us who are "angels" in our paths and seeing opportunities to touch the lives of those around us.

We join Catherine in encouraging you to pursue hope and the One who offers it freely to all. And it is our hope at CRM BOOKS that through our line of Reality Fiction, you will find joy and inspiration in your own experiences of life.

~ C.J. Didymus - Cheryl Karst & Jackie Dasher ~

~~ Questions & Reflections ~~

Whether you are reading these questions individually, or as part of a Bible study or reading group, you are encouraged to let the words and ideas flow freely as you reflect on your own life and situation. In fact, I recommend that you write your answers on a piece of paper and place them inside the back cover of this book. Come back to them - a day later, a week later, a month later, or even years laters. Your words, as Isaac's did to Celia through a letter, will speak so loudly that it will seem God ordained them for that very moment. *-- CR?*

1) In looking at the conclusion of the events of *A Song in the Air*, we see Romans 8:28 in action. What events of your own life can you see that have transpired as ordained by that scripture?

2) Think of all the characters in *A Song in the Air* who served others in various ways. How do you serve others?

3) When situations beyond our control befall, do we recognize that God is with us, and that through Him, we can overcome any obstacle? In what area of your life do you need to recognize that Holy Presence now?

4) Just like a bowl of ice cream, we all need a little Cookie once in a while. We meet people each day - at work, in the mall, on the street - who could easily be someone sent into our lives to help us along our spiritual journey. Who have you run into lately that could have played the role of Cookie; Jeff Frank; Consella Costa?

5) Like we see from the fictional character of Isaac, there is hope in every situation. It is often hard, as adults, to look at and accept things with that childlike spirit. How can you keep that simple faith at the forefront of all your thoughts and decisions?

6) Isaac left behind his two greatest treasures. But more than that, he left behind the gift of himself. What gifts do you leave behind to remind others of Jesus? And what can you do to offer light to someone groping in a world of darkness?

Reality Fiction

The writing style of Catherine Ritch Guess has become synonymous with the term "Reality Fiction" since she opened her own niche in the inspirational market nearly three years ago.

Her novels, most of which are based in real settings, feature realistic characters and situations of contemporary society, and are spiced with historical facts. Although the stories, characters and locales are used fictitiously, her mission is that readers will find themselves within the pages of her writings.

From the letters she receives, it is obvious that her idea of Reality Fiction is working as it ministers to her readers. She intends her work to plant seeds and meet the needs of individuals who would never venture inside a house of worship or pick up a Bible. And for believers, she strives to help strengthen their spiritual lives by weaving a wealth of theology between the lines.

Her message is "if God can love the characters within my pages, he can love everyone." It is her hope and dream that readers will be uplifted in their own individual lives and situations through her characters and their stories.

UPCOMING RELEASES of CRM BOOKS

Let Us Break Bread Together
Volume 2 - Sandman Series
Catherine Ritch Guess

Church in the Wildwood
Catherine Ritch Guess

Hear My Cry
John Shivers

For the Beauty of the Earth
Catherine Ritch Guess

Ain't Another One Like Him
C.J. Didymus
(the writing team of Cheryl Karst & Jackie Dasher)

'Tis So Sweet
Catherine Ritch Guess

About the Artist

Madeleine Nagy is a first-grade student at Cannon School in Concord, North Carolina (the "real" Tillman Academy). She is excited to be making a contribution of her artwork to this literary project. Her artistic skills run in the family as her grandmother is a pastel and watercolor artist.

Miss Nagy enjoys arts and crafts, cooking and playing with her friends. A diligent student in school, she also currently participates in swimming, karate and piano. In addition to spending time with her school friends, Madeleine enjoys playing with her younger sisters, Annabelle and Gabriella.

Madeleine resides in Spencer, North Carolina.

M- 4-1-2015   11/16/04

F
GuE

ASHE COUNTY PUBLIC LIBRARY

Song in the Air

DISCARD

50503300168160

About the Author

Catherine Ritch Guess, also a published composer, spent thirty-four years of her life as an Organist/Minister of Music before creating her niche in the world of inspirational literature.

Guess, who holds degrees in Church Music, Music Ed and a Master's Degree in Christian Education, is a Diaconal Minister of the United Methodist Church, currently appointed as the Circuit Riding Musician. This position allows her to serve globally through her writing, teaching, inspirational speaking and music.

A native of North Carolina, Catherine resides in Cedar Mountain where she is busy completing the third book of this Shooting Star Series, *The Midnight Clear*, and her second Easter novel, *Let Us Break Bread Together*. Between recording two new CDs of her musical arrangements, she is getting ready for the release of three other novels, *Church in the Wildwood, For the Beauty of the Earth* and *'Tis So Sweet*.